D0408715

The
Color
Midnight
Made

The Color Midnight Made

A NOVEL

———

ANDREW WINER

WASHINGTON SQUARE PRESS

NEW YORK LONDON TORONTO SYDNEY SINGAPORE

Excerpt from "Sad Steps" from *Collected Poems* by Philip Larkin. Copyright © 1988, 1989 by the Estate of Philip Larkin. Reprinted by permission of Farrar, Straus, and Giroux, LLC.

Library of Congress Cataloging-in-Publication Data

Winer, Andrew.
   The color midnight made: a novel / Andrew Winer.
      p. cm.
   ISBN 0-7434-3990-2 (alk. paper)
   1. African American neighborhoods—Fiction. 2. Color blindness in children—Fiction. 3. African Americans—Fiction. 4. Problem families—Fiction. 5. Race relations—Fiction. 6. White children—Fiction. 7. Boys—Fiction. I. Title.

PS3623.I63 C65 2002
813'.6—dc21

2001058830

First Washington Square Press hardcover printing July 2002

10 9 8 7 6 5 4 3 2 1

 WASHINGTON SQUARE PRESS and colophon are registered trademarks of Simon & Schuster, Inc.

For information regarding special discounts for bulk purchases, please contact Simon & Schuster Special Sales at 1-800-456-6798 or business@simonandschuster.com

Designed by Joseph Rutt

Printed in the U.S.A.

For my father

The hardness and the brightness and the plain
Far-reaching singleness of that wide stare
Is a reminder of the strength and pain
Of being young . . .

—PHILIP LARKIN

The
Color
Midnight
Made

I

They say I can't see colors. They're lying. I can see colors in *people*. Moms is yellow. Pops is camouflage. Our teacher Mr. Garabedian is tan like a weed. I got a color for everybody. Except me.

I told my best friend Loop he was silver and black, like the Oakland Raiders. Loop gave me a slug.

"I *already* black," he said.

So he went solo with silver.

It started when we had to get our eyes checked by Dr. Chow, Eye Master of the Universe. He was already waiting in the library when we sleazed in. Mr. Garabedian said we had to keep a tight line and walk in pairs. We were a centipede of backpacks.

Everyone talked loud but not me. I always go quiet in the yellow light of the old library. Those books are talking too much already.

Eye Master of the Universe sat near Biography, bald and wearing a white coat. He was testing us one at a time and taking forever. Loop pulled out of line to get a look.

"W'sup with this stupid test?" Loop said. "This is for squids. Only whiteboys get their eyes checked."

"I know," I said. "W'sup with that?"

Yeah, *I* was a whiteboy. Jack London Primary only had fourteen. But nobody, including Loop, thought of me as one. Loop said I musta been black in a past life, so it was cool I was hangin wid the bruthas in *this* one, since I had prior experience and did not be comin at it on the honky-ass tip.

So I was okay.

We were almost to the front of the line. My stomach went tight each time I looked at Eye Master. I had to pass his test in front of Loop and the other gritties, or else I'd look like a squid.

I lifted my eyes up to the library's high arched ceiling and took a deep breath. The hanging lamps glowed softly above me like twelve old suns, and the air tasted calm and quiet and as yellow as it looked. It tasted like books and breath. It smelled older than Earth.

It was our turn and Eye Master made me go first. You had to sit in the chair and cover one eye at a time and read a dumb chart on the wall. I had it all sewed up until from out of nowhere he flashed some cards at me. Each had a bunch of color dots smashed together like grapes. "Tell me the number you see," he said.

The first three cards were easy: Six, Eight, Zero. But the next few didn't have any numbers in them—just colored dots. Behind me, Loop and Clarence and Douglas whispered "Seven!" and "Two!" and every goddamn number but I couldn't see anything.

Come on you dots, I said, You gotta have a number in there.

Eye Master said, "Are you sure, Conrad? Try it again."

I ran my tongue over my back teeth and gave it all my mentals but the dots weren't talking to me, except to say: *Hi, dots ain't in right now but please leave a message, thanks, and yo mama!*

Eye Master picked five special cards out of his stack and shuffled them. It was real important I try my best this time, he said. I squeezed my finger into a sticky gum wad under my chair, and he flashed me all five cards: "Anything?—how about *this?* Anything? *This?*—or this?—or *this?*"

"Nope." "Nope." "Nope." "Nope." "Nope!"

He stuck the last card in my face and gave it a shake. "*No?*—you don't see a number?"

"Nope."

Eye Master's mouth was a straight line.

"Come with me," he said, taking my arm and pulling me past every-body. Loop and the other gritties stepped back. I heard them whisper I was going blind.

In the librarian's office Eye Master closed the door and pulled the shades so the others couldn't see us. The office didn't have the good old smell of books like out in the library—it smelled sharp and mean, like metal and new paint. The light was different too. It sprayed from a white fluorescent tube and ricocheted off the walls and X-rayed everything in the room. If I closed my eyes, I could see the skeleton of the chair and the desk and even of Eye Master, who sat there writing on a piece of paper.

"What's wrong?" I asked him.

With his other hand he pressed his bald head in one spot, leaving a white mark. "You're partly colorblind," he said.

"No I am not."

"Yes you are."

He was still writing. I looked down at his black shoes. "No I am not."

"You're red and green colorblind," he said. "You have trouble with purples, pinks, any hues that contain red or green."

He sounded pretty damn happy about that.

"But I can see colors. I can see red. I can see green too."

"Not the green everyone *else* is seeing. You see colors *differently* than other people. And you have difficulty telling red and green apart."

My throat felt dry as chalk. "I can see colors," I said.

He sighed and turned to me. "Look, the eye detects colors by hav-ing an equal balance of rods and cones, and you have less cones than a person who sees colors normally."

I didn't know what to say about that. Eye Master seemed to have an awful lot to write about my problem, and from what I could make out, the other gritties were right: I was headed for being blind. Today I couldn't see colors. Tomorrow I wouldn't be able to see *things*.

Pops had said fifth grade was gonna grease me.

Eye Master handed me the paper and smiled. "Give that to your parents."

Loop and Clarence and Douglas were waiting out in the library. The way they stared at me you'd have thought I was blind already. "W'sup?" "'Sup?" "'Sup?" they said.

I couldn't look at them. I was a squid.

I walked right out of the library and into the cold blue afternoon light and didn't stop until I reached the basketball courts where I pulled out Eye Master's note and pressed it against the metal post. It was written to *The Parents of Conrad Clay* and said I was not colorblind complete, but pretty damn close.

I stared at the note and swallowed three times. It didn't seem right that a piece of paper could change your whole life. But there it was.

I stuffed the note back in my Raiders jacket and ran all the way out to Naval Housing, where kids screamed and spidered over the monkey bars and a boy with mud on his cheeks pointed a space gun at me. I kept going out to Slime Canal, past the Ferry, and past a ship from China named *Cho Yang.* I watched a pigeon flap out of my way. I wanted to see things like everyone else did. If I practiced my colors enough maybe I'd see them right—like a brutha. Don't worry now eyes, I said, We're gonna set you straight. We just gotta practice:

Yo pigey pidge! I said, You're gray.

Too easy.

I yelled at the ship from China, Yo *Cho!* You're white and red stainy! Get a new paint job please!

Hey you yellow weed, smash! Now you're juice! And what's hangin old black cracky tire?

I pulled out the note from Eye Master of the Universe again. Then I folded it into a spaceship, added a rock for the motor, and launched it into Slime Canal. I didn't wanna worry Moms and Pops with my discount eyes. They had enough trouble. Good-bye note, Peace! I said. Have fun at the bottom of Slime Canal. *Plunk!*

Now you are a sturgeon taco.

2

Gramma was gray.

She had gravy gray skin and gray springy hair she called her "swamp moss," and a shiny gray mole that had started out small when she was ten years old like me and now hung off her cheek like a coat button. There were huge-ass corns hanging off each of her big toes and those were gray too. Gramma talked funny because she came from Exline, Missouri, some tiny town on the other side of America I'd never been to. She was seventy-two and she wore pants.

According to Gramma, she was gonna be in the grave a long time, so she wanted to see a little light while she was still aboveground. That was why we were going for a walk now. We did it almost every day right before the sun went down.

We lived in Alameda, but everybody called it the Island. The only way to Oakland was across Slime Canal on one of the bridges or under it through Webster Tunnel. Mr. Garabedian said that when the Spanish settlers first showed up, giant oak trees covered Alameda, and it was gold-plated for hunting and fishing because of all the deer and ducks, seals, sturgeon and salmon. Even now people still called Alameda *Oakland's Own Hawaii*.

Well there was no Hawaii on me and Gramma's walk. The Naval Station was starting to close down and you saw it all over the neighborhood, from the empty houses to the empty streets. We lived on

Pacific, four houses down from Webster, the busiest street on the Island. Pacific hung off Webster like a dead arm. Gramma said our street reminded her of a boxer's face after fighting Mike Tyson. Houses missing, like knocked-out teeth.

We sleazed past drooping cars and leftover tires, Slurpee cups and underpants. Streetdust soaked up oilspots under buzzing telephone lines, which sagged low and heavy from too many people talking through them. The telephone poles were crooked and burnt black and poked the sky. Empty lots had cracky gray dirt like the skin of an elephant, and trails polished shiny from people walking through on shortcuts to 7-Eleven or Hideout Liquor. Windows were busted out everywhere, even on some houses with people still living in them. The whole street smelled tired and angry.

"Nobody cares about this street," Gramma said.

I cared about it. But I didn't say nothing.

We spotted the old man who had tried to grow a garden in an empty lot next to his house. He was bent down over his sick-ass plants. He'd planted corns and squashes and black-eyed peas, but the plants stuck their heads up complaining or else never grew at all.

"That's what you get for plantin in a *toilet!*" Gramma called out to him.

The man looked up, but when he saw that Gramma's face looked like one big opinion, he turned back to his dying plants and shook his head, sweat drops dripping from his nose. Gramma told me his dirt did not grow plants because it was too busy soaking up pee from the neighborhood dogs. Gramma had a lot of philosophy.

It was getting dark but we took our time and slow-sleazed in the cold air. I didn't tell her about Eye Master and his color cards or about the note I'd launched into Slime Canal. I didn't tell her anything. She said I was awful quiet, just like Granpa used to be. He would walk with her for hours without saying a word.

We turned onto Webster, my favorite street. Since the Naval Station started to close, Webster was the only street still busy and packed with people, and when you walked down it you were in the middle of everything. On Webster, you got straight into life.

Sometimes I'd even spot One-Eye the Pigeon, who was fat and bad at flying and fought cats for food. He mostly tried to keep warm up in the traffic lights, turning his missing eye to the bright hot light. He never chose the green or yellow light. One-Eye roosted in the red.

"Words didn't sit right with your grandfather," Gramma said, looking in the shop windows, "but he was the most generous man anybody ever met. He once got a bonus from John Deere and took a bus all the way to Virginia to visit his family who were very poor. He got on that bus wearing a brand new suit, holding a suitcase full of clothes, and I'll never forget the sight of him two weeks later when I met him at the station."

"What'd he look like?" I said.

"He—" She let out a laugh. "He had on nothing but his T-shirt and a borrowed pair of ragged shorts! And it was the dead of winter! You should've seen those other people getting off the bus, staring at your grandfather like he'd lost his marbles. I could've died right there."

I liked it when Gramma laughed. Her eyes went wet and shiny and you could see the back of her throat wobble.

"He left all his clothes with his family?" I said.

"Right down to his socks. His suitcase too."

"Did you get mad at him?"

She wrinkled her forehead while she thought about it, then her face loosened into a bright, easy smile. "Oh, no. No, no. When I saw your grandfather walk off that bus half-naked and not giving a damn what anybody thought—well, I just loved that man more than anything in the world." She was watching me now. "Too bad he died before you were born."

"He died from cigarettes," I said, remembering what Moms had told me about her pops.

Gramma shook her head and stared down the street. "That ain't it."

"He didn't smoke cigarettes?"

"Oh he *did*—damn him—he did. I didn't allow him to smoke in the house, and one night, it was the coldest Missouri had seen in twenty years, he snuck out to smoke after I was asleep. He slipped on the ice and cracked his head on the corner of the tool shed. By the time I noticed he'd been gone from bed for a while, it was too late. I found him curled up next to the shed. Frozen cemetery-dead."

My skin was all bumpy. The truth about Granpa had me a little scared but I was excited at the same time. The way he died seemed special and important and I couldn't wait to tell Loop and the other gritties about my frozen dead Granpa with a cracked-open head.

Gramma turned to me and let out a sigh. "Yep. That was January of '88. You were still in your mother's belly. I came out here to live with your mother and your father that spring, just in time to see you get born."

We walked a little farther, until Gramma stopped to watch people getting on a bus. They flicked their cigarettes and stepped up into the bone white light inside and I could tell they were after-work people because they didn't smile or look at anyone, just like Moms and Pops when they came home at the end of each day. Once the people got on the bus you could only see them from the belly up. They were unhappy ghosts floating toward the back.

Lately, there were *a lot* of unhappy ghosts walking around Alameda, especially near the Naval Station. More layoffs were coming, and everyone knew the Station was gonna pack it up one day for good. Some people believed it would happen within a year, and they were already moving away to find work. Others said it was gonna take ten years to close down. From what I could see, no one knew exactly which way things were gonna roll, but the workers who were still around, including Moms and Pops, were sticking to the Station like dots to dice.

In four years, Pops was gonna be fifty. Moms was ten years younger than him. Pops wasn't in the Navy anymore, but he still worked on the ships, welding and drilling and bolting and riveting, sometimes even underwater. He'd been fixing ships forever, since he was in Vietnam. When he married Moms, he'd gotten her a job at the Station cafeteria, and even though she didn't like it, she'd been there ever since. She started out serving food. Now she ordered it.

All they seemed to talk about lately were the layoffs. And the talks were starting to become fights.

"Moms and Pops are gonna lose their jobs, aren't they?" I said to Gramma.

"I suppose," Gramma said, as the white bus light flickered off her cheeks.

"What's gonna happen then?"

Her eyes followed the ghosts in the bus. "I'm not sure, Conrad."

She was always sure about *everything*.

"Why not?" I said.

"Because I just don't know."

I didn't like it when grown people said they didn't know. If *they* didn't know, then *who* did?

The bus hacked a cough and hissed and pulled out. Gramma watched it roll away until it was out of sight. "You have to walk a long way through life before you understand things," she said.

"That's why you understand everything now," I said.

"*Me?* Oh Lord, no. I still don't know the half of it, Conrad."

"We better go for more walks, then," I said.

In front of Zeke's Skateshop we went down the line and picked out our favorite skateboards in the window. Gramma said she liked all the colors and I said I did too even though I wasn't sure if I was seeing them right. She stopped in front of an Alien Workshop board with a painting of a silver alien surfing the galaxy. She leaned her forehead against the glass.

"You like that one?" I asked.

She didn't answer. Her face pressed even harder against the glass until her nose was mushed. She closed her eyes.

"Gramma?"

Her fingers spread on the glass like they were trying to hold on. I looked down. Her cracked heels were lifting up out of her shoes.

"*Gramma?*" I said again.

She drank in a big gulp of air and then let it out. "Mmm," she said. She opened her eyes and slowly pushed herself away from the glass until she was standing straight again. "I don't know. I didn't feel so well for a second."

She smiled at me and took another breath. "That's better." She eyed the board in the window. Her face smudge was still on the glass. "That one reminds me of your jacket."

"Yeah," I said, turning to stare at the deck for a second, "silver and black—like the Raiders."

"It sure is shiny," she said.

"I know," I said. But I wasn't eyeing the deck anymore.

I was looking at my Gramma.

Farther down the street we found Pops's Ford truck parked out front of Patti's Bar. I was about to say, There's Pops! but Gramma kept going like the truck wasn't there.

We walked right by it.

Then we passed Suds 'n' Duds, and Gramma said, "You're lucky your head is still small. You won't remember everything."

3

Moms was smoking a cigarette at the bathroom mirror when we came home. She was getting ready to go out, and the mirror filled her face with glowing light. I stood in the hallway to watch her and also to soak in the hot dry air rising up from the heater vent in the floor. Gramma stopped to complain about how hot Moms was keeping the house. She told Moms that she had lizard-blood running through her veins. I figured I did too because I went in for heat just like Moms.

"Why don't you buy yourself a giant heat-rock?" Gramma asked her.

Moms ignored Gramma and brushed out her hair, which was dyed blond, but when I was little I'd drawn it using a yellow marker, so Moms was yellow to me. The way her hair shined now in the bathroom lights, the way it stretched straight with each pull of her brush—that beat out just about anything I'd ever seen and left me feeling all quiet.

Gramma nudged me. "Look at your mother, Conrad," she said. "Ever since she was two years old she's been entertaining herself in mirrors like she was her very own Disney Channel."

I didn't say anything. I liked watching Moms. She entertained me too.

"Should I cut my hair?" Moms said. "Does it make me look like a hussy?"

"Yes!" Gramma said angrily.

Moms put down the brush. She lifted her burning cigarette from the edge of the sink and took a long suck off it, squinting at Gramma the whole while. Gramma couldn't take Moms eyeing her that way and stormed off to her room shaking her head. Moms turned to me for my opinion.

"No," I said.

"Thank you," she said as smoke slipped out of her mouth. "Wanna keep me company while I get ready?"

"Yeah."

I felt the heater vent warming the soles of my shoes as Moms ran the faucet and started telling me about all the problems people at her work were having. As far as I could tell, what Moms mostly did at work was talk with her friends about problems. The more she talked about other people's problems the happier she got.

She splashed her face in the sink and I tried to figure out what problems I had so I could talk to her like the people at work. I couldn't come up with anything except that I was going blind, and I wasn't about to tell her that.

"Where you going tonight?" I asked.

"Your father is taking me to Japanese. He should be home from work any minute."

I almost told her Pops was at Patti's Bar but I didn't want her to start a fight with him when he got home. She didn't like it when he drank and neither did I. When Pops drank it went straight into his fists and his fists sometimes went into me and Moms.

She took a couple sucks off her cigarette, then opened the medicine cabinet and got out her bottle of Actifeds and swallowed a pill with a gulp of Pepsi. Moms was allergic to cigarettes so the only way she could smoke was to take Actifeds. Without the pills she couldn't breathe.

She rubbed some cream under her eyes and patted powder on her cheeks. She drew a dark line around her lips and filled it in with lipstick, then brushed gray over her eyelids. When she was done, she dropped her shoulders and studied her face in the mirror. "Better," she said.

"Do you ever put on red?" I said.

"On my eyes?—no."

"What about green?"

"What am I, Santa Claus?" She let out a laugh and I did too. I was glad she didn't put on green or red.

She checked her watch. "It's almost eight. Why isn't your father home?"

"I don't know," I said. "W'sup wid that?"

She suddenly glared at me. "I don't like it when you talk like that, Con. You're not *black.*"

I felt my face heat up. I was only talking.

She eyed her backside in the mirror. "Where is he, anyway?"

"He's drinking," came Gramma's tired voice from her room.

"How do you know?" yelled Moms.

"He's *always* drinking," Gramma called out. "He'll be drinking till he's a dent in the dirt."

"I don't want to hear it, Mother!" Moms clenched her jaw and threw up her hands.

"Tell me some problems," I said, trying to get her happy again.

She turned to me. "*What?*"

"Tell me about some problems at work."

She picked up her cigarette and took a long puff, then blew the smoke out toward me.

"I'll tell you about a problem," she said. "Your *father* is a problem."

4

It was almost ten o'clock by the time we heard Pops's truck pull up out front. Gramma was asleep in her room. Moms and me were watching television. The front door swung open and Pops stood there blinking at us through his glasses, his dark eyes trying to focus. His camouflage jacket hung crooked on his shoulders and his black and gray curls were flattened back wet. There was a toothpaste plop hanging from his mustache. He always brushed his teeth in the bathroom at Patti's Bar before coming home—he thought it would hide his beer breath.

Pops saw the way Moms was glaring at him, and he turned to me. "She's mad at me, isn't she?"

I didn't know what to say.

He flashed me a smile. *"You're* not mad at me, are you?"

"No."

His eyebrows arched and dropped, like they were figuring out what to do with my answer. He nodded to himself. Then he took a step, stumbled, caught himself on the TV, and kept going towards the hall.

Moms's face looked so angry, I didn't want to be left alone with her. I got up and followed Pops into the hall. He stepped into the bathroom and when he turned to shut the door, he saw me standing there and winked. "Time to pay the water bill," he said, closing the door.

I heard him running the faucet and splashing water. I stood on the heater vent and looked back into the living room. Moms was pointing the channel changer at the TV and flicking wildly through the channels, her eyes cold frozen on the screen.

The toilet seat popped up and Pops started a leak. I liked the sound of Pops's leaks—they were loud and strong and you could hear them from anywhere in the house. When Pops was leaking, everything was all right.

He began to whistle. His leak kept going and going. How much beer could a belly hold?

After almost two minutes it began to be funny. I got the giggles and wanted to laugh, but I knew Moms was mad, so I put it in lay-away. My mouth trembled and my head went hot. I was a meatball and Pops was King Slow-drain.

Suddenly he pulled the bathroom door open. He wasn't peeing at all. He was pouring water from Moms's flower vase into the toilet.

He started laughing and before I knew it I was laughing too. Gramma called out from her room for me to be quiet, but it felt good laughing and I let it out loud.

Me and Pops were busting up together when I opened my eyes and saw Moms standing in front of us. She shook her head at Pops. "You're a shit, Ray."

He seemed surprised. Before he could say anything, she stepped past us into the bedroom and slammed the door shut, locking it.

Pops looked at me. The house heat had steamed up his glasses and turned his eyes into black blurs. "You on my side?" he said.

I was shaking. I didn't know what he was asking me.

He held the vase out. I went to take it, but he moved it just out of my reach. "You on my side?" he said again. He wiped his glasses with his sleeve. His browny black eyes looked far apart, like they were each alone.

"Yes," I said.

He handed me the vase and went to the closed door. "Jan?" he said into the crack.

"Go away," came Moms's voice. "You don't even remember you were supposed to take me to Japanese."

He stared at the door. I could see he remembered now.

"We can still go," he said.

"I don't want to go anywhere with you," she called out. "Just leave me alone."

"Jan," he said. He knocked on the door, then started pounding. "*Open the door, Jan!*"

"Quit it, Ray!" came Gramma's tired voice from her room.

Pops took a step toward Gramma's door and pointed at it. "*No!*" he said. "I won't quit it!" He went back to Moms's door and pounded it so hard with his fist I thought it was going to break. "Open the fucking door, Jan!"

Moms screamed from her room: "*Go away—!*"

"*Open it—!*"

"*Go away! Go away! Go AWAY!*"

Pops let out a roar, then turned and drove his fist through the wall. The whole house shook. His hand was stuck and he had to yank on his arm to free it, pulling out chunks of wall chalk. His knuckles were bleeding. I could hear Moms crying.

Gramma came out from her room and squinted in the hallway light. "You leave my daughter alone," she said in a trembly voice.

Pops got quiet after that. He went into the hall closet, and I listened to him rummage around for a while. I wasn't allowed into that closet. It was where he kept his old things from Vietnam.

When he came out, he was carrying a long brown cloth case and a small cardboard box. I'd never seen either one before. He saw me and pointed at the closet. "You know what I'll do if I ever catch you in there?"

I nodded. He'd beat me black-and-blue—that's what he'd told me a million times. He walked to the living room and sat on the couch and set the box and case on the coffee table in front of him. I went out to watch him. He unzipped the case and pulled out three pieces of a rifle. My heart was pounding.

He clicked the three pieces together.

"Why did you get that out?" I said.

"To clean it."

"Why?"

He took a small can of oil out of the case. "So I can *use* it." He started dabbing the rifle with oil.

"What are you gonna use it on?"

"People."

He opened the cardboard box, which was filled with bullets, shiny and gold and lead-tipped. He took one out and slipped it into the rifle.

"That sonofabitch is gonna get what he deserves," he said.

"Who?"

He cocked the rifle, held it up to his cheek, and aimed it at the television. "The guy who's breaking into houses around here. I saw Sam at the bar tonight. Said the sonofabitch stole his TV yesterday. Right out of his living room."

"You gonna shoot him?" I said.

He turned and aimed the rifle at me.

"Why . . . you afraid?"

The hole at the end of the barrel was staring at me like one of Pops's dark drunk eyes.

"Not me," I said. "No way."

5

"How come Pops doesn't sleep in the bedroom with Moms anymore?" I said.

I hadn't been able to sleep after seeing Pops get out his rifle, so I'd gone into Gramma's room and was lying with her in the dark. We could hear the couch squeak each time Pops rolled over out in the living room.

"Because," Gramma said with a wet, cracking voice, "the spirit left the bedroom."

I didn't know what she meant, only that it sounded like the stone cold truth.

She sat up and clicked on the dresser lamp, then opened the drawer and got out a bottle of dark stuff she kept there. Gramma was against drinking, but everybody knew she liked her "cough syrup," which she also called her Sea of Galilee. She turned away from me and took sips from the bottle and I watched her bent back breathe. A loud snore suddenly came from the living room, and she capped the bottle and put it away. "I ain't the sharpest tool in the shed," she said. "But I know something is brewing, and I want you to be careful around your father."

I felt my chest go tight. "He's just sleeping out there quiet," I said.

"For now, maybe."

She clicked off the lamp and put her head back down on the pillow. "The sun is gonna come up soon and your mother will too if we don't stop talking and go to bed."

I couldn't go to bed now. That rifle was still in my head.

"First tell me the story about the Odors," I said. Whenever I had worries, I asked Gramma to tell me the same story. I liked knowing what was gonna happen.

"All right," Gramma said, "but only if you promise to go back to your room afterwards. Your grandma is getting too old to see the sun come up without having slept at all."

"I promise," I said.

"You have to imagine it was a long time ago, back in the Middle Ages. You didn't put on airs and you didn't think you knew every goddamn thing just because you read your newspaper and got a schooling like the young people do nowadays. You didn't see your greed you got nowadays either because there wasn't much money floating around. And the men weren't losing their britches to get rich quick like every Tom, Dick and Harry is today. Some of the men lived differently. Away from all the ruckus you had in the villages. They lived in a cloister on a high bluff overlooking mountains and valleys and maybe a river too."

"But tell me about the Odors," I said.

"I'm getting to it—hold your *horses*. Well, these men were studying to be men of God. They didn't discuss it, but in their hearts most of the men dreamed of being saints one day; very few ever made it that far. They lived without nothing, and it ought to make us ashamed the way we're livin now. Most days, they ate a dry slice of bread and if they were lucky, a nibble of cheese—"

"What about where they slept?"

"Quit interrupting, *dammit!*" She picked something out of her eyeball. "Oh hell. Where was I? At night the men slept on a stone floor in rooms so small, you couldn't swing a cat by the tail in there. Well, they grew old and did good deeds and studied their Scriptures, but they knew the angel with the sword could stop by any hour of any day, and they waited with joy for God to make his move and take them up to the firmament. And one-by-one, God surely took 'em, and that was when the others—whose time wasn't up yet—knew which of the men had become saints."

"Because of the Odors," I said.

"That's right. The Odors of Sanctity were the sign—made it known to everyone who the saints were. If a man died and his body gave off a sweet odor of honey and lemon trees, then you knew he was a saint."

No matter how many times Gramma told me the story, I always got a scary, tingly feeling all down through me when the men died and their sweet smell said they were saints. It was like they got to live again.

"Now it's way past late and I'm going to sleep," Gramma said. "So don't pester me no more. Love you, Conrad Clay."

"I love you more."

"I love you the most."

"I love you in the whole world," I said.

She pulled the blanket over her.

"That beats me to all hell, so good night."

I didn't go to bed. I snuck into the living room to look at Pops. He was asleep on the couch, using his camouflage jacket for a blanket. The television was firing blue licks of light out into the dark room.

I dropped down on my knees next to him without making a sound. He still had on his socks, and his glasses lay on the coffee table next to his keys. High on his nose were two small bruises where his glasses usually touched. I wanted to reach out with my thumb and finger and touch them too. His nose suddenly blasted a snort and I froze as his pressed lips rose like they were kissing the air. Then his lips parted and blew sour drinking breath at my face. It was my favorite time with Pops. When he was asleep.

His eyes suddenly popped open.

"Hey," he said.

"Hi."

"You watching me?"

"Yeah."

"Good."

He closed his eyes again.

"Still watching me?"

"Yeah."

"Still on my side?"

"Yeah."

A smile broke across his face. "What are you doing up?"

"Nothing. Gramma was telling me a story."

He was quiet. Television light flickered his face.

"You wanna hear *another* story?" he said.

"Okay."

He sat up slow, blinking and wiping his eyes, and turned to face the television. "You can't tell your mother this one," he said.

I looked back into the hallway at Moms's closed door. It suddenly felt like Pops and me were doing something wrong.

"I gotta know you're with me on this, Con. Otherwise I won't tell you this story."

"I ain't telling," I said.

His mouth opened to speak, but nothing came out. It just hung open like a fishmouth, drinking in the blue television light. When he finally spoke, it was slow and careful, like each word was costing a C-note: "This morning, I went in to work and put on my clothes. Our boss Ronald came over with his sheet. He said they'd located rust in one of the *Nimitz'* bilges, probably a hairline fracture. So me and Moose"—he was Pops's best friend from work—"lugged our welding box through the ship. The bilge was a sewer, only *hot*. It was at least ninety degrees in there. Moose and I stood there cussing at the bilge for fifteen minutes. Then we got to work. The job was a nightmare— rust leaking from a quarter inch of old marine paint. Took us all morning just to get the paint off. Had to use acid. Try wearing venti- lators in heat like that. And the sewage smell *still* came through our filters. We had the fracture filed clean by three in the afternoon. Still hadn't had lunch. Moose said, 'Hell, let's just finish it out.' You know Moose."

I *did* know Moose. Pops didn't trust any man on the job as much as him. If something went wrong, like a fire in the engine room, you didn't wanna get trapped with anyone else. In the crunch, Pops always said, you want Moose. I hoped someday me and Moose would get trapped on a sinking ship. I wanted to be in the crunch with Moose too.

"Anyway," Pops said, "Moose and I can lay a weld line any time, any place, better than anyone. We had that sucker sealed clean and ready for the paint crew by *four-thirty*. I told Moose I'd buy us Mexican if he carried the weld box. When we were changing back at the lockers, Ronald came over. Said he wanted to talk to me in private. We went back in the coffee room and he shut the door. He talked a little about the Station closing—same old shit we all know. Then he talked about the 'Second Wave.' What the hell was he talking about?—*I* didn't know. He said I was in the Second Wave. My not being union was the reason. He kept saying we'd *all* be affected eventually. I asked him what the hell was the Second Wave and he poured himself a coffee and without even looking at me he said, 'Layoffs.' I asked him if he was firing me. 'Letting you go,' he said. He was pouring cream into his fucking coffee and he said, 'I'm letting you go, Ray.' He paid me for the work I'd done up through this afternoon. Then I was gone."

Pops sat there for a second, staring at the television, then he lay back down and covered himself with his jacket and closed his eyes.

I was clutching the edge of the couch. I could hardly breathe.

Pops's eyelids twitched in the changing television light. "Go to sleep," he said.

I stood up and headed toward my room, but I stopped in the hallway over the heater vent to let the hot air blow up inside my pajamas. I lowered my face into the dusty black heat and breathed in its baked metal smell. In the living room, Pops was a small dark shape on the couch.

"Good night Pops," I called out quiet.

There was no answer.

6

The windows wouldn't break.

Loop said the Navy had built them extra thick for when the Russians bombed us. I said we weren't using big enough rocks.

It was the day after Pops had told me his story, and me and Loop were in a big gravel lot at the edge of the Naval Station. Rain was coming down and nobody was around. On the other side of the cyclone fence sat three warehouses with a million dusty gray windows ripe for some black holes.

I wished the Russians *had* bombed the Station. It was the Station's fault for firing Pops. They were the ones making him drink. I could just see it: missiles dropping from a cloudy sky, Pops's boss running like a roach, then *BOOM! BOOM! BOOM!*

I yelled a bunch of swears at the Station. Then I picked up a big gravel rock and flung it. *POP!* A window smashed inward and all the glass was suddenly gone, like the building had sucked the window into its black belly.

"Yeah!" we yelled and grabbed some more big ones. We flung them through the drizzle drops, our frozen fingers burning. We nailed thirty. *Pling! Pling! POP!*

"Hey!" came a shout. A workman ran out of one of the buildings and watched my last rock fly over his head and smash another window. "Goddammit!" he yelled.

He ran at us.

Me and Loop grabbed our decks and said, "Mission accomplished!" We tore out across the crunchy lot, wet gravel popping under our soles.

"Book!" I yelled.

"I am!" said Loop.

I looked back. The fence had stopped the man from going any farther. At the street we threw down our decks and cooked out of there. Sail away soldiers!

Me and Loop weren't just any two gritties—we were flatland lowgrounders, since there weren't any hills to deck in Alameda like there were over in Oaktown. Gramma said we had propellers in our rears, but she was wrong or we'd have hopped on our boards a long time ago and flown the hell out of Alameda with the geese.

Every gritty got a name. Loop's real name was Norman, but he became Loop because he could mack two boxes of Froot Loops in one shot. At first Douglas called him Froot Loop, but he kicked Douglas's ass for the *Froot* part, so for the sake of purposes I said, "How about just *Loop?*"

My gritty-name was Con, which I was never happy about until I learned that a *con* was a guy in prison lock-down. Which was cool.

We shredded onto a street pasted with soggy leaves.

"Land mines!" yelled Loop.

You didn't wanna hit a mine or else be a human rocket blasting. Watch out you soggies, we're coming through! We rolled from corner to corner and from street to street. We plowed puddles and ollied gardens and sent flowers flying. We weren't scared of getting caught since the houses slept dark and dead with no people in them. Wake up now houses!

Loop rolled ahead and started a rap: *"Sleazin, sleazin . . ."*

I yelled back, *"We aims to be pleazin . . ."*

"Twistin and twirlin . . ."

"We wants to go girlin!"

Loop's wheels shot a galaxy of silver spray. He said, *"Near and far . . ."*

"We ain't gots a car!"

"Dang," Loop said. "I can't think of the next line."

"*The East Bay Gritties . . .*" I yelled.

"*They needs the titties!*"

I laughed straight out. Loop was a Coupe de Luxe.

I said, "*We eats ham and eggs . . .*"

"*The waitress gots legs!*" yelled Loop.

I said, "*We . . . We . . .*" That was all I could come up with.

"*We breaks plates and dishes . . .*" Loop yelled.

"*Till she gives up the kisses!*"

He said: "*And get her all cryin . . .*"

I smiled and pointed at his back: "*Tell us if we lyin!*"

We lipslided the corner onto Park Street. A bus wheel hit a brown puddle and mudflecked my Raiders jacket but I didn't want to lose Loop and kept going. We passed a bunch of shop windows that said: HELP WANTED HELP WANTED HELP WANTED HELP WANTED.

Give me some help too! I said.

In front of Mission for the Homeless we slalomed the cement-sleepers. We decked side-by-side, splitting apart to go around people, then joining back together. We were water rushing around a rock. Outside Sunshine Market we scared two old wilmas with a 360 at their feet and left them straight-out mad clucking. We backside ollied the bus bench past old fossil Mr. Honig in his newsstand.

"Hey . . . !" Mr. Honig said.

"Hey! Hey! Hey!" we said.

Rain rammed us as we decked down Central, the longest street on the Island. Loop went fast, I went fast. We puffed hot breaths. We were locomotives. I didn't care about my wet clothes soaked cold. I didn't care about anything. Heavy drops hacked my head and filled my eyes and Loop swam blurry ahead and I did too and man was I happy. I wished Central Street was not the longest in Alameda but the longest in the world and kept going past the Naval Station and over the bay and through San Francisco and then all the way to Hawaii. I wished Central took us all the way to Japan. That would take sixty years for me and Loop. Then I could be happy for sixty years.

• • •

We eyeballed the 7-Eleven all lit up and bright across the parking lot. We had three dollars, eighty-five cents. We were starving.

"Let's jack some Skittles," I whispered.

"Skittles be for squids," Loop said.

"I know," I said quickly. "I ain't jonesin for no sea-slug Skittles, noamsayin?"

"Yeah," said Loop.

Loop gave me all his money and said for me to buy some Slurpees. I could see he was up to something. We flipped up our decks and ran across the greasy lot. Water rainbowed silver and blue over the grease. *Splash! Splash! Splash!* We were trouts.

Inside 7-Eleven, Shahid was behind the counter like usuals, keeping a stink eye on everyone who sleazed in. We took a long look at him. He took a long look at us.

I walked up to the counter. "Shahid, give us a Riptide Raspberry, please, and also a Cherry Blast!"

Shahid watched the puddle of water spreading around my feet. His eyes were hooded and his face drooped. He looked tore down. Like a person who was dead and didn't know it.

"Show me your money," he said.

He never believed that Loop and me had cash. Sometimes we didn't.

I slapped two dollars on the counter. He took it and rang up two Slurpees and gave me eight cents change, then went to pour our Slurpees. "Shake it please so no air bubbles," I said.

I turned to see Loop jacking some Hot Tamales. When he stuffed a box of Froot Loops down his jacket, I started getting scared. Any squid could see he had something down there and Shahid was almost done with our Slurpees. I started playing with my zipper, *Zoot! Zoot!*

Shahid spun around and handed me the Slurpees, which shook in my hands like two Cherry Blast volcanoes spilling to the floor. He stared at me, waiting for me to leave. My legs felt weak. I turned slow and followed Loop out of the store. I could feel a spot on the back of my head where Shahid's eyes focused. Suddenly we were outside in the cold again.

"Tuh!" said Loop.

"Puh!" I said.

Loop looked back at the store and flipped Shahid the finger. "C-ya wouldn't wanna be ya!" His voice was trembling.

We stopped at the sidewalk. "Wanna go home?" he said to me.

"Let's drink our Slurpees," I said. I didn't want to go home. Loop had two brothers at his house. He was lucky. I didn't have any.

We crossed the street to the empty self-car wash so we could marinate against the cinder-block wall and watch the rain. Our clothes dripped water onto the smooth cement and we laughed at our purple tongues and pretended we weren't scared anymore. Then we got quiet and stared at the 7-Eleven.

"Nickel-and-dime fake-ass store," Loop said.

"Yeah," I said.

Our finger bones hurt and our faces froze. I blew warm air into my hands but it didn't help. Loop pulled the Hot Tamales and Froot Loops out of his jacket and set them on his skateboard. We poured half the Hot Tamales into my hand and half into his. I popped five in my mouth and slid the rest into my pocket for later. We got busy with the Froot Loops. Loop said he had the purples and asked me if I wanted the greens, reds, oranges, or yellows. I said the yellows straight out, because that was the only color I was sure of. I was glad for the yellows.

We finished out the Froot Loops and stared at the empty box.

"I'm cold," I said.

Loop slugged me in the chest and got up.

"Where you goin?" I asked him, but he disappeared around the corner. I looked up: over my head, water hoses hung down at me like snakes. A blast of wind slapped a nozzle against the metal arm and swung it around to the other side with a long squeak. It was the loneliest sound I'd ever heard and I was glad when Loop came running back.

"Give me all your cheddar!" he said, excited.

I didn't know what havocs he was up to now but I was in on it no matter what. I handed over all the change in my pocket and followed him back out into the rain to a rusty metal coin box that said:

ALAMEDA SELF-CAR WASH
HOT RINSE $1.75

Below, some squid had crossed out WAX and written:

SEX $3.50

Loop concentrated putting coins into the box. It wasn't easy because our hands were cold stiffs. You could tell no one had washed their car that day by the empty *clang* each coin made when it hit the bottom.

"But we ain't got a car to rinse," I said.

Loop looked up at me, all mad. "You cold?"

"Yeah."

"Puh! Then we gonna put *ourselves* through."

He plopped the last coin into the coin box. *Chi-Ching!* The box cranked into buzzing.

"Come on!" Loop said.

Back under the car wash, the overhead pipes hissed and clanged and we stood under them and waited. "It's comin!" Loop shouted, "It's comin!" Steam began to stream out of the pipe holes and float away in the wind. Then drops. Me and Loop let them hit our faces. Warm water dripped down over us and seeped into our clothes, but we were so frozen that we stood still so not a drop would miss us. The water grew boiling hot but we didn't care and hung tough like thawing-out beef patties.

The machine banged and clacked and the water went soapy but we still didn't pull out. We were warm-blooded jumping beans, yelling and hopping up and down under hot misty soapwater.

Then the water stopped. We were still covered with soap, like two white foam puffs.

"Why'd it stop?" I said.

"It's changin over to the rinse cycle," said Loop.

He grabbed the spray gun and blasted me and blasted himself too. I screamed, "Hit me! Hit me!" and he shot the spray at my face, knocking me over. I laughed and got back up and leaned my face into Loop's spray. The water pricked my cheeks and sandblasted me until I felt clean of everything. Clean of our dusty, broke-down streets. Clean of Shahid's staring eyes. Clean of Eye Master's note and of being color-blind too. I felt clean of Pops's beer breath problems and late-night secrets.

Loop handed me the gun and told me to blast him back, and the hot rinse washed us down and warmed us up and we didn't care about anything except it was the best time we ever had.

Ever.

Even after the box clicked off and the buzzing stopped and the spray did too, we kept laughing and falling down because we couldn't stand on happy knees wobbling. Our clothes felt heavy and warm and wet on our skin, and we flopped on the slippery cement like bass pulled from the bay. We slid and rolled around under the rubber snakes until all our laughing evaporated up to the sky.

7

I turned the corner onto Pacific Street and spotted Moose's King-cab truck out front of our house. I could see Pops leaning against it, talking to him through the rolled-down window. Moose was wearing a blue flannel shirt and it looked like he'd just come from work. He was big and brown and had a mustache that flowed over his mouth and hooked up with his beard below. When I was little I'd thought he was a real moose, with secret fur under his clothes.

When I got up close, I saw that they were arguing. Moose was staring at his dashboard and pulling on his mustache with his fingers. "No, it doesn't feel right," he was telling Pops. "Lin's probably waiting for me at home, anyway."

"Come *on*, Moose," Pops said. "Just come in."

Moose looked up and saw me. "Hey, it's Conrad! Looks like you ran into some rain."

"W'sup, Moose?" I said.

He smiled and stuck his hand out his window to shake. His hand was bigger than my head and I took hold of it, expecting him to vice-grip me, but he only gave me a soft shake.

"Are you comin in?" I said.

"No. I just got off—" He stopped and eyed Pops. "*We* just got off work—"

"Con knows," Pops said, nodding at me.

Moose's smile disappeared. His finger tapped the steering wheel.

"*Come on*, man," Pops said to him. "Just this one time."

I could see now that Pops was asking him to come in and pretend that he and Pops had both worked today. I felt embarrassed standing there. Moose finally shook his head and got out of the truck. "All right," he said.

Pops put his arm around him. "That's my buddy."

I followed them into the house. Moms got up from watching television when she saw Moose walk in with us, and gave him a hug. Moose was her favorite. He didn't swear or tell dirty jokes like Pops's other friends, and he was sweet to his wife Lin. Moms asked him to stay for dinner—Gramma was cooking—and Moose tried to get out of it, but Moms won.

Then Pops said he had something to show Moose. For a second I thought he was going to bring out the rifle, but he took Moose into the kitchen and Moms sat back down to watch TV. I ran to the kitchen to see what Pops was talking about. Gramma was just pulling a pot roast out of the oven, and Pops was looking for something under the counter.

"Don't bump into me, Ray, dammit," Gramma said. "It's hot!"

"Need some help, Esther?" Moose asked her.

"No, I don't," Gramma said. "Just stay outta my way."

Moose smiled and stepped aside as Gramma poked the pot roast with a fork. She caught me and Moose staring. "You two look like a couple of starving tapeworms." She took two forks and stabbed some potato chunks and held them out to us. "Here! Don't pester me again till suppertime." Me and Moose blew on our steaming pieces of potato and barely got them into our mouths before she took our forks away. "Now get out, all three of you! And Con, change into some dry clothes before you catch your death."

"Hold it," Pops said. "I'm showing Moose my new tea."

He pulled a big glass bowl out from under the counter. It was filled with black liquid and covered with tinfoil. I'd never seen it before.

"What the hell is that?" Gramma said.

"It's Kombucha tea," Moose said.

Pops set the bowl on the counter and removed the tinfoil, and we all gathered around to look. A huge blob of fungus floated on top of the black liquid. It smelled moldy and sharp, like rotten bread and burning matchsticks. Gramma pinched her face. "You're drinking *that?* Looks like mold to me."

"It is," Moose said.

Gramma eyed Moose and put her hands on her hips. "You got Ray drinking this crap?"

"I know it looks bad. But Lin's been drinking it for years," Moose said. "I used to make fun of her, but then she got me to try it. I swear I never felt better. It actually doesn't taste bad. You just drink the tea, not the mold."

"They've been drinking this for thousands of years in Japan," Pops said. "Supposed to make you live longer."

Gramma gave the fungus a good looking-over. "Yeah, well you ain't getting me to drink it. My mother lived to be ninety-seven drinking nothing but creek water and homemade whiskey and she would've cracked you over the head with an iron skillet if you told her drinking moldy tea would make her live any longer. So how do you like *them* apples?"

She was waiting for an answer. Pops and Moose looked at her. They didn't seem to know what to say. She eyeballed them a second longer, then got busy whipping together ketchup and mayonnaise for the salad dressing.

Pops and Moose turned back to the tea. Pops filled two cups with the stuff, pouring slowly so the fungus didn't spill out. The fungus jiggled on top of the water like a pile of pudding. He handed a cup to Moose, who drank it down in three gulps, then set the cup on the counter and ran his tongue around his mouth. Pops watched him closely.

"Well?" Pops said.

"Hm," Moose said.

"Right?"

Moose let his head fall to both sides like he was weighing things in either ear. "Yep," he said.

"Huh?" Pops's lips were working on a smile.

"Uh huh."

"What'd I tell you?"

"Yeah," Moose said, licking his lips.

"I got it right, didn't I?"

"Not bad."

Pops smiled proud. He picked up his cup of tea, looked into the black juice, then poured it down his throat. He slammed the cup down and smiled at us.

Gramma eyeballed him like he was crazy. "Well," she said with a grumpy voice, "Feel any younger?"

"Like a newborn baby," Pops said.

Gramma had dinner ready by the time I changed into dry clothes and came back out to the dining room. Everyone was seated at the table, and she slapped slices of roast onto plates and handed them out.

"Mmm," Pops said, taking his plate, "Sure is nice to have a home-cooked meal."

"Why, thank you, Ray," Gramma said.

"This looks great, Esther!" Moose said.

Moms stared at Gramma. Then at the roast. "At the cafeteria today we cooked roast turkey for three hundred people," she said. She was trying to start a fight with Gramma. She was doing that a lot lately.

Gramma looked at her, then got up and went into the kitchen. Pops gave his neck a crack. Nobody said anything. From where I sat, I could see Gramma getting a pack of processed turkey out of the fridge. She slipped it into her apron pocket. Whenever things got greasy at dinner, Gramma always tried to make me feel better by sneaking me processed meat slices. Processed meat was my favorite because they worked on it more than normal meat, so it tasted better. Right on the package it said what they did to the meat:

CUT

CHOPPED

SMOKED

PRESSED

COOKED

Normal meat just said USDA CHOICE on the package, which to me meant they were too lazy to do any work on the meat to make it taste better. They hadn't given it a *process*.

Gramma came back in with a pot of beans, which she pushed toward Pops. "Here, Ray, try some green beans."

Moms watched Pops fork a few. "Those don't looked cooked enough, Mother."

"I cooked 'em just fine," Gramma said.

She and Moms locked eyes. Pops cracked his neck again.

Moms turned to him. "How was work today, Ray?"

My heart almost popped out of my chest. I picked up my fork and pressed it against my cheek. Gramma dropped a slice of processed turkey onto my plate while no one was watching. I folded it and stuck it into my mouth.

"*Ray?*" Moms said, hawking him with her eyes.

He ignored her and took a bite of beef and turned to me. "What'd you do today, Con?"

"Nothin. Just school. Then we decked out to the Station."

"Who's *we?*"

"Probably that friend of his," Moms said. "What's your friend's name—Scoop? Poop?"

"*Loop,*" I said, staring at my food.

Moms gave Moose a look. "His friend is black."

Gramma slipped a slice into my hand under the table.

Moose smiled at me. "What part of the Station did you guys skate-board to?"

"Out near Ale's Bar."

"*Ale's?*" Pops said. He jabbed Moose. "Remember that place? Moose and I used to have some wild times there."

"Naw," Moose said, chewing a chunk of meat.

"Sure we did," Pops said. He turned to me. "Did you know Moose used to be the meanest sonofabitch in Alameda?"

Moose looked up at me and dipped a shoulder toward Pops. "He's just playing with ya."

"Oh, come on!" Pops said. "I could tell some stories—"

"Ray, stop!" Moms said. She glared at him. "Moose doesn't want to hear your stupid stories. Nobody does. Can't we just talk normally?"

Pops's face filled with blood and his eyes narrowed on her. He looked like he was going to hop the table and pounce on her. She ignored him and sipped her glass of Pepsi.

"This pot roast is great," Moose said with his mouth full. He pressed his knife and fork down on the table in order to shift in his chair.

Gramma turned to Moms. "Aren't you gonna try the roast, Jan?"

"Huh?" Moms said.

"The roast," Gramma said. "Why aren't you interested in your food?"

Moms's forehead wrinkled. "I work with food all fucking day, Mother. Just give me a chance, okay?"

"You don't have to cuss," Gramma said.

"Why not? *You* do."

Pops stood up. "Want a beer, Moose?"

"Mm!" Moose said. "That sounds real good."

Gramma's hand was waiting for me down low where no one could see, holding another slice of processed turkey. I waited until nobody was looking and stuffed it into my mouth.

"So how was work today, Moose?" Moms said.

"Oh, you know." Moose didn't look up. He shoved more food into his mouth and said, "Same old, same old." He pointed his knife towards Pops in the kitchen. "We had to recut some pipe. Water pump. It was rusted straight through. That's about it."

He was covering Pops's back, but I could see that Moms was starting to sniff. She had a way of pulling stuff out of you without you even knowing it. If she wanted to find out about something, she never asked you direct. Moms came at things sideways.

When Pops sat back down she watched him real close. He set two bottles of beer on the table and we all stared at them for a while. Finally, he and Moose reached out and twisted the caps off. They lifted the bottles to drink at the same time, taking long gulps until their bottles were high in the air. The bottles came down and they wiped their mouths.

Moose licked his lips and said, "You all are invited to a barbeque tomorrow. Lin and I are cooking up ribs." He nodded at me. "Con," he said. Then he looked at Gramma. "Esther." Then Moms. "Jan." Next he turned to Pops's bottle of beer. "Ray—you're all invited to come eat barbeque."

He lifted his bottle and finished his beer. We were all quiet until Moms said, "Well, thank you, Moose. That's sweet of you."

Pops cracked his neck. Then he got up and brought back more beers—a six-pack this time. I could see Moms wasn't happy about it. I wasn't either.

He and Moose slurped their way through the beers and told stories about work while Moms sat across the table, eyeing them. Pops said what about the time a rudder broke out of Guam and everyone thought it couldn't be fixed in the middle of the seas? He and Moose had to swim underwater and weld the rudder back together while sharks tried to eat them. Pops said that was the first time in the history of the Navy anyone had ever welded a two-ton rudder on the open sea. He and Moose banged their beers together and Pops said they were the best welders in the goddamn Navy and how come they weren't being paid more? *"You know?"* he said to Moose. "I mean, why aren't we paid more? You know what I'm saying?" He looked so concerned about it that I was sure he'd flat forgotten he wasn't welding for the Navy anymore at all.

Moms got the bottle of rum from the kitchen and poured some into her glass of Pepsi. She took a small sip and stared at Pops with a tight straight mouth. Pops didn't notice her, but Moose's eye kept sliding over to meet hers. He looked nervous. Pops put an arm around him. "You can't tell me I don't lay the best bead in Alameda," Pops said. He pulled Moose's face until it smashed against his chest. Moose was looking at Moms. "You know it, don't ya?" Pops said to him.

Moose pushed Pops away. "Ahh," he said.

Moms took a sip from her drink, watching them.

"I'm the best," Pops said to Moose, "and you know it. You know it's true. Give me an arc welder. Give me goddamn Elmer's glue. I'll put any two things back together."

"Except your life," Moms said.

Pops flashed a wide smile and he held it up for Moms to shake her head at.

"Well," Moose said, standing up. "I should go."

I was real sorry to hear that, and it looked like everyone else was too.

"Naw," Pops said to him, "You don't have to go."

"Yeah. I do."

Pops took Moose's arm. "C'mon, Moose—"

Moose yanked his arm back and glared at him. "I do, Ray. Lin's waiting for me. Jan, Esther, thanks for dinner. See you tomorrow at the barbeque. Bye, Con."

He left the dining room. We sat at the table and listened to him open the front door. When he was gone, Gramma said she was tired out and had better start cleaning up. Only me and Moms and Pops were left at the table, and I kept my eyes on my plate.

Pops suddenly stood up. *"Sick* of it," he said under his breath. He left the table.

Me and Moms looked at each other. Her eyes were wet. The screen door slammed and we heard Pops out front.

"Sick of it!" he yelled.

I was woken up that night by the sound of running water, and I got out of bed. The house was completely dark except for a light coming from the kitchen.

Pops stood at the sink, still wearing his camouflage jacket. He was running the faucet at full blast. The bowl of fungus tea was on the counter.

I could tell by the sleepy sunk look in his face that he wasn't in one of his hitting moods, and I went and stood next to him. He smelled of cigarettes and beer.

He looked at me for a second, then went back to staring at the water. "You have to run the water for five minutes," he said.

"Why?"

"Get all the pollutants out. From the pipes."

He turned the water down to a trickle, then picked up the bowl of tea and filled it until the jiggly blobs of fungus were almost level with the top of the bowl. He set the bowl back down on the counter.

"Is it making the tea now?" I said.

"No. You have to put it in the dark and wait for the fungus to grow back."

"Why?"

"So the byproduct will leak down into the water."

We stared at the chunks of floating fungus for a while.

"You have to let it sweat," I said.

Pops let out a tired chuckle. "Yeah, that's right."

"When's the sweat gonna come out?"

"Couple days, maybe." He pressed the tinfoil back over the bowl, then slid it under the counter and shut the cabinet. "Keep an eye on it."

"I will."

8

Moose and Lin expected us at noon. Pops filled a cooler with beers and Pepsis and carried it out to the living room where Moms was brushing her hair. Gramma came out of her room, wearing a white hat and a bright smile, ready to go. "Alrighty," she said.

Moms eyeballed her. "Just the three of us are going today, Mother."

"*Jan*," Pops said. "Moose invited her too."

Moms and Gramma glared at each other.

"Just the three of us today," Moms said.

Gramma was silent. Moms raised an eyebrow at her. Pops looked like he didn't know what to do. Why was he letting Moms be so mean to Gramma?

"Oh *hell!*" Gramma said finally. She headed back to her room. Moms's eyes followed her until she was out of sight.

"Let's go," Moms said, turning to me and Pops. She walked out the door.

"Come on, Con," Pops said, picking up the cooler.

Moms was waiting in the Celica, eyeing herself in the rearview mirror. Pops put the cooler on the backseat and I squeezed in next to it, then Pops got in and started the engine.

When Moms caught me looking at her in the mirror, she squinted at me. "Your grandmother thinks that just because she cooks dinner on Friday nights she's the mother of the house," she said. "Well, *I'm* the mother." She lit a cigarette, sucked on it, and studied herself in the mirror again. "I should have worn my blue dress," she said, filling the car with smoke. "Don't you think?"

I didn't know who she was asking.

"It's fine," Pops said.

He backed us out onto the street and eased us toward Webster. I saw his hand move over to her knee. He'd already forgotten about Gramma.

Moose's driveway was long and we pulled all the way in and parked beside the backyard. Pops's other friends from work, Frog and T.C., were helping Moose with the barbeque. Moose held his baby, Freddy, who was wrapped in a brown blanket like a slug. They all turned and smiled when we got out of the car. I didn't like them smiling at us. They still had their jobs.

T.C. said hello. Frog breathed in, puffed out his chest, and made a loud bullfrog sound. Moms went to sit with Moose's wife, Lin, on the back steps. Lin was Japanese.

Me and Pops carried the cooler over to the guys at the barbeque. Moose set Freddy down on the grass to play, and everyone grabbed beers and popped them open. T.C. kept one hand in his pocket and slouched his skinny stomach forward. He didn't seem to have a chest. He sipped his beer and eyed Pops. Frog did too.

"How's it going, Ray?" Frog finally said.

"Yeah," said T.C. "How're you doing now, Ray?"

Pops looked at them like they were crazy. "What d'ya mean, 'How am I doing *now?*' I'm doing *great!*"

Frog started to say, "I just meant with you getting laid off—"

"Everything's great!" Pops said. "Everything's fine. Right?"

The men all stared at him and nodded their heads. I could see they knew Pops was lying. I saw fear in their eyes too. It was only a matter of time before they lost their jobs just like he had. I stuck my face over the barbeque and breathed in the hot smoke. It burned my throat.

"I'm starving," Pops said. "Con, move over."

He threw some ribs and hamburger patties on the fire and we all watched them sizzle.

"Freddy!" came Lin's yell.

We looked down. Freddy had a charcoal brick in his mouth. His hands and face were black and dark drool had dribbled over his T-shirt. Lin ran out and scooped him up. His arms and legs drooped down like he was a soft stick of butter. She pulled the charcoal chunk out of his mouth and flung it at Moose, yelling that it was his fault for not keeping an eye on Freddy and now it was his turn to give him a bath. She handed Freddy over to him, and Freddy's face mushed into Moose's belly, rubbing black charcoal all over it as Moose tried to get a grip on Freddy's flab. Freddy was a jellyball.

"But I'm barbequing," Moose said to Lin, giving Freddy back to her.

"Eeeeeee!" said Freddy.

"*Moose*," Lin said. "I'm talking to Jan—"

"I'll do it!" I said.

Everybody turned to me.

"There," Moose said. "Con'll do it."

Lin gave him a mean look. Then she blew out some air. "Come on, Conrad," she said. "I'll show you how."

I followed her up the steps past Moms.

"Careful, Con," Moms said.

"I know."

Moose and Lin's house was filled with pillows and cushions and paper kites from Japan. I liked being in there—it smelled old and salty and solid, like a thousand dinners had been cooked in it.

In the bathroom Lin ran the tub and I took a big breath. I was glad to be away from Moms and Pops. Lin had me grab the towel off the door and spread it on the toilet seat. She lay Freddy on his back and told me to take his diaper off while she filled his plastic bath in the tub.

"How do I undo his diapers?"

"There," she said, pointing to Freddy's sides. "Peel it off."

Freddy said, "Eeeeee!" and kicked his feet while I pulled off his diaper. It was clean.

"Now what?"

"Did you get his shirt off?"

I lifted Freddy's shirt up over his head and his big round eyes watched my face.

"Okay, bring him over," Lin said.

"Pick him up?"

"Don't be afraid."

I put my hands under his arms. "Here?"

"Yep."

Freddy watched me while I lifted him. He was heavy as a watermelon. I moved him over to the tub and his legs hung straight down like King Kong being lifted by a helicopter.

"All right, set him down in the tub."

I did, but when I let go, Freddy slipped under the water.

Lin's hands shot out and lifted him right back up. "Oop! Can't let go of him!"

Freddy went in for a shock. He looked at Lin. He looked at me. Then he broke out crying.

"Ohh, you're okay, big baby!" Lin said.

"Sorry, Freddy," I said.

Lin handed me a cloth. "The soap is over there," she said. "Put a little on the washcloth and gently rub the dirt away."

Freddy stopped crying when I rubbed the cloth over his face.

"Try to keep the soap out of his eyes," Lin said.

I soaped him up complete and covered his head in bubbles, being careful like she said.

"You can't eat the barbeque, Freddy," I said.

He stared up at me with an open mouth.

I splashed water on his shoulders and wished that he was my younger brother so I could teach him how to deck and give him more baths.

We set him up on the sink and toweled him dry and put some baggy pants on him.

"Check out the baggies," I said. "Now you lookin *tight!*"

He just stared at me.

"Freddy's got a new best friend, doesn't he?" Lin said.

Freddy and I looked at each other. I made a silly face. He took it serious.

Lin poured Freddy's tubwater out. "All right," she said, "time to eat and get messy all over again."

"Cool!" I said, smiling.

Freddy smiled too and said, "Eeee!"

Lin picked him up and carried him out. The bathroom suddenly felt empty. I could hear Pops telling jokes to the other guys in the yard. It was a lonely sound. A sound that made me want to stay inside.

When we were done eating, Moose disappeared into the house and came back out with a Nerf football and a bunch of baseball caps. "Who's gonna throw the Nerf with me?" he said.

I got up. "Me!"

Pops said he was gonna play too. T.C. put both hands in his pockets and said, "No thanks." Frog burped like a bullfrog.

We put on our caps. Pops took off his camouflage jacket. He had on his black Merle Haggard T-shirt, which was a size too small. The seams dug into his armpits and the sleeves barely covered half his shoulders. He was wearing his black work boots, and he rolled up his jeans to make them look like football pants. His hairy white ankles poked out and Moms laughed at him but he didn't care and ran around the yard lifting his feet high off the ground like a silly dance. I laughed at that.

He and Moose held cans of beer in one hand and caught and threw the Nerf with the other. I told them that wasn't how you played football but they didn't wanna put down their beers. Every time Pops threw the ball his glasses slipped halfway down his nose and he used the top of his beer can to push them back up, making a metal *click*.

I threw a spiral to Moose and of course he missed it because he only had one free hand and the ball rolled under the back of Moms's Celica. Moose walked over and stared at the rear bumper. He gulped his beer until the can was empty, then crumpled it with one hand and threw it into the bushes.

Then he reached down, put his hands under the bumper, and lifted the back of Moms's Celica off the ground.

Moms and Lin stopped talking and stared at him. Frog put down his hamburger and said, "Jeez." T.C. looked embarrassed and lowered his eyes.

Moose shifted sideways, one step at a time, taking the car with him. The tiger tattoo on his arm jiggled tight. He swerved Moms's car to the side until the football was out in the open. It sat in a black oil spot. Moose lowered the car and it let out a groan as it came to rest on its rear tires again. He looked at his hands and wiped them on his jeans, then snagged the ball and threw it to me.

Pops said *that* deserved another beer and popped open a new can for Moose.

Lin stood up, holding Freddy, and yelled at Moose about how it was a stupid thing to do and he could have hurt himself and Moms's car too.

But Moms was smiling. She leaned back on her hands and smiled like she was five years old. It was okay, she told Lin. She liked Moose lifting her car up. "No one's ever lifted my car before," she said. "Thanks, Moose."

Moose tipped his Yankees cap to her and took a gulp of beer. Lin stared at him, angry.

Moms got up and walked around the back of her Celica. She bent down and put her hands under the bumper exactly where Moose had picked it up. She tried lifting the car, but of course she couldn't. She straightened up and rubbed her hands.

"Do it again," she said to Moose.

"No!" Lin said straight out.

Moose looked at Moms. So did me and Pops. What was she doing?

"Moose, *no*," Lin said.

"Jan—" Pops said.

Moms looked at him. "*What?* I liked having my car picked up."

"All right," Moose said.

Everybody turned to him, except for T.C., who was staring down at his own shoes. Moose held up his can of beer to salute Moms, finished the rest of it, then dropped the can on the lawn. He walked over to the Celica and Moms stepped back. She watched carefully while he bent his knees and put his hands under the bumper. Her mouth curled up into a smile.

Moose slowly straightened his knees. The car squeaked. Lin said something in Japanese and ran into the house with Freddy. She slammed the back door.

The car lifted off the ground.

Moms's lips parted and her mouth hung open. She watched Moose straighten his back and shift sideways. His legs were wobbling. He set her car back down in the middle of the driveway where it had been. She was hopping up and down and clapping before the tires even touched the ground.

Pops pushed his glasses up with his pinkie finger.

He was staring at Moms like she was someone he'd never met before.

9

M r. Garabedian lowered the lights and showed us a video tape of President Clinton. The week before, Garabedian had asked us why we thought Congress was trying to impeach the president, and we all yelled out "Sex!" That was why we were getting a lesson on impeachment today.

"I'm concerned that there's a misunderstanding in this room about what's going on right now in Washington," Mr. Garabedian said. "The president is not necessarily in trouble because he had sexual relations. He's in trouble because he withheld the truth. Because he may have *lied*." Garabedian pointed at the monitor. "Look at Clinton's face during his grand jury testimony. Can you tell that he's a troubled man, here? A man carrying dark secrets?"

We all leaned forward to get a closer look at the screen. President Clinton looked tired and worn down as he answered the questions people kept asking him.

"Well?" said Garabedian.

"He's straight up wicked-ass guilty!" yelled Douglas.

"How do you know? What are the signs telling us this?"

"He white!" said Loop.

Everybody laughed. I laughed too.

"Seriously, now," said Garabedian.

We focused on the video again. Clinton seemed nervous. He kept doing things with his hands, and crossing his arms in front of him. He answered another question, then forced his face to smile, but his eyes were blinking a lot. I didn't like looking at him.

"His eyes keep turning down," said LaTonya.

"Good," said Garabedian. "What else?"

"His smile!" Loop shouted.

"What about it?"

"It's all fakey," said LaTonya's twin sister, Rashelle.

"Okay. Why is he faking it?"

"'Cause he got realities," said Clarence.

"*Realities?*" Garabedian said. "What do you mean by 'realities,' Clarence?"

"'Cause my pops said he's caught in a lie with no way out."

"Good—"

"Pops said he can't understand why everyone's all lunchin about it," Clarence said, "since all he was doin was hittin his ho on the side and besides, white people been lyin to us all along anyhow."

The room busted up. I wasn't laughing now. I was staring at Clinton.

"*Shhh.* All right," said Garabedian. "What about *you*, Conrad?"

I turned and blinked at Mr. Garabedian, surprised. How did he know I was also carrying secrets? He couldn't have found out about Pops getting fired. Had Eye Master told him I was colorblind? I swallowed.

"*Well,* Conrad?" Garabedian said.

He paused the video and flicked on the lights. Everyone turned to me. I couldn't speak. It was like I was going to be impeached too.

Garabedian saved me by saying it was time for math, but for the rest of the day I couldn't get President Clinton out of my head. I needed to talk to someone about my secret and the only person I could think of was Midnight. He was Loop's oldest brother and he was blind.

Midnight also knew how to take care of problems. He got rid of what he didn't like, and what he didn't like was light. Before he lost his sight, Midnight was famous for turning his street into the Black Hole—that's what everyone called Cypress Way since it didn't have

lamps anymore. The last one broke when me and Loop were in third
grade. Midnight took care of it with his Glock.

Long before he ever got a gun, Midnight had tried to turn Cypress
dark. When he was ten he threw rocks at the lamps. Then golfballs,
baseballs, softballs, and footballs. Later, he fired BB's, then slingshot
fish sinkers, and even flung steel-tipped darts. Once he dragged out
his pops's Black & Decker and drilled into a lamppost. His pops beat
his ass for that one, and for a lot of other things too. The lights all
kept shining and everyone figured Midnight had given up on getting
the street black.

Then one day Alameda woke up for a shock: all twelve lamps had
been blown out on one of its blocks. Some said a UFO had landed on
Cypress. Gramma said it was God sending a message that the city better do something about all the dog crap and garbage nobody bothered
to clean up.

No one had to tell me it was Midnight. I knew he'd finally found a
way to darken down his street.

That's when the fight began. The city put in new lights to calm
everyone down, but Midnight took his Glock and shot them out
again. People were full of vinegar about that. The city fixed three
lamps and posted cops to watch over them at night. Midnight just
waited until everybody forgot about the problem and the cops
stopped coming around. Then he shot the three lamps dead.

After that the city didn't give a crap about the Cypress Way lights
anymore. They only fixed one, which shined until Midnight took me
and Loop up onto the roof one night and handed me his gun.

"Take a crack at it," he said.

I'd never shot a gun and I was afraid, but Midnight and Loop were
already eyeballing the glowing lamp across the road and waiting for
me. The Glock was heavy and it wobbled when I lifted it with both
hands and aimed. I pulled the trigger. Ringing rammed down my ears
and the gun jerked my hands back over my head, leaving them stone
cold bruised. The lamp was still shining.

When Midnight took the gun from my hurt hands, I couldn't look
him in the eye. I had missed. He let Loop take a shot but he missed
too. Midnight grabbed the gun and on his second shot he took out

the lamp. I never heard it explode, only the ringing slam of the gun firing. The light was out like it never was there in the first place.

Midnight put the gun in his pocket and looked out at the blackness like there was still something to see. I could only see emptiness, but it grabbed my heart and pounded it until it was popping. What Midnight had done pretty much paved over anything I'd ever seen. Downstairs, he gave me a hand slap and said I was his boy for helping out, then he and Loop went inside and I headed home down Cypress through the new dark Midnight had made. Midnight was gold-plated now and this was his work and the cold black around me might as well have been bright yellow sun shining.

That summer, when the streets were tired and yawning and hot even at night, Midnight had an accident. He'd been playing around with his gun when it blew up in his face. Everyone thought he was gonna get nuclear about being blind, and later on he did. But when they first brought him home from the hospital, Midnight bragged that he never liked what he saw anyway so he was better off not having to see it.

I made sure Loop wasn't home when I went to see his older brother. I knocked on the door and heard Midnight call out "Yo!" The door was open and I went in. The house was tiny and brown—brown carpet, brown walls, and a brown vinyl couch, torn-up and shiny from too much sitting. The kitchen counters were brown and the television was brown and so was Midnight sitting blind in his corner. He aimed his sunglasses at me as I walked over. "Con! My man," he said. He could always tell who you were by the sound of your steps.

"W'sup?" I said. "What you doing, 'Nite?"

"Nothing but being blind."

He *was* doing something, though—he was gluing bottle caps together, like usual. When Midnight had first gone blind, he wasn't able to run around like he used to and he started agitating, just lying around the house all day with nothing to do. He yelled at people for no reason, saying he was gonna kill everybody and Watch out! He challenged people to fight him, even though he couldn't see them. After that, Loop's moms, Mary, stopped having people over, and at school we all talked about how Loop had a brother going crazy.

When Mr. Garabedian found out one of his favorite old-time students was losing his brains, he visited Mary and said he had an idea. That's when Loop said we had to start saving plastic bottle caps from our Pepsis for Loop to take home to Midnight. "Why?" I asked Loop. "What's Midnight doin?"

"He gluing."

Which was true: Midnight was gluing the white caps together—it was Garabedian's idea. Midnight had started out making straight sticks. But they grew so long there was nowhere to put them, and he had to break them in half so they could lean up against the corner of the room behind his chair, like giant elephant tusks. Mary told him he'd better make them curve and that's when Midnight's sticks became shapes. At first he made giant white bullets, using his fingers to feel if they were the right shape. Next he built white cars. The more he made, the less screaming he did until finally he wasn't mad at everybody anymore.

After a while Mary let people come over again, and Garabedian was one of the first. Nobody could believe it when they saw what Midnight was doing. Then Midnight heard a show on television about how to make furniture. That's when he started making chairs. His chairs looked exactly like normal chairs, only made outta bottle caps. He had me and Loop sit in them to test their strength, but every chair broke. Mary bought him a better glue called poxy, but when we came in for the test, his new chairs broke just like the others. Midnight stopped talking to anybody and didn't make anything for three weeks.

Then Mary said, "How 'bout a lampshade?" and that got Midnight going strong. He made the first lampshade and Mary bought him some metal wire so he could hang it on the lamp beside him. The next one was better. He kept making new lampshades. He wouldn't quit. Mary complained to everybody that there were too many lampshades in her living room, but she was afraid to tell Midnight to stop. So she took him down to the flea market one Saturday to see if he could sell the lampshades. He sold every one of them and people asked for more. He started making nightstands and breakfast trays and even coffee tables. From that day on Midnight sold his bottle-cap furniture at the flea market every weekend.

Right now he was building a big white bowl for Mary's beauty shop, to hold brushes and combs and scissors. His hand reached out and found the glue tube.

"So whatchoo comin over here solo for?" he said.

I didn't know how to start. I said, "I don't wanna get in trouble."

He tilted his face up at me. "Trouble?"

"Yeah, like Clinton."

Midnight's voice went low. "*Ohh*," he said. "Like Clinton."

"Yeah."

"You in some deep down *serious* kind of trouble."

"Yeah."

He squeezed a glob onto his bowl. "So, you gonna tell me 'bout this trouble you in?"

I suddenly froze up scared. If I told him, how could I be sure he would keep it a secret?

"Well?" Midnight said.

"It's a secret," I said.

"*Secret?*"

"Yeah," I said. "But if you tell me a secret, then I'll tell you mine."

"All right," he said. "What secret you want me to tell you?"

Midnight hated his real name, and long ago he'd made Loop and everyone in his family swear to always keep it a secret.

"Your real name," I said.

His face went stone cold. "*Nobody* knows that."

"Nobody knows my secret either," I said.

We were both quiet. I saw him thinking.

"I think you wanna tell me your secret," he said.

"No I don't."

He fell quiet again and pressed another cap onto the bowl. "Since I stopped seeing," he said finally, "I've heard more things than you could ever imagine. This house would've fallen apart a long time ago if I'd let out even a half-dollar's worth of the secrets I got locked up in my head, noamsayin? Lotta the time I'm just tryin to stay on point around here—keep my shit together. But you know me: problem gets in my way, I swat it down. It's just water off a duck's ass." His fingers felt to see if the cap was glued on smooth. "All I'm saying is, you got something you wanna talk about, it's safe with me. I wouldn't drop a dime on ya, and I ain't gonna play wid ya either. I'll give you the reel-to-reel, see, 'cause I'm just checkin your flow."

There were goosebumps all over my skin. I had to tell him now. I leaned over and whispered into his ear that I was colorblind.

His eyebrows dipped down. *"Yeah?"*

The way he said it, I could tell he thought I really *was* in some serious trouble. I said, "You ain't gonna tell anybody, right?"

He suddenly pulled the sunglasses off of his face. His sunken eyes jerked side-to-side. "Whatever you just told me," he said, "is as gone as the light from my eyes."

I felt the hairs on the back of my neck rise. He put his glasses back on. *"Hey,"* he said. He held up his bottle-cap bowl. "What color's this?"

"White."

He pointed at the floor. "The carpet. What about the carpet?"

"Brown."

Now he pinched his sleeve. "How 'bout my shirt? What color's my shirt?"

I stared at it hard. "Green . . . no, gray. Or red? I don't know, what color *is* it?"

"How should *I* know?" he said. "I never seen it."

His face got all serious. "You telling me the truth about being colorblind?"

"Yeah."

"No leg pulls?"

"Uh uh."

"Sweet," he said, smiling wide. He held out his hand and slapped me five. "Now you halfway to being cool!"

IO

Later that week, Moms's Celica wouldn't start and had to be towed to the shop. When the mechanic called to say the engine was blown, Moms started crying and said we couldn't afford a new car. Pops said "Like hell!" and called a bunch of numbers in the used car section of the paper. He found a car for only six hundred dollars and circled the ad twice with a pen.

On Saturday the three of us piled into the truck and headed off to buy the car. For some reason it was hot out. Moms rolled down her window and said it was an Indian Summer.

Pops checked the address he'd written down next to the car ad, then tossed the paper onto the dashboard.

"What's this guy's name?" Moms said.

"Chuck."

When we drove down into the Webster Tunnel, I turned to Pops. "We're going to Oakland?"

"Mm-hm."

I grabbed the seat with both hands and stared ahead at the tunnel lights snaking by like lightning bolts. We were leaving Alameda. We were going on an adventure.

We flew up out of the tunnel into the white Oaktown light. It seemed brighter than the light back in Alameda. The buildings were taller and there were Chinese signs everywhere. The sidewalks were filled with people buying vegetables and fruit and fish.

"Look at all of them," Moms said, excited.

"Are they from China?" I said.

"Some of them, I'm sure."

"But not all of them?"

"Probably not."

I looked at the people real close, trying to tell which were the ones that had come all the way from China. It seemed impossible to come that far.

We turned away from the tall buildings onto streets filled with old houses painted blue and yellow and black. I spotted two street gritties decking down the sidewalk in the heat. They had taken off their T-shirts and stuffed them into their back pockets. Now the houses turned into auto body shops and liquor stores.

"We're going the wrong way," Moms said. She grabbed the paper from the dashboard and checked the address.

"No we're not, the numbers are getting smaller," Pops said.

The shops turned into houses again, and Moms leaned back. "You talked to this guy?" she asked. "You sure about the car?"

"Read it," Pops said, eyeing the paper in her lap. "Seventy-six Chevrolet Impala. Runs good. Engine perf. Brakes perf. New tires. Six hundred firm. Call Chuck."

"Seventy-six? That's more than *twenty* years old, Ray."

"Trust me—it's built better than anything they're making today. Besides, what do you expect for six hundred dollars?"

Moms shrugged and looked out her window. The farther we drove, the more the houses looked like the ones on Pacific Street. There were even empty lots between. Almost every house was covered with graffiti tags I didn't recognize. Men sat on porches, kids played on the sidewalks and streets, cars had flat tires and slumped to the side.

"Looks like our neighborhood," Moms complained.

She looked at Pops. He was ignoring her. She turned her eyes back to the street.

"It's all blacks," she said.

"Yeah," Pops said, looking out his window.

"Is this where Chuck lives?" she asked.

"Mm-hm."

Moms let out a long sigh.

We pulled up in front of a building called Creekside Luxury Apartments and Pops turned the engine off. The three of us stared at the beat-up building. It was painted bruise yellow, and brown water stains sunk down the walls under each window. A couple of wood beams had been nailed to the front to give it a fancy look, but you could tell from the leftover nails where other beams had fallen off a while ago. In the dirt yard some kids had laid black Hefty trash bags in a row, with rocks in the corners to weigh them down. A small naked girl held a hose so the water shot down the line of bags while the other kids ran and jumped and slid on their backs across the wet plastic.

"Can I go over there?" I asked.

"No!" Moms said. She looked at Pops. "I don't think we should go in, Ray."

"What about the car?"

"I don't care. Can't we find one somewhere else?"

Pops looked out at the building. "We're not going to find a lot of cars for six hundred."

He and Moms looked at each other.

"All right," she said. "Come on, Con."

We got out of the truck and the kids stopped sliding on the bags to watch as we knocked at door number Three.

"Yes?" came a man's voice.

"We're here to see the Impala," shouted Pops.

A man in a white T-shirt and tan work pants answered the door. He was about as old as Pops, with light brown skin and white hair. His round face glowed and seemed happy even though he wasn't smiling. He took a look at us, then stepped back. "Come in," he said.

Moms pushed me forward first and I stepped past the man into his apartment, which smelled like flowers. Golf was playing on a big-screen television. A giant bookcase was lined with books and vases, old plates and golfing trophies. The carpet, the walls, the furniture, even the bookcase—they were all white. So many lamps filled the apartment with bright white light that everything seemed to glow and shimmer. It was like the whole living room was at the bottom of a sunny swimming pool.

"Come in quick," said the man, "Jack-the-cat will escape otherwise and then drag in mud."

Moms and Pops crowded behind me and I moved in past a white leather couch to a shiny glass table with more vases—each one filled with flowers. Moms and Pops stared at the leather furniture and the big case full of fancy stuff.

"You have so many *flowers,*" Moms said.

The man shut the door and looked at his flowers. "My wife Jess used to grow them out back and bring them in every morning. I kinda got used to it. Jess used to say that our lives are like a flower—we grow and bloom, then dry up and die." He winked at me: "The only difference is that *we* make a lot of noise."

Moms said, "She's—"

"Been gone four years now," said the man.

"I'm sorry," Moms said.

The man smiled. "I have no complaints." He fished a dead flower out of a vase. "I still buy flowers at the store every couple days and bring 'em home. Keeps me and Jack from getting too lonely." He held out his hand to Pops. "Chuck."

Pops looked a little rattled as he shook Chuck's hand. "Ray."

Chuck looked at me. "That your son?"

"Yeah," Pops said. "Conrad."

"How you doing, Conrad?"

"Good," I said.

"Well, the car's out back under the port," Chuck said. "Hot out. You all thirsty?"

"A beer sounds great," Pops said.

"Sorry," Chuck said, heading past us to the kitchen. "I have a bottle of wine somewhere, but that's about it. How about soda? I have Diet Coke, and some ginger ale, I think."

I looked at Pops and suddenly felt embarrassed to be with him. Wherever we went, his drinking dragged close behind.

"Ginger ale sounds all right," Pops said. "Jan?"

Moms was still looking at all the flowers. "No thanks," she said.

"How about you, Conrad?" called Chuck. "Ginger ale?"

"Okay."

I followed Pops into the kitchen. Chuck poured us sodas and we drank them down while he watched us.

"So, you're from Alameda," he said.

"Yep," Pops said.

"Too bad about that Naval Station."

Pops stared down at his shoes. "Mmm," he said.

We stood there quiet then, nobody saying anything, taking sips of soda. Finally, Pops eyeballed a set of golf clubs in the corner next to the refrigerator. "Play golf?"

"Oh yeah," Chuck said. "Almost every day, when my knee isn't killing me." He reached to rub his knee, then straightened up. "Well, wanna take a look at the car?"

The Impala was long and wide and painted baby-blue like the sky. It sat under the carport next to a silver BMW that Chuck said was his.

Moms and Pops stood there looking at the BMW.

Chuck ran his finger across the dust on the Impala's hood. "This was my dad's car."

We all turned to the Impala. Pops reached out and opened the passenger door, then shut it. I liked how solid the door sounded when it slammed shut. He walked around and did the same on the driver's side. Chuck stood back, following him with his eyes.

"Aren't you gonna look under the hood?" Chuck said. "Kept her in perfect condition ever since Dad died. I don't have much use for her, but I've been keeping the battery up. Drive her down to Charlie Brown's Steakhouse Thursday nights, that's about it."

Pops lifted the hood and disappeared under it while we all waited. The hood came down and Pops opened the driver's side again and got in behind the wheel.

"How does it run?" Moms asked. She went around to watch Pops and I went with her. "I'm going to be driving it to work."

"Oh, you don't have to worry," Chuck said, sounding kind of sad. He took out a handkerchief and blew his nose and rubbed his eyes. For the first time, I saw that they were wet. For some reason I wanted to tell him how pretty the Impala's blue paint was.

Pops pumped the gas pedal, hit the ignition, and the car roared. A cloud of brown exhaust blew out the back and hit Chuck, who was putting his handkerchief back in his pocket.

"Ray!" yelled Moms. Pops looked up and she pointed back at Chuck. "Turn it off!"

Pops killed the engine.

"God, I can't believe you," Moms said in a hushed voice so Chuck couldn't hear.

"What?"

Moms could see Chuck's wet eyes now. She whispered to Pops, "What are we going to do?"

"You want it?" he whispered back.

She looked down the side of the car. "It's so big."

"The engine sounds strong," he said. "Looked clean too." He eyeballed Chuck in the rearview mirror. "I don't know. I trust this guy."

"He's *crying*, Ray," whispered Moms.

Pops checked the rearview mirror again, then looked at me. "Let's just get it. We're not going to find anything better."

"All right," she said.

"Should I try to get him to knock off fifty bucks?"

"Don't you dare."

He got out and took his wallet from his pocket and walked back to Chuck. Me and Moms followed. Pops pulled a bundle of hundred-dollar bills from his wallet. I looked at Moms. She didn't know yet that Pops had lost his job. I wondered if those hundreds were the last bit of money he had.

He held the wad of cash toward Chuck. "We'll take it," he said.

Chuck turned his eyes away from the money. He didn't seem to like Pops holding it in front of his face. Pops lowered his hand.

"Might as well hold your money till I've signed over the pink slip to you," Chuck said. He went to get it from his apartment, leaving us under the carport.

Pops gave Moms a confused look. *"Christ."*

"I don't think he wants to sell this car," she said.

"Then why'd he put an ad in the stupid paper?" Pops kicked the ground with his boot.

"Maybe he needs the money," Moms said. "I feel sorry for him."

Pops looked at the apartment building. "Jesus Christ."

Chuck came back with a pink piece of paper in one hand and a pen in the other. He pressed the paper down on the roof of the Impala and signed it slow. Pops stood near the rear tire, waiting. He seemed to be holding his breath. Chuck's eyes were still wet as he gave the pink paper to Pops.

When Pops handed him the money, I looked away. A girl was staring down at me from a high window of an apartment building across the alley. The way she eyed me made me feel like we didn't belong there. Like we were taking something we shouldn't take. I turned back to the Impala.

Chuck was getting something out of the glove compartment. He looked around the inside of the car, then stood up with a piece of binder paper in his hand. "I'll just write up a couple sales receipts real quick," he said to Pops. "Then you can take her."

He held the paper against the car window while he wrote. "My dad," he said. "He . . . When he died thirteen years ago, Jess and I flew down to Tucson to sort out his things. He'd had this car a number of years and was proud of it. Nicest car he'd ever owned. Anyway . . . Jess and I decided rather than sell it, we'd drive it on back, make a trip out of it." Chuck smiled, stopped writing. "That was fun." He nodded at the Impala. "She didn't give us any problems either. No overheating. Even out on the Mojave, and it was the middle of summer too." He finished writing the receipt and handed the paper and pen to Pops. "Here, you have to sign it twice."

Pops just stared at the paper and I thought for a second he wasn't going to sign it. He looked at Moms, like he needed her help. She tried to smile at him, but the ends of her mouth couldn't seem to lift. He grabbed the paper and signed it quick. Chuck ripped the paper in two and gave him half.

"That's it, I guess," Chuck said. He stepped back from the car, and we all stood under the carport and stared at the Impala. "My father's been gone a long time," he said.

Pops lowered his head. I followed his eyes to the license plate frame: *Stenson Motors of Tucson.*

Chuck said, "This car—" Then he couldn't seem to talk anymore.

Pops turned to him. "I hope we'll do it justice," he said. He held out his hand. "Well, thanks."

Chuck shook Pops's hand without raising his eyes.

"Con, get in the car," Pops said to me. "We'll drive around to the truck out front."

Moms patted Chuck's shoulder. "I'm sorry," she whispered, and got in the passenger seat of the Impala and pulled the door shut. I slid in the back. The air smelled like plastic and vinyl and coconut sunscreen. Moms stared straight ahead and we sat without talking, then Pops got in and started the engine.

Chuck stood under the port and watched while we backed out. His eyes weren't on us—they were glued to the front grille. We left down the alley and I looked back. Chuck had walked out into the middle to watch the Impala leave. Pops turned the corner and Chuck was gone.

Out on the street in front of the building, Pops pulled up behind his truck and turned off the Impala. The kids were gone. They'd left a wrinkled trash bag in the middle of the yard.

Moms and Pops were staring at the back of the truck. Nobody said anything. The Impala's engine made ticking sounds as it cooled down.

"Well, we got it," Pops finally said.

Moms started crying. My mouth began to tremble just watching her. I curled my hands around my eyes like binoculars and looked out at the trash bag lying by itself in the yard. Then I lay across the backseat and pushed my finger up into the soft cushion roof.

After a while, Moms wiped her eyes. "At least I can drive to work now," she said, sniffling. "I just wish it wasn't so big."

I was glad the car was big. Moose wouldn't be able to lift *this* car. I put my hands behind my head, and propped my shoes up against the opposite window. Pops looked in the rearview mirror and saw my shoes touching the glass, and he turned around with a face so filled with anger that I thought he was going to pummel me right there.

"Get your feet down, Con!" he yelled. "Don't you have any respect?"

II

That Friday during recess, Loop and the other gritties were suddenly looking at me funny. I sleazed over to get a drink at the fountain, and when I finished, a whiteboy everybody hated named B.L.T. was standing there smiling at me. His real name was Brian Lane Tucker, but we called him B.L.T. because those were his initials and besides he was fat. He was so big, his cheeks had muscles. He stopped eating one week but he was still fat and it was clear to everyone he was built to bloat.

"What's it like being colorblind?" he said to me.

My face went hot. "I ain't colorblind," I said, bending down to take another drink.

"Everybody knows about it. Why do you think they're all staring at you?"

I looked at Loop and the others. They *were* all staring. The only person I'd told about being colorblind was Midnight. Had he said something to Loop, even after he'd promised to keep it a secret?

"If you ever want to scare those guys," B.L.T. said, "I know how to build a bomb. I got a book."

I eyed B.L.T. He was serious.

"Are you whacked?" I said.

I looked at the gritties again. The way Loop's eyes were hawking me, I could tell he wasn't happy that I was talking to B.L.T.

I ran the fountain and pretended to drink. "Loop is my best friend,"
I whispered to B.L.T. "Don't come near me again."

After school, I walked across the field to the Secret Bush in the back
of the school where me and Loop sometimes stashed our skateboards
before class. I found Loop standing there, holding my deck in his
arms.

"W'sup?" he said.

"Nuffin," I said.

"I heard you colorblind."

"Who told you that?"

"Someone."

"Well I ain't," I said.

He suddenly put his chest in my face. "You friends with B.L.T.?"

"Puh!" I said. "Not me, nope."

He kept eyeballing me so I said, "If I am, then you can call me a
squid and throw me in Slime Canal."

"You gotta prove you one of us, then," he said.

"How?"

"By touching a dead body."

"Where we gonna find that?"

"I know a place."

"No you don't," I said, getting scared. But I was curious too. *"Where?"*

"Where my cousin Malik gots a job at Lincoln Morgue. He cleans
up all kinds of dead peeps and he eats the guts straight outta their
bodies."

I'd never met Loop's cousin Malik. When I didn't say anything
straight out, Loop shoved my shoulder. "You an arch chicken."

"No I ain't."

"Tell me if I lyin."

"You lyin," I said. "Let's sleaze over and see the deads. Puh! Ain't no
arch chicken."

I *was* an arch chicken but I sure as hell did not tell Loop. I wasn't a
chicken about anything in the whole world except Loop's cousin
Malik suckin the guts out of deads. I'd never heard of anything like
that. I'd heard of suckin the taco out of a Taco Bell taco. I'd heard of

suckin the Pepsi out of a Pepsi. I'd sucked the chicken out of a Swanson's chicken pot pie many times. But *this* was hardcore and my neck froze up and my legs went dead and I couldn't breathe thinking about Loop's cousin Malik.

It took us forever to deck down to Lincoln Morgue. Loop banged on a metal door in the back where he said the deads got carried in. The door creaked open and Malik stepped out, looking surprised to see us through his thick black glasses. He had on white doctors' clothes and hi-tops, and his head was shaved shiny.

He and Loop high-fived. Malik looked at me, then told Loop to come inside with him for a second. I waited in the alley, staring at the Dumpster and wondering if there were old body parts in there. Malik finally appeared and waved for me to come in. My breath caught in my throat. I leaned my deck against the wall outside next to Loop's. As I went in, Malik put a finger to his mouth and said, "Shhh."

Loop was waiting in the hall. Malik took a long look outside and slammed the door shut behind us. We were in the dark now. Daylight crawled inside the door cracks and shined like knife points off the black cement floor. The ceiling pushed clam-cold low on us and drippy pipes held on overhead. Me and Loop folded our arms. We were meat-locker steaks.

Malik pushed open a door that said WARNING! and we followed him into a room of bright lights and a gas station smell. There were three steel beds. One waited shiny clean. White sheets covered long lumps on the other two. Deads.

I shivered.

"Gentlemen, welcome to the Operating Room," said Malik, waving his arms around and flashing a smile like he was King of the Deads. He put a hand on one of the covered bodies. "Wanna see it?"

"Yeah, yeah, yeah!" Loop said.

Malik eyed the white sheet and his smile disappeared. He grabbed the corners and yanked the sheet off like a whip crack.

The dead was laid out naked across the table. His skin was brown and patchy. Loop walked up to the table. I followed, breathing fast. Loop moved down the table, looking the body over, and I stayed right next to him. We circled the dead while Malik leaned against the counter and lit a cigarette and watched us.

A long scar rode silver over the dead's belly, like a train track around a black mountain. Short black curls of hair covered his legs. You could see his penis. His fingernails were yellow and the bottoms of his feet were hard and white like an old leather drumskin. The toes were cracked and thick at the top and crunched together like mushrooms. We moved to the head. There was a heavy gold ring in one ear, and the face stretched long and pocky. The eyes were closed.

I didn't like how quiet the room was. You could hear the buzzing of the lights, a pipe clanging, even Malik blowing out smoke. My legs were so wobbly I almost wished that *I* was the dead on the table instead of having to be standing there looking at him.

Loop went and stood next to Malik. "You gotta touch it," he said.

"I will," I said, playing it wide like I wasn't scared.

I reached out to touch the stomach with my finger. . . .

The skin seemed to twitch before I even touched it! I started to pull away, but a hand suddenly grabbed the back of my neck. The hand was attached to an arm, and the arm belonged to the dead! The arm pulled my head toward the dead's lifeless face. I tried to break out of the hand's grip but its long fingers had a hold on me.

I cried "No! No! No!" Loop and Malik backed away against the counter. Malik was saying, "Holy shit! Holy shit! . . ."

The dead's face suddenly lifted from the table! His eyes popped open, and his hand jerked my head toward them until my nose pressed into his nose, and his veiny eyes were in my eyes, and his sour breath surrounded me. I screamed. Loop and Malik were yelling. Something crashed to the floor. The dead's mouth opened to speak, but only a raspy, stinky hiss came out. Then it whispered: "Sing."

I was sure that's what it had said.

The dead's mouth closed, swallowed and spoke again. "Sing," it said.

I let out another scream, and the dead's hand shook my head like a coconut.

"Sing me Marvin Gaye!" the dead shouted.

I didn't understand. The hand shook my head again and everything went blurry.

"Sing Marvin!" said the dead.

I cried out that I didn't know any Marvin Gaye songs, and I closed my eyes. I was meat.

Then I heard laughing. I opened my watery eyes—the dead was laughing at me. He took his hand off my neck and laughed so hard he had to lie back down on the table, the silver scar on his chest heaving up and down.

Loop and Malik were pointing at me and laughing too. They had to lean against each other so they wouldn't fall. I still didn't understand.

Loop said, "Damn, Con, you King of the Squids!"

The dead sat up and held out his hand to shake with me. "We had your ass goin big time!"

Malik pulled some work clothes out of a cupboard and threw them at the dead. "Here," Malik said to him, "I'm tired of looking at your naked ass. Get back to work."

Now I could see that I'd gotten my chain rattled.

Malik came up to me and held a hand out to shake. "It was my idea—saw you out there lookin scared already and thought we'd have a little fun witchoo. That's why I called Loop in first. Hope we didn't scare you too much. It's all good."

It wasn't all good. I didn't shake his hand. I made a loud sound like the horn on a Navy boat blasting. Not a scream or a yell, but an animal roar aimed at Malik and Loop.

Malik just stood there looking surprised.

I ran out of the Operating Room and down the dark hall and out of the morgue, where I grabbed my deck. I couldn't breathe and my eyes were watery and I ran up the street. Half of me was back in the morgue getting laughed at by Loop and Malik and the dead. Half of me was running across Webster and through the Safeway parking lot and across Kwik-Stop Gas. I ran until I stopped crying. I ran until I was me again.

• • •

I needed to make a wish. In KFC, the girl behind the counter had a nametag that said RHONDA. "Give me a wishbone and a extra-large Pepsi please, Rhonda," I said.

"A *wishbone?*" she said.

"Yeah, I gotta make a wish quick."

She looked over the register for the wishbone button. "We ain't got wishbones."

"Tuh!" I said. "You got chicken?"

"Original and Crispy."

"Then you got wishbones," I said. "You can't have a chicken that doesn't got a wishbone in it."

She gave me a long look and shook her head. "You have to order something from the menu."

"Then just give me whatever chicken part has the wishbone."

"I don't know what part that is."

"Then how much is a whole chicken?"

"We don't sell a whole chicken. We got a bucket. That comes with thirteen pieces, plus four biscuits and your choice of four side dishes."

"What about a wishbone?"

"I don't think so."

I was about to tell her to forget it and just give me a Pepsi, but the manager came out from the back. He was at least eight feet tall. His head rubbed the ceiling. His nametag said LEBRANDO.

"What's the problem?" LeBrando asked Rhonda.

"He wants to order a wishbone, but I told him we ain't sellin none."

LeBrando leaned over the counter and looked down at me. "What's the problem, sir?"

"I touched one of the deads," I said, "but he came awake on me and I found out he wasn't a dead for real and my road dog, his name is Loop, he played a joke on me with his cousin Malik so I ran all the way over here—"

LeBrando's eyebrows shot up. "Wait a minute. You sayin you ran your ass all the way over here?"

"That's right—"

"Just to get a wishbone?" LeBrando asked.

"Uh huh. See, they said I was the King of the Squids, so I gotta make a wish—"

"'Cause you ain't no squid, right?" he said.

"Right."

LeBrando straightened up and turned to Rhonda. "Clearly we need to get this young man a wishbone right away."

I was glad LeBrando said that and I could see why he was the manager and not Rhonda, who didn't even have enough philosophy in her to know where on the chicken was the wishbone. He pushed Rhonda aside and held one of his long fingers over the register.

"Let's see here . . . wishbone, wishbone . . . Ah! One wishbone." He pressed a key and rang up my wishbone. Then he leaned over again. "Will that be all, sir?"

"And a extra large Pepsi please, LeBrando," I said.

"One extra large Pepsi . . ." He plinked another key. "That'll be a dollar ninety-seven."

I handed him two dollars and he gave me three cents, then disappeared into the back. After a minute he came out with a box.

"One special order wishbone," he said, handing me the box. We slapped hands high and Rhonda passed me my drink and I left.

I slurped the Pepsi all the way down Webster. By the time I rolled up to Slime Canal I'd drunk sixty-four ounces complete. Clouds hammered the sun down to a gold line behind the Bay Bridge. Slime Canal was black as tar. I crawled down to a flat rock covered with crabs.

Hey crabbies! I said.

Give it a name and watch out for our pincers! said the crabs, sleazing sideways but keeping two eyeballs on me like John Wayne shuffling across the street with guns out.

I set down my wishbone box and peed into the black water the Biggest Leak of Pepsi in the History of the World. Get some pep now you fish!

Soon as I finished leaking I went dizzy—maybe because I'd lost so much Pepsi. I lay down on the cold salty rock and rolled onto my stomach and stared at a floating dead perch being picked at by a school of tiny fish. The small fish flashed, took bites, then looped around for more.

I sat up. Docked on the other side of the canal were two white ships, *Vancouver* and *Ottawa*, both with giant maple leaves on their smokestacks.

I opened the box LeBrando had given me. There it sat, wrapped neatly in wax paper: a good greasy wishbone. I held it up and wished for Loop never to trick me again. I made a wish for Pops to find a job and stop drinking. I wished to find my own color. And also for the Raiders to beat Denver.

Then I said, All right crabbies, take your end and pull! They said, *No thanks, we got some barnacles to eat or else we'll watch from down here in the cracks, so go ahead make your goddamn wish, Conrad.*

My left hand pulled for the crabbies, my right for me, and the wishbone went *Snap!* My right hand held the long piece. Loop was still my best friend and Pops was gonna get a job. The Raiders were in luck and so was I.

I made a secret wish also: that I could swim out to the Maple ships and sail away from Alameda and from Moms and Pops and from Loop too. Then I'd mail a letter:

Dear Loop,

You are still my best friend even though we are enemies. I'm standing on the highest mountain in the world, nine million feet, and an eighty foot killer bear ate all my food before I wrestled him over a cliff and I didn't eat for seventy-six days except for some tarantulas which tasted like a Sloppy Joe. I bit the head off a eagle for dessert and gave the body to my new best friend who's a wild wolf and I ain't gonna tell you where I am. Tell my Moms and Pops what I did and tell them you can have my Raiders jacket and they can have my helmet collection, only tell them they have to share it fifty-fifty, Moms gets the AFC and Pops gets the NFC. Tell them I ain't coming back forever until I'm old, probably when I'm eighteen.

Signed Your Secret Agent,
Conrad Clay

P.S. I am not a squid.

12

Pops's truck woke me up that night. It was the sound of rocks and pieces of glass crunching under tires as the truck pulled up to the curb out front.

Before he even made it into the house, I knew he was drunker than normal. It took him too long to get from his truck to the porch, and even longer to unlock the front door. I lay in bed, listening through the wall, my eyes open to the dark. He stumbled into the living room and fell onto the couch. It was quiet again except for the buzzing telephone lines outside. After a while I closed my eyes.

I began to hear voices. I was still awake enough to know they weren't real—they were coming from my own falling-asleep head. One voice belonged to Pops and it was saying, *Don't you have any respect?* His voice changed into B.L.T.'s: *If you ever want to scare those guys, I know how to build a bomb.* And then it was Loop: *Arch chicken arch chicken arch chicken* . . . His voice faded away until finally it was nobody, and I was nobody, and my head got dizzy and I was done.

Then, I heard a soft banging noise like a distant drum. My ears weren't connected to my dead sleep self, and the banging sounded like someone else's ears were hearing it. As far as I knew it was all part of my dreams. But the sound grew louder and closer and became more and more a part of me until it was clear my own ears were hearing it and I came right up and out of my deep down sleep. I opened my eyes and sat up in the dark.

Someone was pounding on the glass outside my window!

I jumped out of bed. The shade was pulled down and I couldn't see outside. I suddenly remembered what Pops had said about a burglar breaking into houses on our street and my chest started thumping. I crouched on the floor beneath the window as the glass above me rattled.

Then the pounding stopped and the window frame began to crackle and creak. Someone was yanking up on the frame, trying to lift it. I was about to run for the living room and wake Pops when the creaking stopped cold and everything went quiet. I didn't dare move. I waited and listened, but nothing happened for the longest time. The burglar must have given up. I got to my feet and gave the window shade a tug and it snapped up.

He was in the window! We both jumped away from the glass!

As I tripped backward over a shoe, I realized that the frightened, wide-eyed face I'd just seen belonged to Loop.

I flicked on my bedroom light and ran to the window, pressing my face against the glass. Loop was flat on his back on the wet grass, looking up at me confused. I waved and he smiled and waved back and I sure was glad to see him. For a few moments, we just stared at each other. In the yellow light from my room his skin glowed and shined so much he almost looked wet. He was an ice-cream scoop sent to me from the night.

I motioned with my hand for him to wait and I'd come out and meet him. He nodded and got to his feet. I threw on my pants and shirt and snuck out into the living room, barefoot. Everything was dark. I stopped for a second to make sure Pops was still passed out on the couch, but the couch was empty. I tried to see into the dark shadows around me. Where was he?

A black shape moved in front of the window. Pops. From his outline against the streetlight I could tell his back was turned to me. He was looking out the window.

"Pops," I said. "It's my friend Loop."

He didn't seem to hear me. He shifted a little, so that I could see his whole shape now. He was peering out through the left side of the curtains. He had the rifle.

"Pops!" I called out. "It's Loop! It's just my friend!"

He moved to the right side of the curtains and looked out through the opening. His eyes were shiny in the light, and moving around wildly. His lip snarled at one end.

"*Pops!*" I said.

"Shut the fuck up," he whispered without turning.

He went to the front door and opened it without making a sound, then stared out through the screen door. The rifle was shaking in his hands. Suddenly there was a crackling sound outside in the front yard. Pops raised his rifle and his body stiffened.

"No!" I shouted.

"Shut—up!" he said.

He pushed the screen open and stepped out onto the porch. There was another crackling sound on the lawn and then I saw Loop, standing in the middle of the yard. Pops took aim and I bolted past him and onto the wet grass straight at Loop. Loop smiled and walked toward me. "W'sup—" he started to say.

"*Run!*" I screamed.

Loop just stared at me, confused and surprised. I waved my arms and shouted, "*RUN! RUN!*"

Loop looked over my shoulder and his face suddenly filled with fear when he saw Pops. He turned and booked across the neighbor's lawn, then out to the sidewalk. For a flash, he passed under the bright light of the street lamp, then disappeared into the darkness of the street.

A door opened at one of our neighbors' houses, and a man stood there watching me.

"What's happening?" came Moms's voice.

Moms was at the screen door behind Pops, who stood on the porch holding the rifle at his side. "*Ray?*" she said to him.

He ignored her. His face was in shadow.

"Tell your friend," he called out to me, "that he's gonna be sorry if he tries to break into my goddamn house."

He opened the screen door and Moms stepped aside to let him enter. She looked out at me for a second. "Come inside, Con," she said, then followed him into the living room. I heard her asking him questions.

I stayed right where I was, breathing quietly in the middle of the lawn. My head was filled with flashes of rifles and shouting and shadows and wild eyes, and I was so bursting with anger I couldn't think straight, except that I hated Pops for scaring Loop away.

The house was quiet when I woke up the next morning. Pops was passed out on the couch naked except for his underwear. The rifle leaned against the coffee table, right in front of his closed eyes.

I put on my clothes and jacket, then snuck into the hall and into Pops's closet. It was the first time I'd ever been in there. I closed myself in the dark, feeling the blood pumping through me. There was a bad smell and all I could think of was sweaty skin.

An unlit bulb hung over my head like a dead fruit. I reached up and pulled the string and, in a flash of bare bulb light, the closet suddenly came alive around me with knives and giant feet and monster faces. I almost let out a yell, until I saw that the knives were really shiny tent spikes, hanging down at me on a string from the shelf above, and the giant feet were only Pops's army boots. The monster faces were two gas masks, hanging on a nail. Hoses shot out from their noses, making them look like giant mosquitoes. I turned both masks to face the wall so their bug eyes weren't watching me. I wanted to find what I came for as fast as I could and then get out.

There were two steel ammo boxes in the corner and I snapped their lids off. They were both filled with drills, screw drivers and wrenches. I closed them back up.

A cough came from out in the living room, and I froze and listened. Nothing. I grabbed the shelf above me with both hands and lifted myself high enough to see what was up there: a folded camouflage tent, some rope, an old sleep sack. I let myself back down.

My eyes fell on a canvas duffel bag leaning against the wall. I lifted the bag. Very heavy. I unsnapped the flap and threw it open. Bingo.

At the bottom of the bag were eight boxes of bullets.

I closed the flap and turned off the light.

Pops was still snoring and I got the bag past him with no problem. I carried it through the kitchen and out the sliding glass door.

It was a cold gray morning outside. Around the side of the house, I stuffed the duffel bag down into the bottom of the trash can. Then I covered it with a bag of rotting food just to make sure Pops didn't find it. He'd kill me if he did.

When I came back into the kitchen Pops was standing there waiting for me. He'd put on his clothes. His eyes were bloodshot and his hair was flattened to one side.

"What are you doing?" he said.

"Nothing." I swallowed the word.

"Nothing?"

He was studying my face. I was blinking too much, like Clinton. I tried to stop.

"Just taking out the trash," I said.

His eyes narrowed, moving back and forth between mine. Then he slowly turned to the trash bag in the corner. It was filled complete. On top, a broken eggshell balanced on a crushed milk carton. Some egg white had dripped off the edge and onto the floor.

We both stood there, staring at it. He finally pointed at the bag.

"You gonna take that one out too?" he said.

13

I didn't go back in the house after taking out the trash. I didn't want to. It was Saturday and there was no school and I stood on the sidewalk, looking around. Clouds covered the day cold, and the dirt gray street didn't send any light back up to the sky. The Impala's windows had frosted over, and I used my finger to write my graffiti tag on one of them. Every gritty at Jack London Primary had their own tag— mine was *Escaped Con*. I'd watched *Escape from Alcatraz* thirty-six times on video, and I renamed it *Escape from Alameda* and pretended I was the guy who sleazed out the tunnel and swam away from the island. Our tags weren't for real, only dreams. That's why I put *Escaped* in mine.

I wrote my tag on all the other windows too, going around the whole car. Then I ran around and around the Impala fast, keeping my eyes on the windows. I got dizzy and everything was spinning and all I could see was:

ESCAPED CON ESCAPED CON ESCAPED CON ESCAPED CON ESCAPED

When my scrambled head straightened out, I grabbed my deck from the porch, threw it down on the sidewalk and pushed off. I said Hey! to the fat cat crouching under Pops's truck, and Run cat run! to the other cat booking away, *Whack!* to the empty lot weeds, Ho! to the houses hanging, Yo! to the cold fences fencing. I said Get you on my way back! to some pennies lying on the asphalt like fish scales glittering. I was glad to be away from Pops.

The tide was low and the air along Slime Canal was heavy with the deep sour smell of motor oil and barnacles and rotting seaweed. I decked out to the end and sat down on a cold wet rock. Long fingers of fog crawled over the bay and high above, the clouds had black ink bellies. It was still early and across the canal, lights lit up the giant loading cranes, whose hungry heads reached out over a ship and ate away at its cargo bins. The cranes had four steel legs. They were dinosaurs coming down from the Oakland hills for a drink of water.

I shouted the name on each cargo bin as it was lifted up off the ship.

"A-P-L!" . . . "HYUNDAI!" . . . "SEA-STAR!" . . . "LINDA MEXICANA!"

A wind blew in off the bay and stung my cheeks. I couldn't smell anymore, and tried blowing my nose clean but it was stuffed with cold nose clog. I looked along the canal—the dark sky seemed to sag down to the rooftops of the old wood warehouses. I shivered and pulled my jacket up over my chin, and put both hands in my pockets. Then I leaned my head back against the rock and closed my eyes. I thought about Pops some, and about Loop too. Then I got to wondering who had told everyone I was colorblind. . . .

I must have fallen asleep, because a bright light suddenly glowed through my eyelids. I opened my eyes. The rocks around me were covered with curtains of black flies. A ragged tear of light had ripped the black clouds until they showed a great gray hole of day behind the Oaktown hills. Across Slime Canal, the ship was gone and the loading dinosaurs slept with their lights turned off. Seagulls were picking mussels off nearby rocks, then flying over the road and dropping them on the pavement so they cracked open. They swooped down and fought over the yellow meat inside.

Down the canal, a Chinese man in a Raiders ski hat sat on an old tire, smoking and watching the tip of his fishing pole. He gave me a quick look, then turned back to his pole.

The wind picked up, bringing a drizzle with it. The Chinese man pulled his jacket hood over his hat. The wood warehouses on the other side turned black from the rain and the signs looked like gravestone words. It was the all-time loneliest feeling I'd ever had, and the wind whipped right through me and pushed me down low until I was a wet weed in the crack of the rock.

I wondered what Loop was doing. I wanted to go see him but I was afraid after last night. He probably thought Pops tried to shoot him for tricking me at Lincoln Morgue. Maybe he thought I was his enemy now.

The rain stopped after a while, and I hopped up the rocks to the road, pulling a twenty-foot piece of seaweed with me. I got on my deck and decided to drag the seaweed behind me down the street. If the pavement broke it apart before I got to the Ferry Terminal, then I would go home. If it lasted, I'd go see Loop. And maybe I'd find out if Midnight was the one who'd ratted out my secret.

The Chinese man looked up when he heard the seaweed scraping the road. I kept going.

A car full of high-school squids honked and tried to run my seaweed over but I pulled it in quick. The car swerved and roared away with hands hanging out the windows.

At the Ferry Terminal, my seaweed string was still going strong.

Maybe I hadn't given it a hard enough test. I took the seaweed down Main. Cars blew by and steamed faces stared at me from inside frosted-up windows. The cold wind that was whipped up by the passing cars left loneliness all over my face, but I took the feeling in and kicked it down into my leg and out onto the pavement, leaving it behind in a million frozen footsteps.

I kept going on Main, then across the dirt lots of Atlantic, until the seaweed became dusty and dry halfway down Webster Street and I let it go.

Don't stop, I said. Don't stop till you get to Loop's.

I smiled when I saw the Christmas lights on Loop's house. Loop's dog, Tugboat, was laid out on the doorstep and his fat belly was a big bag breathing and blowing swirls of steam away from the house like a factory smokestack.

Hey Tugboat, I said, don't bother lifting your fat head, I know you're too heavy.

Tugboat's eyebrows went in for a shift. *Don't worry, I ain't gettin up for your ass, but Hey! Conrad, Hey!*

I was about to knock when I heard the television inside and I suddenly got all chicken. What if Loop *was* mad at me? I went around to the front window and leaned over the juniper bushes and pressed my nose against the glass. I couldn't see much through the curtains except the fireplace glow and part of a blue television screen.

"See anything good in there?" came a voice behind me.

I spun around. Loop's neighbors Moon Dog and Cinci stood there with a bag of Doritos and a six-pack of Diet Coke. They were coming over to Loop's.

Moon Dog and Cinci had been big-time wrestlers. Now they cleaned carpets for banks and offices at night and helped out Mary and Midnight by watching Loop's baby brother Termite during the day.

"No," I said. I felt like a Peeping Tom getting caught outside Loop's window.

"Well," said Moon Dog, his white face beaming at me, "why don't you come in and help Mary?" He tugged at his long beard. Since the last time I'd seen him, it had turned yellow, like starved grass. "She's bleaching my beard this afternoon."

Cinci cupped his mouth and whispered to me: "He thinks it'll make him look pretty."

"You shut up," Moon Dog warned him. Then he turned back to me: "Well, are you coming in?"

"No," I said.

"You *aren't?* Why not?"

"Me and Loop are enemies."

"Well, *hell!*" Moon Dog said, winking at me. "So are Cinci and I here, and look at us—" He pressed the Doritos bag into Cinci's big belly: "*We're* still together!"

"Drop it," Cinci said to Moon Dog, smacking away the bag of Doritos.

Cinci was big and bald and black as a tractor tire and he always wore black suits, which had been his wrestling trademark back when he was "Cincinnatus X." People had to be warned never to stand behind Cinci, because he'd lift you off the ground with one hand and set you back down where he could see you. Sometimes I stood behind him on purpose. I liked being lifted.

"You better just come in without any hassle," Moon Dog mumbled to me. "Cinci's in one of his moods today."

Moon Dog put his arm around me and I could smell his after-shave spice. He was the biggest man in Alameda: almost seven feet tall and four feet wide. He even had fat on the back of his head. He told me I could get big like him if I ate lots of green vegetables, but I always saw him down at KFC sucking down a row of ten biscuits with two buckets of chicken.

I went with the wrestlers into Loop's house where the air was smoky and hot from the flapping fire. Mary had already put up her Christmas decorations, including Jesus in the manger, which was on top of the television. Midnight was in his corner, and Mary was in the kitchen, mixing a big bowl of the purple cream she used to bleach Moon Dog's beard. I didn't see Loop.

Moon Dog pushed me right up to Mary. "Look who we found standing outside, peering into your window." He looked around. "Where's Termite?"

"In his crib taking a nap," Mary said. She had on her usual overalls, and her hair was buzzed short like a man's. Mary always said hell if she was gonna mess with her own hair after doing everyone else's all day. She gave me a good looking-over. "You're lookin fuzzy, Con. 'Bout time for your next haircut, ain't it?"

"Yeah."

"You thinking too much lately?"

"No."

"Well you must be, because the hair keeps coming out of your head day and night. You come by the shop Monday after school gets out. Won't be so busy then." She gave the bowl of cream another stir. "I'll get rid of some of that fuzz on your head."

"Okay."

She kept looking at me. "What were you doing out there?" she said. "Why didn't you just come in?"

I didn't know what to say.

"Is something going on at home, Con?"

That took me by total surprise. Before I knew it my lips were trembling.

"Con?" she said, setting down the bowl. "What is it? Your grandmother?"

I shook my head.

"Everything okay with your folks?"

I pressed my lips together tight. She put her hands on my shoulders. "You don't have to tell me. You're always welcome here—you know that, right?"

I nodded. She gave me a hug, then picked up the bowl again. I turned and looked into the living room. Cinci was in his usual chair by the fireplace. Moon Dog had planted his blubber into the sleeper chair.

Midnight was listening to the television. I was pretty sure he *was* the one who'd told Loop my secret, especially since he hadn't trusted me with *his* secret, his real name.

I was about to go over and ask him about it, but Mary stopped me by putting her hands on my shoulders again. "Now," she said, "maybe you can tell me why Loop nearly jumped through the ceiling when he heard you coming in. He ran his booty into the bedroom and shut the door like you were the *devil* coming to get him."

I lowered my eyes.

"*Loop!*" she called out. "*Come out here!*"

She took my arm and brought me out to the living room, and I wished I'd never come since it was clear Loop didn't want to see me. Mary yelled for him again and he finally walked out. His face was knocked clear of any expression one way or the other. He was a mud puddle.

"What up with the two small-fry homeys?" Midnight called out.

"Looks like they're in a feud of some kind," Moon Dog said.

"*Yeah?*" Mary said. "Well they better *un*-feud their little butts this minute, 'cause I don't have patience for any feuds in *my* house." She turned to me: "You two still friends?"

"No," I said.

"Nuh-uh," Loop said.

"All right," Mary said, "I've seen you two McNuggets grow up together since your hardwood heads weren't even touching my kneecaps! You two think you're all high and mighty enough that you can get along without each other? Let me tell you something: don't get carried away with yourselves, thinking you're royal blood, thinking you came from the finest rosebush. For better or worse you two are both just a bunch of crabgrass, and that's why you need each other . . . so Loop"—she put an arm on his shoulder—"are you gonna apologize for whatever you did to Con? Because I *know* you did something."

Loop wouldn't apologize and I wouldn't either. We stood there facing each other like two boxers. Mary and Midnight and the wrestlers all tried talking us into making up and shaking hands but we held tough and stared each other down.

Then a funny thing happened. The more we stared at each other, the more I saw that we were on the same slope, just like Mary said. We just needed a way to break our stand-off.

Mary said, "I'm gonna brown 'n' serve you two like a couple of crispy links if you don't quit it. Now which one of you is going to help me bleach Dog's beard?"

"Me!" I said.

"Me too!" said Loop.

"There we go," Midnight said, pointing a finger in our direction. "Now give each other some skin and let's get on with it."

Me and Loop slapped each other high. *Smack!*

"Oh yeah, that sounded *good!*" said Midnight. "Don't nothing gonna get in your way! Let me hear you two homeboys smack it again."

Me and Loop slapped each other low this time—*Smack!*

"Sweet!" Midnight said with a wide smile.

"You two friends again?" Mary said.

"Puh," Loop said.

"Tuh," I said.

We looked at each other and smiled, all embarrassed. Loop was my link.

A cry came from the bedroom.

"Now look what you did," Moon Dog said to us. "You've gone and woken up Termite from his nap."

Cinci got up. "I'll get him."

"You sit back down, Cinci," Mary said. "You two been baby-sitting him all week long. Termite's given you enough trouble." She disappeared into the back room.

"Trouble?" said Moon Dog, getting all puffy in his chair. "Termite isn't any trouble. Isn't that right, Cinci?"

"Mm," mumbled Cinci.

"We practically have to beg Mary to let us come over and take him for the day." Moon Dog shifted in his chair and stared at the television. "Poor woman works so hard cutting all those people's hair. Tell them, Cinci."

"Drop it," mumbled Cinci.

"I feel bad enough asking her to bleach my beard every month. Poor girl."

Mary brought Termite out of the bedroom. He clung to her shoulder and stared at all of us. His eyes were big and round and his mouth hung open. His real name was Kenneth, but when Loop's pops saw him come home half-size from the hospital with big bug eyes and looking like an eggplant, he told everyone, "That ain't mine! That ain't mine!—he look like a *termite*." So Kenneth became Termite. That was before Loop's pops left for Atlanta and never came back.

"There's my favorite!" Cinci said, smiling at Termite.

Mary set Termite down on one of Cinci's thick legs, and Termite hugged his leg like a possum in a tree. Then he climbed up onto Cinci's belly, his tiny hands disappearing into Cinci's pudge. Cinci smiled down at him: "You're almost getting too big for this, aren't you?" Termite's knee slipped and nailed Cinci where it counted. "Ow!" Cinci cried out.

"Careful of his apparatus there, Termite," Moon Dog said. "That's my pride and joy."

"Oh *Dog!*" yelled Mary.

"Well it *is*," Moon Dog said all proud.

"Watch your language," Cinci said, eyeballing him.

"Yeah," Midnight said, "don't wanna be givin the boys any ideas."

"We don't need to hear anything from *your* mouth either," Mary said to Midnight.

I didn't know what they were talking about. *I* hadn't heard any bad language.

"I think Termite is hungry," Cinci said.

Mary brought Cinci a jar of mashed pumpkin, then walked over to the TV and grabbed Baby Jesus out of the manger and handed him to Cinci. "Ever since Termite discovered Baby Jesus," she said, "he won't eat anything unless Baby Jesus is dunked in it."

Cinci dipped Baby Jesus into the jar of mush and then put him in Termite's mouth. Termite sucked the sauce off of Baby Jesus, and soon his face was covered with pumpkin. Everyone laughed and I did too and I sure was glad to be at Loop's. People were happy here.

It was time to do Moon Dog's beard. Mary brought out the bowl of Purple Crap, which is what she and Moon Dog called the bleach cream. Moon Dog lay back in the sleeper and Mary set the bowl on his chest and handed me and Loop each a comb. We stood on either side of him and dipped our combs in the Purple Crap.

"Now get it on quick," Mary said. "It has to be on his beard for twenty minutes."

We combed the Purple Crap down Moon Dog's beard, beginning at the top. The cream smelled like flowers mixed with gasoline. I liked the smell of gasoline and I liked the smell of flowers, so I didn't mind.

"Watch his chest, Conrad!" Mary called out when I dropped some cream onto Moon Dog. She brought over a paper towel and wiped it up. "You two wanna keep helping, you gotta do it right."

"It's okay, Mary," Moon Dog said, "they're doing a great job."

We finished spreading the Purple Crap on his beard and Mary took the bowl into the kitchen. Now we just had to wait. Loop sat down to watch television. I decided to go talk to Midnight.

"Yo, 'Nite," I said.

Midnight's head turned in my direction. "Wha's up, lil' bro?"

"Nuffin."

"Sweet," he said, smiling.

I leaned toward him and lowered my voice: "Did you tell anybody?"

"Huh?" he said. "Tell anybody what?"

"What I told you last time I was here," I whispered.

Midnight seemed to think about it for a second. He opened his mouth, but before he could say anything, Moon Dog called out: "Midnight, it's time for wrestling!" Since he went blind, Midnight controlled the television and if you wanted the channel changed you had to ask him to do it. Midnight's mouth was still about to tell me something. He seemed frozen.

"Well, 'Nite," said Mary. "Are you gonna change the channel or do we have to wait till Christmas?"

He turned in her direction. "We watch that shit every day. What if I don't feel like it?"

"'Nite," Cinci said, wiping Termite's chin with his handkerchief.

Midnight's fingers found the changer and switched the channel to wrestling. Cinci sat up and held Termite tight. "All right!" Moon Dog said.

Midnight was already listening to wrestling. "Who's on?" he called out.

"The Iron Sheik," said Moon Dog. "And Abdullah The Butcher."

"Sweet!" Midnight said.

I gave up on him and sat down with Loop to watch. Loop looked at me, then turned back to the TV. After a while, he whispered to me: "Why your Pops tried to shoot me?"

"He didn't," I whispered back. "He thought it was a burglar trying to break in."

"Oh."

I waited a little, then checked Loop's face. He didn't seem mad about it.

I took a big breath and watched the wrestlers on TV. Abdullah The Butcher clotheslined The Iron Sheik, then The Sheik body-slammed him back and lifted him up by his ankles to put him into a pile driver. Abdullah's head thudded into the mat.

Moon Dog pointed at the television. "*Get* it, girl!"

Abdullah pulled The Sheik down and got him into a figure-four leg-lock.

"*SHOW* you right!" yelled Cinci.

"Kaaaaa!" screamed Termite. His arms were flappy.

"Those men are gonna get hurt," Mary said, but everyone ignored her.

Every time the men on television did a body slam or head butt, Moon Dog and Cinci yelled at them to *Get it!* and *Go on, girl!* I couldn't understand why they kept calling them girls.

A commercial came on. Loop asked Moon Dog if he and Cinci were better than Abdullah The Butcher. Moon Dog was still excited and wiggled his head. "Girl, we were the *best!* Tell them, Cinci."

"Yep," Cinci said. He wiped his sweaty head with his handkerchief.

"Did you wrestle in your black suit?" Loop asked Cinci.

Moon Dog laughed. "Honey, the ring was the only place he *didn't* wear his suit."

"Drop it," Cinci said.

"He sleep in it too?" Loop said.

"Ha!" Mary said.

"He sure does," Moon Dog told Loop.

Me and Loop both turned to Cinci. "*Do ya?*" asked Loop.

"Yeah," Cinci said.

"Well . . ." Moon Dog said. "There is *one* other occasion when he'll take his suit off."

"Don't even go there, Dog," Midnight said.

"Drop it," Cinci said. He gave Moon Dog a mean eye.

Me and Loop searched their faces. "WHEN? WHEN? WHEN?" we yelled.

Cinci glared down at us. "When I take a shower."

"Oh," said Loop.

"Oh," I said.

Wrestling ended and Midnight started flicking channels. Mary took a wet towel and wiped off Moon Dog's beard. Now it was even whiter than the color of his skin. He went to check it out in the bathroom mirror, then came out smiling. "Much better," he said. He looked at me and Loop. "Thanks, you two. Thanks, Mary."

"It's getting to be nighttime, Con," Mary said. "Don't you think you better get on home? Your mama's probably worried about you."

I swallowed. I hadn't thought of Moms or Pops the whole time. "Okay," I said, although I didn't want to go home. I didn't want to leave Loop's. Not ever.

I said C-ya to Loop and he went into his room, and then I said good-bye to everyone else and slowly picked up my deck and headed for the front door.

"Hey Con!" came Midnight's yell.

I stopped at the door and looked back. Midnight's face was turned toward me.

"Come here a second," he said.

I looked at Mary—she and the wrestlers were busy talking in the kitchen. I leaned my deck against the door and walked over to Midnight. In his lap was the bowl he'd made for Mary's shop. It was upside down and his hands palmed it like a basketball. "You here?" he said.

"Yeah?"

"Come closer."

I moved toward him a step.

"How close are you?"

"Two feet."

"Make it one foot."

I stepped forward until I could feel his breath on my face.

"You there?"

"Yeah."

He made a fist and held it up right next to his cheek. I watched it tremble there. He turned his face just a notch so his sunglasses pointed straight at my eyes.

"See that ring?" he said.

On the pinkie finger of his fist was a thick gold ring. It had a blue stone so dark it was almost black.

"Yeah."

"That's a special sapphire," he said. "Now get real close and look into it. Get up close, until your eye is almost touching it. Look right into it."

A speck of light sparkled in the middle of the dark blue. Like a shiny star at night.

"Okay," he said, "Are you looking?"

"Yeah."

"You see it?"

"Uh huh."

"What do you see?"

"Midnight."

I felt his warm breath as he whispered in my ear:

"Willis."

14

Even though it was stormy and dark, even though rain soaked me like I owed it twenty dollars, I left Loop's happy. Midnight had trusted me with his name, and that meant my secret was safe with him—he wasn't the one who'd ratted me out. I dropped my deck and rolled along with the gutter water. Besides his family, I was now the only gritty in Alameda who knew Midnight's real name and I felt like a fish egg floating.

Who *had* leaked my secret?

I was still trying to figure that out when I shredded onto Pacific and a pair of headlights came up behind me. I heard a honk and rolled to the right to let them pass, but they slowed down beside me.

It was Pops in his truck, pointing for me to stop.

I came to a halt, and he pulled the truck up even with me. His camouflage jacket was zipped up to his chin and a cigarette hung from the corner of his mouth. He leaned over and struggled to open the passenger door. I walked toward the truck, but when he pushed the door open and I saw what sat on the passenger seat, I froze.

It was the canvas duffel bag—the one I'd thrown in the trash.

"Recognize this?" he said.

I nodded.

"You know where I found it?"

I felt my throat tighten. I couldn't even open my mouth to speak.

"I said do you know where I found it?"

"Yeah," I finally sputtered.

"Where?"

"In the trash."

"How did it get in the trash, Conrad?"

I stayed focused on the bag.

"How—did—the—FUCKING—BAG—end—up—in—the—TRASH?"

"I put it there," I said, afraid to look at him.

The windshield wipers were squealing.

His hand suddenly grabbed the duffel bag and flung it at me. I jumped back and it hit the ground and boxes of bullets slid out onto the wet pavement with a scraping sound. Raindrops pelted the bag.

"Pick it up!" he said.

I bent down and put the boxes back into the bag.

"Bring it here."

I stayed crouched on the asphalt. I couldn't move.

"Pick the bag up and bring it here," he said. *"Now!"*

I slowly lifted the heavy duffel bag and carried it over to the seat. His cigarette smoke spidered down my throat.

"Don't put it on the seat—it's all wet." He pointed to the floor of the truck. "Down there."

I struggled to get the bag down to the floor and when I was done he reached out and grabbed hold of my wrist. I yelled and he yanked me up into the truck and my ankle caught the door and smacked against the metal. His arm reached past me and pulled the door shut so I was trapped inside with him. He slid to the middle of the seat and forced me down across his lap. I screamed but he turned me over onto my stomach and put a hand on my back and pressed me down so hard over his thigh I couldn't breathe. His other hand reached under me and ripped my fly open and pulled my pants and underwear to my knees.

I let out a yell.

Nothing happened. The air was cold on the bare skin of my rear.

Then came a loud smack. My skin screamed with a million stinging jolts. Pops sank his hand down into the middle of me, filling my insides with fire. I choked and sucked for air as his hand came down again and again, again and again and again.

He jerked my pants up and pushed me out of the truck, then pulled the door shut. The truck roared off down the street past our house to the corner of Webster where it turned out of sight.

I stood there heaving. The stinging got worse, then worse again, like I was pressing my rear against a hot frying pan over and over. I slowly picked up my deck and headed home. I was halfway across our front yard when the sight of our house stopped me cold. After what Pops had done to me, I wanted to burn the house down. I wanted him to come home and see nothing there but smoking ashes. I'd be just like Midnight. He took care of what he didn't like. He blew the lamps out . . . *I'd* burn our house down. Or maybe I'd ask B.L.T. about the bomb he said he could build. I'd hide it under the middle of our house. Then *BOOOM!* It'd be louder than a rifle shot. I'd make an explosion so big all of Alameda could hear it. *That* would stop Pops from giving us any more grease.

I went inside. Gramma was watching TV with the sound turned down low. "There you are," she said. "Your father went out looking for you."

I didn't say anything. She caught me staring at her Sea of Galilee bottle on the coffee table and she started to hide it, then stopped. "Oh hell, you know I take a sip of this every night—I don't know why I'm hiding it. It's time to go to sleep anyway." She started to get up.

"Can't we watch TV?" I said, trying to stop her. I didn't want to be alone in my room.

She sat back down. "Well, all right. An old *I Love Lucy* rerun is coming on—we can stay up till the end. Come sit down quiet—your mother's got a headache and is trying to sleep."

I eased down onto the couch next to her. My rear end suddenly let out a stinging scream, and it took me a while to find a way to sit that didn't kill.

"What's the matter with you?" Gramma said. "You need to make a bowel movement?"

"No."

She turned back to the TV, then reached for her bottle and took a sip. When she was done she licked her lips and held the bottle up so she could look at the TV light through it.

I Love Lucy started. Lucy and Ricky were like Moms and Pops. They ran around yelling at each other. Except Ricky smiled at the end and said, "Oh, Lucy!" And Ricky didn't have any bullets in the closet that I could see.

Me and Gramma made a bet: who could last until the end of *I Love Lucy* without breaking down and yawning? Each time a commercial came on, Gramma said, "Lordy, lordy, I'm so tired." Then she eyeballed me to see if I was gonna lose it and yawn. She had tactics.

I hung tough through two commercial breaks. Then KFC came on. When Gramma saw my mouth fall open for a two-piece Crispy with biscuit and mashed potatoes, she went in for the kill, letting out a fake gold-plated yawn a mile wide. She had me. I yawned way back and stretched my arms up high.

"If you were at an auction, you'd have just bought it," she said. She let out a cackle and I started laughing and then she burst out laughing too. She took another swig from her bottle and almost rolled off the couch from laughing so hard.

"Why do you always say funny things?" I asked.

"I've been talkin funny since I was two years old, Con. I suppose when I'm six feet under I'll still be telling you funny things, and you'll laugh at my tombstone and everyone will think you've lost your marbles."

I was quiet. I didn't like it when she talked about being dead.

There was a sound from the hall. Gramma grabbed my wrist. "Shhh," she whispered. We listened. Nothing.

Then Moms's voice came through her door: "*Con!*"

"She wants you," Gramma said.

"*So?*" I wanted to stay right next to Gramma. I stared at the TV.

"Con, come here!" came Moms's cracked voice.

Gramma shook my arm. "Go see your mama."

Moms called for me again just as I opened her door. The room smelled like a dirty wet towel. She sat up in the middle of her giant bed, covering her chest with a blanket. Her Siamese cat lamp glowed on the carpet and shined off her wet cheeks from below, making her look like a jack-o'-lantern. Black makeup seeped down from her eyes, and her lips were smeared fat with lipstick like she'd been punched. Her long yellow hair was pulling the brown roots out of the middle of her head and forming a dark stripe. A pillow-wrinkle ran down her forehead between her eyes. She looked split.

She pointed to the dresser. "Bring me my Actifeds."

I brought her the bottle and she popped the lid and poured pills onto the bed. Her fingers found a pill and lifted it to her mouth and she swallowed it dry.

"I don't want you spending so much time with Grandma," she said.

"*Why?*"

She raised an eyebrow at me. "Because she's getting old, *that's* why. She's filled with weird thoughts and I don't like you hearing them, do you understand?"

I didn't say anything.

"Close my door on your way out."

I snuck back out to the living room and sat down slow and careful.

"She doesn't want me talking to you," I whispered to Gramma.

Gramma heaved a sigh and waved an angry hand in the air, then uncapped her bottle and took a sip.

"How come she doesn't like you anymore?" I said.

"She likes me," Gramma whispered. "She just doesn't want me seeing her life fall apart. From the time she was a little girl, she thought she was a princess in a fairy tale. That's why she married your father. When he joined the Navy and found out he was being transferred to California, she thought he was her prince, sweeping her away from Missouri. She's always been stubborn—doing things her way. I told her she was making a mistake. She can't stand seeing that I was right."

"*Are* you right?"

She looked at me and squeezed my hand. The lines in her face deepened. "Time to go to sleep."

She stood up and I did too, only a lot more slowly.

I caught her eyeing me. "Let me look at your rear end," she said.

"No."

"I want to see it, Con."

I turned around.

"I mean drop your trousers. Come on now, I ain't gonna bite you."

I slowly undid my pants and pulled them down. She let out a gasp.

"What in the world *happened* to you?" she said, staring at my behind.

I looked to see. My whole rear was bruised.

"Did your father do that?" she whispered.

I nodded.

"My *Lord!*"

"He painted my butt black," I said.

"No he didn't," she answered. "He *beat* it black."

In my room I pulled off my pants and underwear real slow, then climbed up onto my bed. I didn't get under the covers. I eased onto my stomach and lay across the giant smiling Raider pirate on my blanket, spreading my arms and legs out to the four corners, fitting them exactly to the sword and crossbones. I pretended I was floating on a raft in the bay, following the tide under the Bay Bridge, past Alcatraz, past the San Francisco piers, under the Golden Gate Bridge and over the hungry sharks, the seagulls fighting to follow. And me, riding my Raider, cold floating it and doing a buck-fifty straight for Hawaii.

I got up and flicked off the light. On my bed, I rolled carefully onto my side. Then I closed my eyes and went to sleep curled up in a ball like a dead bug.

15

At lunch on Monday I found B.L.T. alone in the bathroom, washing his hands at the sink. I asked him where he'd heard I was colorblind, and he looked me over before saying that Eye Master was the one who'd dropped a dime on me. According to B.L.T., Eye Master had told Chocolate Chip—a tiny bald gritty who always wore homemade clothes and sat in the back of our class—that he needed glasses because he'd failed the eye chart test. Chocolate Chip had started crying, and Eye Master tried to make him feel better by saying he wasn't the only one with half-price eyes. Then he told Chocolate Chip that I was colorblind.

When B.L.T. was done telling the story, he dried his hands on his pants and turned to leave.

"What about that bomb?" I said.

He stopped and looked back at me. "You wanna get Chocolate Chip?" he said, his voice trembly.

"No!" I wasn't gonna hold it against Chocolate Chip for leaking my secret—the other gritties always called him *homemade* and they'd been giving him so much lip about his new glasses that telling them all about *my* eye problem was probably the only way he knew to fly past it. I'd just wanted to know more about the bomb. "Forget it," I said, kicking the tile floor.

B.L.T.'s eyes got all serious. "It's called a pipe bomb," he said.

I looked out the door to the blacktop to make sure nobody was coming. "How come?"

"That's what you make it with."

"What?"

"A *pipe*. I got instructions from a book in my brother's room. He's a artist, but he went away to college. I go into his room and read all his weird books and my mom doesn't care—she thinks I'm learning something. I got lots of stuff." He smiled at me. "Hey," he said. "We could build a bomb together."

His wet mouth was breathing hard between his puffy cheeks. I felt my own breath coming quickly.

"Maybe."

"I can see you're not telling me everything," Gramma said.

She'd forced me to go on a walk. We stopped in front of Zeke's Skateshop. I didn't say anything.

"Am I right?" she said.

"No."

She looked me over. "Well," she said, "I think you've got too many worries on your mind, and I want you to sell all your fears to me."

I had no idea what she was talking about.

"I'm gonna buy your fears from you," she went on. "It's an old Southern trick my own grandpa taught me when I was your age. You don't have to *tell* me your fears—just *sell* them to me, then you'll feel better."

"For how much?"

She pointed to the Alien Workshop board in the window. "How much does that skateboard cost?"

"Sixty-nine ninety-nine."

"Sixty-nine *dollars! My Lord!*"

She cussed out the greedy aliens who'd made the skateboard, but we went inside to buy it anyway. At the counter she reached into her purse and pulled out a roll of old twenty-dollar bills, tied together with string. Her hand was shaking and she couldn't undo the knot, so she handed it to me. I untied the string and gave the money back to her. The bills felt thin and wet, like they'd been stored in some dark and damp place for a long time. We paid for the deck and I carried it out under my arm.

"There," Gramma said once we were out on the sidewalk.

I lifted the deck to my nose. I was breathing in its oily smell of varnished wood and rubber wheels when I heard Gramma sniffle.

"Gramma?"

She didn't answer. Her eyes were filled with tears.

"What's wrong?" I said.

She tried to hide her face from me. "I'm scared, Conrad."

"Why?"

"For what's going to happen to you when I'm gone."

"Where are you going?"

The tears were running down her cheeks now. She wiped them with the back of her hand. "That's just it, see—I'm scared for myself too, Conrad. I'm scared of where I'm going. Every day I'm alive, I'm one day farther from your grandfather. But as sad as that makes me sometimes, it's not what I think about the most. See, your old grandmother is selfish. What scares her the most, what wakes her up in the middle of the night until she thinks she can't stand it anymore, is knowing that she's one day closer too."

"Closer to . . . *Granpa?*"

"Yes."

I wanted her to stop crying. I didn't like seeing her so afraid. *"I* don't think you're getting close to Granpa," I said.

"Well, I am. And I have to face it. My dough ain't gonna rise again." She turned and started walking home and I followed her with a knot in my stomach. We'd bought the board, but I still had the fears.

Back on Pacific Street, we could hear Moms and Pops yelling and giving each other cancer from three houses away. We stopped out on the sidewalk and stared at the warped sides of our house. Rain had sunk stains into the dirty wood walls, and the front bulged at the bottom like a big pot belly. Chips of paint were nibbled off the corners. The house looked like a barnacle out on Slime Canal, clinging to a crusty old rock.

A door suddenly slammed inside, and Gramma shook her head.

"That house," she said, "is an ark of ache."

• • •

Inside, we found Moms standing in front of the television, screaming at Pops, who was trying to watch it. She'd found out from Lin that he'd lost his job and she was angry he hadn't told her. He was sitting on the floor against the couch without a shirt on. There were five empty Coors cans on the coffee table.

"You're blocking my show," he yelled at her. "Move!"

"No! Why did you lie to me, Ray? Moose doesn't lie to Lin. He's thinking ahead too—"

Pops was pointing at her now. "Get out of the fucking way, Jan!"

"—Lin told me he's already looking for a new job—"

He suddenly jumped up and took Moms by the arms. He shook her hard. "Fuck Moose!" he yelled into her face. "Why don't you go live with him!"

There was a knock at the door.

Pops turned and looked at me. Gramma clutched my wrist.

Another knock.

"That's probably the neighbors coming over to complain," Gramma said.

"Shhh!" Pops said.

The knocking came again, this time loud.

"Who is it?" Pops yelled.

No answer.

Pops still had Moms by the arms. "See who that is," he said to me.

I went to the window and pulled back the curtain. A brutha stood on our porch with a folder in his hand. He had short buzzed hair and ears sticking out like satellite dishes. He wore black shoes and black pants and a brown jacket.

"Who is it, Con?" said Pops.

"I don't know," I said.

Pops let go of Moms and came to the window and leaned over me to see out. The man on the porch pulled a Kleenex from his jacket pocket, blew his nose loud, then folded the Kleenex into a tight square and dropped it back into his pocket.

"Who the fuck is *that*?" Pops said.

He went to the television and lowered the sound. Gramma was still standing near the door. "Go to the couch, Mom," he told her.

Gramma shook her head and did as he said. Pops opened the front door.

"Yeah?" Pops said through the screen.

"Mr. Clay?" the man said in a deep voice.

"That's me."

The man pulled open the screen door enough to hand a piece of paper to Pops. "Mr. Riggs. From Best Rental Properties."

Pops took the paper and read it.

"What does he want, Ray?" Moms called out.

Mr. Riggs heard her. "I'm serving you with a warning of possible eviction," he called in through the screen door. "You're already behind two whole months on the rent, and here it is—almost a week into December—and Best Rental still hasn't seen a check."

Moms went to the door and looked at Pops. "You haven't been paying the rent, Ray?"

"Stay out of this!" Pops said, glaring at her.

"Why haven't you been paying?" she said.

"I said shut *UP!*"

Mr. Riggs was staring at them and they both suddenly looked embarrassed. Pops lowered his eyes to the paper. His lips moved while he read and his eyes closed a little more with each line until he was squinting. I wished he had a shirt on.

"You don't have to do this," Pops said to Mr. Riggs.

"Mr. Clay. My job is to make sure the owner gets his rent on time. If people can't make the rent, it's my duty to find someone who can."

Pops smiled. "Come *on*," he said.

I couldn't watch anymore. I wanted a different Pops, one who went to work like normal men and didn't stay home with no clothes on. One who paid the rent and never had to beg.

"Mr. Clay," said Mr. Riggs. "I'm gonna be straight with you. I'm an ex-Marine. I'm different from the woman who used to handle your account. I've been hired because I have specific qualities and training. To be blunt, I don't take bullshit. Which is what Best Rental seems to have accepted from you for quite a while. This isn't the first time you've been late on your rent—I looked up your records. I can't believe you haven't already been evicted. If it'd been up to me, you wouldn't still be standing on that side of the doorway."

I turned to see what Pops was going to do. His eyes narrowed on the man. "You don't have to talk to me like that."

"Mister, I'm speaking to you about a business matter. I haven't lost my temper. Believe me, I could have." He pulled out his handkerchief again and blasted his nose. "Excuse me."

"When do you need the money?" Pops asked.

"Three months rent, by the twelfth of December—that's a week from today. Otherwise, I'll recommend to the owner, Mr. Kalt, a course of eviction."

"You would evict us right before *Christmas?*" Pops said.

Mr. Riggs didn't answer. Moms and Pops both stared at him. A car roared by outside.

"How about a beer?" Pops said finally.

"Mr. Clay—"

"Why don't you come in?"

"Let him go, Ray," Moms said.

"I'd prefer to stay out here, Mr. Clay," said the man.

"Please," Pops said. He lowered his voice: *"Please.* Will you tell Mr. Kalt I'm looking for another job. He must know what's happening at the Station. I just need an extension. A couple weeks at the most."

"Kalt is very ill, Mr. Clay. He's living in Florida and he's fighting cancer. Believe me, he doesn't care about any Navy base closing down—"

"Can't he give us until after Christmas? Is our rent really going to make a difference to him?"

"Mr. Clay, I'm not in the business of asking owners for favors on behalf of their tenants. Good day." The man walked out to the sidewalk and Pops slammed the door.

"*Great!*" Moms said.

"Just be quiet," Pops said.

"That was so humiliating—"

Pops pointed his finger right at her eye. "SHUT UP!"

"No, Ray, I'm not going to shut up." Her eyes welled up with tears as she walked away from him. His finger was still in the air. He watched her disappear into the kitchen, then he started after her.

"Don't you hurt her, Ray!" Gramma called out from the couch.

He stopped and pointed at Gramma. "You shut up too!"

Gramma's eyes turned mean. "Don't you dare speak to me that way."

Another loud knock came from the front door.

I went to the window, hoping it was Mr. Riggs again—anything to stop Pops from hurting Moms.

It was a boy about my size standing on our porch. His skin was blood dark and his shoes were brown and floppy, the kind old men wore. In one of his hands, he clutched a wrinkled Hefty bag.

I went and opened the door. "W'sup?" I said.

He just stood there looking at me with his dark watery eyes.

"W'sup?" I said again.

He held out a small white card with writing on it. I pushed open the screen door and took it. It said:

> You have CRABGRASS. I can take it AWAY.
> I am Sammy, THE CRABGRASS KILLER.
> —Fifteen CENTS per bunch—
> I can't HEAR you. Please WRITE to me. I can READ.
> I can take your CRABGRASS away.

"Is that asshole back again?" came Pops's yell behind me.

"No," I said.

"Then who is it?"

I looked at the boy. He waited there, watching me with his inky eyes. "Just a boy," I said.

"What does he want?" came Moms's sniffling voice.

"He wants to take our crabgrass away."

Moms came to the door. "How much?" she asked the boy.

The boy just stared at her wet cheeks.

"He can't hear you," I said.

Pops stormed up and pushed Moms aside. "We don't want anything!" he said to the boy.

"*Ray!*" Moms said.

The boy saw Pops's steaming mad face and he bolted off the porch.

"You scared him off!" Moms said.

"So what? We can't afford to throw money away to any kid who knocks on our door."

"Where's *your* Christmas spirit?" she said.

He took hold of her arm. "Don't give me that!"

"It was only fifteen cents," I said.

He turned to me, still gripping her arm. "*What?*"

"He was only charging fifteen cents a bunch."

He let go of Moms and glared at me like he was going to hit me. I backed away from him.

Moms suddenly held a dollar bill out to me. "Con, go after that boy and give him this. Now!"

I looked up at her, afraid to leave her with Pops.

"Please," she said. "Go."

She and Pops both watched me grab my deck and walk out the door. It slammed shut behind me. I waited on the porch for a second, listening. Nothing. I dropped my deck on the walkway and pushed off.

The boy was halfway down the block, walking up to another house. When he saw me rolling toward him, he dropped his Hefty bag and tore off across the yard and out into the street.

"Hey!" I yelled, waving the dollar at him. I pushed hard after him. His floppy old shoes clomped the asphalt and I couldn't believe how fast he ran in them.

At the corner of Webster I almost had him. Then he threw a bunch of paper cards in my face. I fell off my board and rolled onto the sidewalk. By the time I looked up, he had disappeared into the Webster Street crowd. I sat there rubbing my bruised knees and catching my breath. All around me on the pavement were the white cards, each with the words: I am Sammy, THE CRABGRASS KILLER.

16

Moms was in her room when I got back to the house. I didn't see her again until the next morning, when I was leaving to go to school. She was standing at the end of the hallway. There was a cut across her cheek, and bruises on both of her arms. She disappeared into the bathroom before I could say anything.

When I came home later that afternoon there was a cloud of blood in the toilet. At the bottom of the bowl was something white and stained with blood—toilet paper, maybe. I flushed it, and even more blood swirled up before it all got sucked down. It sent a chill right down through me. Pops must have hit Moms's stomach so hard she was bleeding inside. Now it was leaking out of her body.

I knocked on Gramma's bedroom door. "Gramma?" I said into the crack.

"What do you want?" came her weak, oily voice.

"Aren't you coming out?"

"I need to rest, Conrad."

I knocked again. There was no answer.

"Gramma?" I said.

The bed squeaked, there was some shuffling, then the door opened. Gramma was still in her pajamas. Her eyes were wet and filled with crust, and I could see she was shaking.

"Why are you so shaky, Gramma?"

"Me? Oh, that's just my loose fat jiggling."

I couldn't take my eyes off the skin below her jaw. It hung there, trembling and white.

"Now what did you want?" she said.

"There's blood in the toilet."

"Blood? It's all right. It's just your mother. Now, let me sleep." She closed the door and I heard her get back into bed.

Wasn't she even worried?

"But she's bleeding bad," I said through the door.

"It's all *right*, Conrad," came her voice. "It's just life going on."

On Saturday, I waited in the Impala while Moms asked the bank for a loan to pay the rent. When she finally got back to the car, she lit a cigarette and didn't say anything.

"Did you get it?" I said.

She blew out smoke. "They said our credit wasn't good enough."

I looked at the bank. What did they know about us?

Moms drove us down Webster. I kept eyeing the cut on her cheek, which she'd tried to cover with a Band-Aid.

"What's wrong with Gramma?" I said.

She shrugged. "I don't know—what's wrong with her?"

"She's always lying in bed. Even in the day. Her skin looks funny."

"Grandma is getting old."

"So?"

"She might be dying, Con."

My throat went dry as bone. "No she's not," I said.

"She's sick, Conrad."

"So? She's not dying."

She turned to me with an angry face. "Look, I'm not going to argue with you, all right? I've got bigger things to worry about, like paying the rent. If we can't come up with the rent it won't matter if your grandmother is dying or not, because she won't even have a place to live and neither will you!"

She pulled over to the curb in front of Hideout Liquor and went inside. I felt knotted up about everything. I wanted to know how we were going to find money. I wanted to know what that blood was doing in the toilet. And was Gramma *really* dying?

Moms came back with a new pack of cigarettes. She lit one up and sat there smoking.

"Moms?"

"What now?"

"Is life still going on?"

She squinted at me. "What did you just say?"

I lowered my head. She sounded angry again and I was sorry I said anything. Then I felt her fingers on my chin—they lifted my face up to hers. "Tell me what you just said, Con."

"I said . . . Is life still going on?"

She looked at me like I was speaking Spanish. Then the ends of her mouth curled up and she nodded.

"Yeah," she said. "Yeah, it is."

I went into Gramma's room that night to make sure *her* life was still going on. We lay on her bed and talked and talked until we both must have fallen asleep, because the next thing I knew it was the middle of the night and Gramma was thrashing next to me on the bed. She was having a nightmare.

"Con? . . . Con? . . . Con!" she cried.

"I'm here, Gramma," I said.

"Hold me, Con! Hold me!" Her eyes were open but she wasn't seeing me.

I took her in my arms. Her skin was cold, and she was so thin I could feel all her bones. Her breath smelled like old food.

"Hold me while I fall asleep," she said. "Hold me down to the earth!"

"I'm holding you, Gramma."

"I'm not ready to see him again—"

"Who?"

"I miss him, but my love is tired!"

"*Granpa?*" I said.

She didn't answer. Her eyes stared at the ceiling. One of her arms fell loose and I took hold of it. "I got you, Gramma."

She finally closed her eyes and I stayed there next to her, holding both of her arms, wishing I had more hands to hold onto her. I had to keep her from going up to be with Granpa.

After a while, her mouth fell open and blew bad breath at my face but I didn't mind breathing it.

She was my Gramma.

When I woke up the next morning I was still in Gramma's bed.

She was gone.

I jumped up and ran into the hall, out of breath. Moms was putting on makeup in the bathroom. "Gramma went to heaven!" I said.

"No she didn't," Moms said. "She went to the kitchen to eat."

I ran for the kitchen. Gramma was at the dining room table chewing on a piece of toast.

"Didn't eat hardly anything last night and I woke up this morning starving," she said. "This is my fourth piece."

I went right up to her and gave her a big tight squeeze.

"There's another one in the toaster if you're hungry," she said.

I *was* hungry, but I didn't dare let go of her.

17

"How much is the rent?" I asked Pops.

"Too fucking much!" he said.

We were driving to Moose and Lin's to ask Moose for money. Pops didn't say anything about what he'd done to me the last time we were both in the truck. Neither did I.

We parked on the street. "This will be quick," he said.

I rolled down my window and watched him disappear into Moose and Lin's house. After a while he came back out with Moose and they stood on the porch talking. Moose didn't look happy and he didn't wave to me like usuals. He was listening to Pops, shaking his head once in a while and pushing leaves off the porch with the toe of his boot. Finally Pops held his hands out like he was saying, "*Well?*"

I looked away, embarrassed for us. Nobody wanted us around. We were pests.

When I looked again, Moose was handing Pops a check. Pops slapped him on the back, but Moose's mouth was a straight line. He shook Pops's hand, then went back into his house and closed the door. Pops eyed the check on his way to the truck, then stuffed it in his shirt pocket before climbing in.

"Is it enough?" I said.

"No."

• • •

When we came home, I decided to write to the owner of our house, Mr. Kalt. If Mr. Riggs wouldn't ask him for more time, then I'd ask Mr. Kalt direct. I didn't know his address in Florida, but I had a plan, which started with my letter:

TOP SECRET LETTER

Dear Mr. Kalt,

My name is Conrad Clay and I live in 2042 Pacific Street so you own my house. Also I am ten years old and my Pops did not pay rent for two months I am sure you are pretty mad about that. Since I would be mad too. The Naval Station fired Pops because it is closing down. He needs a little more time to find a new job. Then he is going to pay you for everything! Do you want to do a trade with me? I can trade you this 1977 Topps trading card if you can wait a couple more months for Pops to pay the rent. It is autographed and it is worth the most of anything I have, even my NFL helmet collection. I know you live in Florida so you probably like the Miami Dolphins but I like the Oakland Raiders. This card is of #60 Otis Sistrunk. He is my all time favorite Raider player ever since Pops gave me this card on my 7th birthday. Otis was the first pro player to shave his head. He played before I was born but I saw him pummel players in my Oakland Raiders Commitment to Excellence video and I met him onetime when he came to Jack London. It was a cold day and there was steam coming off his big bald head. He told us to keep on the straight track and stay in school so we would not have to go to the University of Mars like he did. For 1973 he was lineman of the year and All Pro in 1976. Other players said he was so big it was like running into a soda machine with a head. See how it says Just Win Baby! on the front of the card? that was the Raider motto back then so that is why. Pops said Sistrunk was a classy guy but what I like about him the most was how he played a whole season with a broke arm. To me that makes him the baddest brutha of all times and you can ask anyone at Jack London or anyone in Alameda. Don't waste your time asking in Oaktown. Nine for ten is going to say Otis was the man! and if they do not say it they are rattling your chain. Or else you found a squid to ask and squids do not know anything so you got unlucky. Please do not tell Mr. Riggs I tried to trade you. He was in the Marines and he doesn't like any hassle. And also don't

*tell my Pops please since he gave me this card for my birthday so he can't
find out I'm trading it away. I hope you feel better and beat out your cancer.
Please write me back. To let me know.*

Sincerely,
Conrad Clay

P.S. Here is a drawing of a Raider helmet.
Sorry I messed up the facemask.

I folded the letter and slipped it into a blank Christmas card envelope I got out of Gramma's dresser. Then I pulled out my Otis Sistrunk
trading card from the place in my desk drawer where I'd kept it safe
and hidden for almost three years. Since my seventh birthday I must
have pulled the card out and studied every detail of it five hundred
times over. Now I held it up to look at one last time. In the photo,
Otis is squinting and smiling over his shoulder without his helmet on,
his bald head shining under the sun. I suddenly felt a burning in my
throat. When Pops gave the card to me, I'd wanted a big shiny bald
head too. The card was the beginning of football for me, and the start
of my Raiders worship.

The next day after school I decked out for Best Rental carrying the
letter for Mr. Kalt. I knew where Best Rental was from all the times
Pops had made me wait in the truck while he dropped off the rent. It
had all windows in the front, just like a Laundromat, and sat in the
Safeway parking lot between Heng's Donuts and Nashional Furniture.
When I shredded up this time, there were Polaroids of houses and
apartments taped near the door. I put my face to the glass and peered
inside. A woman with yellow hair like Moms's sat at a desk. Behind
her were four empty desks. No sign of Mr. Riggs.

A bell jangled when I opened the door and the yellow-haired
woman smiled. The nameplate on her desk said PHYLLIS SMITHER.

"Can I help you?" she said.

I walked up to her desk and held out the sealed envelope. "I wanna
send this to Mr. Kalt."

She took the envelope and flipped it over a few times, looking at it, and then her face lit up. "Oh, is this a Christmas card?"

I nodded, holding my breath.

"Well," she said, giving the envelope a little shake, "I'm going to make sure this gets to him right away."

I told her thank you and I left before she could ask me any more questions. Outside, I took a deep breath and pushed off across the parking lot, hoping I hadn't mailed Otis away for nothing.

The next day was Tuesday. I told Loop I needed money fast. We were standing under a ledge outside the cafeteria after school, watching the rain coming down. He wanted to know why I needed money and I said it was to give Moms a present for Christmas. I wasn't lying really. My Christmas present to Moms was gonna be money to help pay the rent.

Loop wanted to help. He came up with the idea to jack some dough from his moms's shop. It would be a secret mission to steal bars of gold outta the Pentagon. We would go in undercover, he said. I was an expert lock picker and code breaker. He was a highly trained Kung Fu-ass criminal from Hong Kong.

I just hoped we wouldn't get caught.

By the time we made it to Mary's House of Hair, we were frozen wet. Loop stopped me right before going in. "I know where she keeps the cheddar so don't be lookin everywhere," he whispered. "She'll see we up to shit in a flash."

The shop was hot and steamy and smelled of burnt blow dryers. Mary was brushing out the hair of a pretty woman who I could tell wasn't from around the neighborhood. She had gold sparkles on her eyelids and her smooth hair dripped down her head like black ink. She was carrying class.

Mary's partner Roz sat in an empty customer chair reading a magazine and ignoring the hair clippings all around her on the floor. Roz was as big as Moon Dog or Cinci, and wore huge flapping dresses. Long corn rows hung off her wide head and her beads clicked whenever she moved.

"Well look what the cat dragged in," Roz said when she saw me and Loop.

"Hey Roz," Loop said.

"Hey Roz," I said.

Mary eyed our wet clothes. "Couple of water-rats, looks like to me," she said, running a comb through the woman's hair.

Me and Loop stood there. Loop's eye looked all over. My eye followed his eye around the shop. The plastic blue waiting chairs had nothing but magazines. The black counters were covered with pins and brushes and bottles. No cash anywhere. Not even a penny. Loop's eye came back with nothing.

Mary stopped combing her customer's hair. "All right, what are you two McNuggets up to? Cuz I know you up to *something*."

We didn't answer. The woman in the chair looked us over. "That your son?" she asked.

"Yep," Mary said.

"He's so cute."

"He ain't cute," Mary said. "He's up to something."

"Aww," said the woman.

"Ain't you," Mary said to Loop. "You two got your greedy little eyes on the lookout for *something*. *What* is it?"

"We need some money," Loop said.

I wished he hadn't said that. I didn't want Mary asking me questions.

"For what?" Mary said, combing the woman's hair again.

"Some snacks."

"*Snacks?*"

"Yeah, that's all."

I breathed easy.

"What—you hungry?" Mary said. "We got some bananas in the back, don't we, Roz?"

Roz didn't look up from her magazine. "*Mmm-hmm*," she said.

"Oh they just want some candy," said the classy woman. She grabbed her purse off the counter and pulled out a wallet with her long thin fingers. "Here," she said, holding out a ten-dollar bill toward me and Loop. "Why don't you get yourselves something good to snack on."

"Damn," mumbled Roz.

"Cool!" Loop said.

I suddenly had four extra eyes in my head and they were all focused on that ten-dollar bill. Loop stepped forward and took hold of it.

"No!" Mary shouted.

"Why not?" Loop said. He and the woman both had their fingers on the ten.

"He can have it," the woman said, smiling. Loop backed the bill out of the woman's hand, but not all the way. He looked up at his moms.

Mary's eyes were big balls. "I said *no.*"

Loop pushed the ten back into the woman's hand. I watched her put the bill back in her purse.

"Now, you two plant your pee-wee butts over there in the corner," Mary said, "and just dry out a second while I finish straightening Sandra's hair."

We sat in the waiting chairs and Loop whispered in my ear, saying to pretend we accomplished our mission anyway. I didn't care about any mission. I was still thinking about that ten-dollar bill.

"I didn't mean to get them in trouble," the woman named Sandra said.

"Don't worry 'bout it, honey." Mary eased Sandra's head forward. "But I couldn't let you give them ten dollars."

Me and Loop looked at each other. "Tuh," he whispered.

"Luh," I whispered back.

"Check out the dress this skinny girl got on," Roz said, holding the magazine.

"Mm-hmm," Mary said, finishing up Sandra's hair.

Roz looked at the magazine again. "That dress, though! If I had them shits, I'd be like, *damn!* noamsayin?" She turned to Mary. "You want this *Cosmopolitan?* If not, I'll take it home."

"What do I want with that?" Mary said. "It's just a white girl's guide to getting more sex. What's their problem?" Then she mumbled, "I get enough of *that* with Bobby around." Bobby was Mary's new boyfriend.

Sandra let out a laugh and Roz gave her a mean look before flicking some more pages.

I whispered to Loop. "Your Moms has sex."

"No she don't," said Loop. He let me have a shoulder slug.

Mary eyeballed us. "You two better not be listening."

"We ain't," Loop said.

"We ain't," I said.

"Why don't you two go skateboard outside until I finish up Sandra?"

We didn't move. We wanted to hear more about sex.

"Dean came over last night," Roz said, flicking a page, "all horny with that look in his eyes like I'm his rag doll or something."

"Lucky you," Sandra said.

"She ain't lucky with this joker, trust me," Mary said.

"I'll pretend I didn't hear that," said Roz. "Anyway, I say to Dean, 'Haven't you had enough? We done it almost every night. You got me open like a 7-Eleven, so whatever you think you gettin tonight, you *ain't* gettin it.' You know what he say? He was talkin about, 'I'm a get me some of that *ass*, is what I'm gettin.' I say, 'Nuh-uhh you *ain't!*' but he was all sprung over me and you know what he say?"

"What'd he say?" Sandra said.

I was glad she asked that.

Roz looked at Sandra. "He was talkin about, 'Turn around, sistah, you *know* I wanna see the junk in your trunk.'"

"What's that mean?" I whispered to Loop.

"I think he talking about getting some," Loop said out of the side of his mouth.

"Dean sound just like Bobby," Mary said. "All lips and lungs."

"Well, *I'm* jealous," Sandra said to Roz. "At least you got a man paying you some attention."

"*You* jealous?" Mary said, watching Sandra in the mirror. "Girl like you with your fancy executive job over at Macy's. All them sexy men in suits working there. Why would you be jealous, honey?"

"There may be lots of men," Sandra said, "but when have I had time to see 'em? I haven't had a date in six months. I'm just so tired of working all the time. Besides, it ain't no fun working there. No one I can talk to, really. I like talking with you all here better than the friends I got at Macy's."

"You're sweet," Mary said. She pulled the apron off of Sandra and told her she was done. Sandra said her hair looked perfect and gave Mary a hug. Then she paid her with a big ball of cash, and my eyes were glued.

Sandra put on her black leather jacket and asked Mary if she wanted to go see a movie some time or have dinner. Mary said she never went out much, but she'd like that. On her way to the door, Sandra rubbed both mines and Loop's heads. I watched her heels click across the floor and out the door. She was leaving, and so were my ten dollars.

"That woman is stuck up," Roz said, after Sandra was gone.

"Well, if she is," Mary said, sweeping up, "I can't see it."

I couldn't see it either. Sandra had tried to give us money.

"No," Mary said, "I can't see it. You hear how lonely she sounded when she asked me to a movie? She's always been nice to me. And she tips good too."

Mary stopped sweeping and turned to me, swinging the empty chair around. "Your turn, Con."

I stood up suddenly. "I can't," I said.

"Well, why not? Look at that fuzzy head of yours."

"I have to go home," I said.

Mary looked at me kind of funny. "*Okay,*" she said. "So you'll come by when you can."

I ran outside without even saying good-bye to Loop. Sandra was just getting into a Lexus down the street. I ran over and knocked on her window and accidentally scared her. She looked up, surprised to see me standing there. The window rolled down.

"Hello?" she said.

"Hi."

"Can I help you?"

My whole body was hot and shaking. "Can I have that money?" I sputtered.

Her forehead wrinkled. She seemed confused. "Huh?"

"The ten dollars you were gonna give us," I said.

She pulled her chin in and looked at me weird. "*Oh,*" she said. "Sure . . . okay." She turned and dug into her purse. Cars passed behind me and people were staring. I felt like a beggar asking for money.

"I don't have the ten-dollar bill anymore," Sandra said. She turned around with a twenty-dollar bill in her hand. "I only have this twenty."

Her hand wasn't holding it out to me, but it wasn't putting it back in her purse either. I didn't know what to do.

"I guess I could give you this," she said.

"Okay," I said.

Her hand shot forward, then stopped, then finally held the bill out for me. "Just take it," she said, sounding frustrated.

I reached out and took the bill. "Thanks," I said, unable to look at her face. My eyes burned as I stared down at the blurry pavement.

"Well," she said, rolling up the window. "Spend it on something good."

I swallowed. "I will."

18

Our neighbor Ms. Van Pelt was the Second Most Beautiful Woman in the World.

Moms was the First.

Ms. Van Pelt was also rich. Richer than us at least. Her father died and left her enough money to quit her job at Ross Dress-For-Less and buy a brand new Chrysler drop-top. Which was why I decided to break into her house. We needed money more than she did. Whatever I took, I'd give it back when we were doing better.

There was a hole under her porch, and I got on my hands and knees and crawled through it under the house to see if I could find a way to get inside. The wood floor creaked above my head. She was home.

I was going to crawl out, but then I heard the sound of water running. It seemed to come from a shaft of light leaking down into the dark between some wood posts fifteen feet away. I felt my way through the spider webs toward the light, following a rusty pipe. The light was pouring down through a wide crack next to a heater vent and I put my eye up to it.

She was in a bathtub. I could only see her head, and the white shampoo foam streaming down her long brown hair. Her head suddenly dipped down below the edge of the tub with a splash, and when she came up again, her mouth was open and her eyes were shut tight

and happy. Her hand reached out for the soap but kept missing. If I'd
had ten-foot arms, I would have reached into the bathroom through
the crack and grabbed the soap and put it in her hand. Her fingers
finally found the soap and slimed her face with it. She was getting
clean.

When she was done, she stood up. For a moment, I could see her
white legs through the crack, then they were gone. On my hands and
knees, I tried to follow the creak of her footsteps above me, but nails
and cement crumbs kept digging into my knees and my head banged
against a post. I gave up and crawled out from under the back porch.

When I stood up, I didn't want to go back home. I couldn't understand it—I'd come to steal some money and there I was, frozen in that
backyard with a runaway heart banging in my chest for Ms. Van Pelt.

I went around the house, peeping in all the windows until I spotted
her in the kitchen, washing dishes at the sink. I climbed the high
wood fence in order to see better. She had a towel piled on her head
and she was wearing a silky smooth robe. Her eyes were focused on
the dishes in the sink. She reached for a dirty glass and when she held
it up to the light, she caught me staring at her from up on the fence.
Her mouth opened and said something. Then she shook her head at
me and disappeared into the house. I was caught.

Before I could get down from the fence, she leaned out from the
back of the house, holding the top of her robe closed. "Are you in the
business of giving women heart attacks?" she called out.

"No."

"Want to come inside?"

"No."

"I have lemonade in the fridge."

"Okay."

I jumped down and walked over to her slow, dragging my fingers
along the side of her house. When I stopped in front of her she
reached out and pressed my nose with her pinkie.

"Spying on me?" she said.

"No."

She smiled, and the sun filled her cheeks with light. "Come on," she
said, turning, and I smelled something flowery coming off of her. I

breathed it in and followed her to the back porch, watching her heels
lift soft and sticky off the steps. They left wet pear shapes on the
painted wood. At the top of the porch, she wiped her feet on a mat
where three pairs of shoes were lined up in a neat row. "You have to
take off your shoes," she said.

"Why?"

"House rules. I have carpet."

We had carpet at our house too but I'd never heard of taking off
your shoes just to go inside. I kneeled down and pulled off my shoes,
eyeing her shiny brown painted toenails.

"I gotta take off my socks too?" I asked.

"If you want. It feels better."

I pulled off my socks and we stepped in. She was right—her thick
white carpet felt soft and tickly on my feet. She entered a bedroom at
the end of the hall. "I just have to put on some clothes, I'll be right
out." She closed the door and I tried to picture her taking the robe off.

The door suddenly swung open. She was smiling and wearing a
light blue dress. The wet ends of her hair were pressed smooth against
her skin. I couldn't stop looking at her.

"You've never been in here before, have you?" she said.

I shook my head.

"How about I give you the special tour then?"

I nodded.

She took my hand and pulled me into the room she'd just changed
in. The shades were pulled and the air was damp and thick with that
same flowery smell. "Now, this—" she said, stepping over some shoes,
"is the master bedroom." There was a mattress on the floor with messy
bunched-up blankets and the robe she'd been wearing. On the floor
were melted candles and wine bottles and a plate with some dried-up
cheese. But what grabbed my eyes were the photos of noses on every
wall in the room.

"Why do you have those?" I asked, pointing at the photos.

"I like noses," she said.

I had nothing to say about that.

I stepped in further, stopping at the edge of the mattress. "Is that
where you sleep?" I said.

"Mm-hmm. Come on, I'll show you the rest of the house."

She pulled me through the living room, the bathroom, and even a closet where she put all her junk. There were noses everywhere in the house—plastic ones, metal ones, even a coffee mug with a nose on it.

"How's your mother doing?" she asked me.

"Okay," I said, feeling dazed. Then I remembered why I'd come in the first place—the money. "Why don't you and her become friends?" I said.

She let out a laugh and tugged at my chin. "You're a real joker," she said. "Just like your father."

How did she know anything about Pops? As far as I could remember, I'd never seen Pops talking to her, except for calling out hello once in a while when she happened to be leaving her house.

The tour ended at the refrigerator where she pulled out a pitcher of lemonade and poured me a huge glass. I drank it down in one shot.

"You don't have any manners, do you?" she said, but she seemed to like it.

She poured me some more and watched me drink and I felt all warm being there in her house filled with noses and flowery smells. I finished the second glass.

"Boy, you drink like you just crawled out of the Saharan Desert," she said, smiling. She filled the glass with more lemonade.

"I ain't gonna drink anymore unless you have some too," I said.

She looked at me, surprised. "Did your father teach you that line?"

"No."

"Well, I hope you don't use that on the girls at school."

"I don't."

"Yeah right."

"Are you gonna have some lemonade?" I said, picking up my glass.

She tapped my nose with her finger. "Nope. I've got my own drink." She opened the cabinet, and I lowered my lemonade and stared.

On the shelf was a big glass bowl of fungus tea.

I suddenly had the feeling that I was doing something wrong being in her house, that maybe Pops wouldn't be so happy if he found out I was there.

When I left, it was dark out. I stopped on the sidewalk and eyed our house and Ms. Van Pelt's. I'd already swallowed some of Pops's secrets, and he'd made me swim in his flow of lost jobs and late night drinking, his hitting and his rifles, his bullets and bottles of beer. Now it was his fungus tea, and he was working on Ms. Van Pelt. He'd already planted his mold in her house. I just hoped it wouldn't grow.

19

By Friday, the day Pops owed three months of rent, we hadn't gotten a call from the owner, Mr. Kalt—either he'd never gotten my letter, or he didn't want to do a trade.

Pops came out of his closet that morning wearing clothes I'd never seen before: a gray jacket, striped tie, dark slacks. He told me to dress up too—I was going with him to see Mr. Riggs at Best Rental.

I didn't wanna have to go to Best Rental when we didn't have money. Then Phyllis, the woman who'd taken my letter for Mr. Kalt, would see me with Pops and know it hadn't been a Christmas card after all. I took the twenty dollars Sandra had given me from where I'd hidden it under my bed and gave it to Pops. "Would twenty dollars help?" I said, hoping I wouldn't have to go anymore.

Pops stuffed the bill into his pocket. "It won't help for shit," he said. "Get dressed."

We took the truck to Best Rental. Mr. Riggs was talking on the phone at a desk just behind Phyllis. Phyllis saw me and smiled, but when Pops told her his name she suddenly got confused. She looked at me, then at Pops, and then at me again, only this time with big sorry eyes and a wrinkle in her forehead like I was the saddest squid in all of Alameda. My stomach tightened into a ball of shame, the way it had when Pops begged Mr. Riggs on our front porch. I couldn't look at Phyllis anymore.

"Please take a seat," she said to us. "Mr. Riggs is almost done with a call, then he'll be right out."

I couldn't understand what she meant by "right out" since Mr. Riggs was sitting at a desk directly in front of us. He finished on the phone and Pops stood up and I did too, but Mr. Riggs flipped through some files on his desk like we weren't even there. Finally, he stopped on a file and by the way he pulled on his nose, I knew it was ours. He clapped his hands, stood up, and walked around his desk. "Come in, Mr. Clay," he said.

We took the two chairs right in front of us and watched him go back around his desk and sit down. He stared at our papers again.

"We need a little more time," Pops said.

Mr. Riggs started shaking his head.

Pops pulled a check out of his shirt pocket. "I can give you five hundred today," he said. "The rest in a couple weeks."

"Mr. Clay," said Riggs, still looking at our file, "that won't be necessary."

"C'mon," Pops said, shaking the check at him. "It's five hundred!"

Mr. Riggs eyed the check in Pops's hand. "Put it away, Mr. Clay."

"*Why?* You can't kick us out when I've got money right here."

"I'm not kicking you out."

Pops stared at him, confused. "You *aren't?*"

Mr. Riggs slid his jaw to the right, then to the left. "No, Mr. Clay, I—am—not."

Pops still didn't understand. Neither did I, but my heart was racing.

"When I conveyed to Mr. Kalt the fact that you hadn't paid your rent in almost three months," Mr. Riggs went on, "the man, against all my advice, allowed his heart to get in the way of business. He decided to wipe your delinquent rent from the record."

"Jesus," Pops said.

"Yes!" came a voice behind us. It was Phyllis, pumping her fists in the air for us.

"Ms. Smither!" Mr. Riggs yelled at her.

"*Sorry,*" Phyllis said, turning back to her work.

"Mr. Clay . . ." said Mr. Riggs, "I cannot believe what I am about to say to you." He pulled out a handkerchief, blew his nose loud, and put the handkerchief away. "Never in my ten years in real estate have I been forced to do what I am about to do. It goes against all my training, and believe me, nothing like this would have ever happened in the *Marines*." He pulled an envelope out of the folder on his desk. "Mr. Clay. Kalt is a very sick man and his judgment has clearly been affected. Yet as handlers of his property, we must represent and carry out his wishes and"—his eyes squinted at the envelope in his shaking hand—"it is with great regret, Mr. Clay, and only because it's my official duty, that I hand you this check, at the request of the owner."

Pops took the envelope, then opened it and read the check. He looked up at Mr. Riggs. "This is for two thousand dollars. I don't get it."

"Frankly, I don't either, Mr. Clay."

"You're *giving* me money?" asked Pops.

"No, Mr. Clay, Best Rental is not in the business of giving money to its renters—we *take* money from them. I am merely acting as an agent for the owner of the rental unit. *He* is giving you money in order to—in his words—'*help you and your family get back on your feet*.'"

Pops looked at the check again. "I have to call him. What's Mr. Kalt's number?"

"Mr. Clay," said Riggs, "you know Best Rental does not divulge information like that to its renters."

"But—he's given us this money. I want to talk to him. I've gotta thank him."

"I will convey that information to the owner," Mr. Riggs said. He closed the file on his desk and told us that Best Rental would be expecting a check for our next rent on the first of next month. He picked up his phone, and reminded us that he was in the business of rental properties, not charity, and had business to do.

Pops stood up and headed to the door and I followed him, my skin feeling warm and bumpy all over. Phyllis was beaming at me as we passed her desk. She whispered to Pops, "Mr. Kalt is a saint."

Out in the parking lot, Pops stared at the check. "*Jesus!*" he said. He handed it to me. "Take a look at that."

The check said: *Pay To The Order Of Mr. Raymond Clay—$2,000*.

"Ever seen that much money before?" Pops said. He took the check back and read it again, then he put it in his wallet.

"Now we won't be kicked out, right?" I said.

"*Hell* no!"

Pops said we had to celebrate. At Safeway we bought a two-liter bottle of Pepsi for me and a six-pack of Coors for him, then we sat in the truck out in the parking lot and slurped on our drinks. It felt like we'd just won a war. Pops handed me his beer and told me to take a sip. It tasted horrible, but I swallowed a gulp anyway because I was so happy. Mr. Kalt had traded with me. He'd even given Pops money! It was stone cold clear that he was an Otis Sistrunk fan like me.

I finished half the Pepsi, until my bones were vibrating. Pops made it through five bottles of beer. He had to take a leak and I did too—I was popping with pee. We got out and he scanned the parking lot: nobody was around except an old wilma sitting in a car staring at us. Pops eyed her for a second, then said, "Oh well," and unbuttoned his jeans and let it rip. The old wilma shook her head but I couldn't hold it any longer and I peed with Pops.

From the truck we spotted a Christmas tree sale across the parking lot. Pops opened his wallet and handed me thirty dollars to go pick out a tree. Then he reached into his pocket and pulled out Sandra's twenty. "Keep that for yourself," he said, giving it to me. He sunk in the seat and closed his eyes.

"Aren't you coming?" I said.

"I'm just gonna rest a little. Pick a good one for us."

The Christmas tree lot was packed with squids and their parents, all of them smiling and excited from the fresh smell of seeping sap and branches and cut tree trunks. A man wearing a Santa's hat stood by the cash register, puffing on a cigar. He had a round chest, round face, and a big flat nose. His eyes were brown and friendly. "Lookin for something, son?" he said to me out of the side of his mouth without removing the cigar.

"A Christmas tree," I said.

He blew out some smoke and looked me over. "Where your folks at?"

"Out in the truck sleeping."

"*Sleepin?*" He pulled his cigar out of his mouth and looked out at the parking lot. "*Both* 'em?"

"Only Pops."

"Oh, I see—he got you in here doin all the hard work."

"That's right."

"Well," he said, puffing his cigar and watching me, "let's find you a tree."

He put his hand on my shoulder and we walked down the rows of trees while he pointed at different ones and said what kind they were. I liked the way his sweet cigar smoke mixed with the cold smell of trees—it reminded me of the pipe-smoking men trying to survive in the Alaska wilds, which Mr. Garabedian made us read about in a book by Jack London called *White Fang.*

We got to the end of the row and turned around to look back at all the Christmas trees.

"Those are my trees," the man said. "Which one you want?"

"Where are they from?"

"*From?*" said the man. "They from the forest, where you think they from?"

"Which state?"

The man looked down at me with a wrinkled eyebrow, then looked back at the trees. "Well now, I suppose they from California."

"You don't got one from Alaska?"

"*Alaska?*"

"Where White Fang is from."

"Well, okay," he said. "Okay." He pulled the cigar out of his mouth. "How much money you got to spend?"

I showed him the thirty dollars Pops had given me for the tree.

"I see," he said. "That oughta be enough for the one Alaska tree I got."

Behind the lot were a bunch of trees still tied up and lying on their sides. Over by itself, on a piece of black plastic tarp, stood one tall Christmas tree.

"There's your Alaska tree," said the man.

He didn't have to tell me that tree was from Alaska—it was fatter and taller than any of the other ones, and covered in white complete. He grabbed it by the trunk and lifted it up onto his shoulder, and I led him out through the parking lot to the truck. Pops was asleep with his head pressed against the window, his hair matted up against the glass in all directions like an old bird's nest.

"Looks like your father need to take it on home for some rest," said the man.

I suddenly wished I hadn't brought him back to the truck. I told him me and Pops were celebrating because Mr. Kalt had given us money and said we didn't have to pay rent. "Mr. Kalt is a saint," I said.

"He *must* be a saint," said the man, setting the tree down in the back of the truck carefully so Pops didn't wake up. "I never heard of no owner who didn't want the rent, let alone giving money back." He shook his head. "I could use a landlord like that."

"Mr. Riggs won't give out his phone number," I said.

"Damn straight he won't. That kind of thing get out, everybody be rioting in the streets trying to get at him." He shook his head again and mumbled to himself, "Just my luck."

I gave the man the thirty dollars and he told me to get Pops on home and in bed where he belonged. Then he walked back into the Christmas trees.

I saw Pops through the rear window. He was coming awake and didn't know I was watching him. He lifted the last bottle of beer and gulped it down, and I suddenly wanted to run back into the trees and find the Christmas Tree Man again.

20

Moms and Pops stopped fighting. We'd gotten money from a saint, Pops had time now to find a new job, and the house felt lighter and quieter. Pops even patched the hole he'd punched in the wall. It was like we'd flown past something bad and now we could all breathe. At least a little.

The days drizzled down. Gramma didn't feel good and slept out most of them. It was her job to decorate the Christmas tree, and she kept saying she'd get to it when she had a little more energy. For now it sat near the front window, white and empty and undecorated.

When Pops and me went to give Moose his money back, Moose was so glad about it he sent us home with a whole silver salmon he'd caught on a boat. He wrapped its fat body in newspaper and handed it to me. In the truck, I held the cold fish in my lap and stared at its head, which stuck out of the wrapping. The mouth hung open and the wide eyes were frozen with the fright still locked inside them. You could see all the thinking the fish had been doing. It must have known it was dying.

In the kitchen, I watched Pops cut the head away from its body. I picked up the head and weighed it in my hands. For a head filled with dying thoughts, it felt light.

Pops took the head from me and tossed it in the air a few times, catching it with one hand. "Too bad we have to throw it away," he said.

"Yeah," I said.

He looked around the kitchen. His eye came to rest on the pot and pan rack over the stove. He hung the head on an empty hook, so that it was watching over the kitchen.

"There," he said.

When Moms came home, Pops pulled her into the dining room. She tried to slip out of his grip, but he wouldn't let her go and made her sit at the table. When he set a plate of broiled salmon in front of her, he didn't have to ask her to stay anymore. She stared at the salmon slab and the ends of her mouth curled up into a smile. The sun was going down outside and her face seemed to fill with glowing light.

"Go get Grandma," Pops said to me.

Gramma was laid out asleep on her bed, still in her clothes, and I tiptoed up to her. Her face looked thin and her cheekbones stuck out. After a while, one of her eyelids twitched and opened. "How long you been cooling your heels in here?" she said.

"Pops told me to come get you," I said. "Dinnertime."

"I haven't been hungry all day," she grumbled. She sat up slow and called Pops a bunch of swears for making her get out of bed. I walked with her into the dining room. When she saw the salmon waiting for her with a lemon slice, she stopped. "*My,*" she said.

The four of us ate at the table. Gramma said it was the best salmon she'd ever had, and Moms said so too. I was just happy we were all together.

After dinner Moms and Pops went out for drinks. It was the first time I'd seen them go out by themselves in a long while.

Gramma and me stayed up late watching television. When we went to bed, Moms and Pops still weren't home.

In the middle of the night, I heard Gramma crying out. I jumped from bed and ran to her room. It smelled different somehow, like rotting earth. I clicked on the lamp. She was rolling in bed, side-to-side, moaning about dirt and dust. I tried grabbing her arms but they pulled loose. "We all live down in the dirt and the dust!" she was saying.

I rushed to Moms's room. Her bed was empty. The living room

couch was empty too. I heard Gramma groaning something about oranges, about how she missed the shine of them and wanted me to bring her one.

I ran to the kitchen. The salmon head was still hanging above the stove, its black unblinking eyes busy with death. I felt a chill sink down through me, right to my toes. In the fridge, I found two moldy oranges. I grabbed one, rinsed it off, and took it back to Gramma.

She cradled it in her arms like a baby, cussing and telling me to leave her alone. "I just need my goddamn sleep, dammit!" she said. She rocked back and forth with the orange in her arms. "I can't get any goddamned-sleep. . . . *Hell!*"

She was finally quiet. She lay on one side, curled around the orange, breathing deeply. I watched her for a while, then clicked off the lamp and went back to my bed.

Somewhere in the night, somewhere in my sleep, I heard Moms and Pops come home, but I didn't get up. I was busy dreaming of Gramma and me, sharing a shiny orange under a white sky with a sun floating in it like a lazy Frisbee.

The next morning, the sun woke up, but Gramma did not.

She was dead.

I was asleep when Moms came into my room and pulled my window shade up with a snap.

"Con, get up. Gramma has died."

I opened my eyes. Moms stood over my bed with a cigarette, blowing smoke into the air. Her bloodshot eyes were staring at me, but they weren't focused. I jumped off my bed and ran for my door to go see Gramma, but Moms dug her nails into my arm and held me back. "The men are taking her away, Con."

I went to the window. On the sidewalk, Pops was following two men as they carried a stretcher out to an ambulance. Gramma was covered by a sheet.

"How did she die?" I said.

Moms cleared her throat. She could barely talk. "They think it was her heart."

"It broke?"

She nodded.

"Was it because she didn't have Granpa anymore?"

Moms took a suck on her cigarette. "Maybe." She sighed smoke at the window glass. "I guess fifty years with someone will do that to you."

I decided right there not to ever be with anybody for fifty years so I wouldn't get taken out by them.

Pops was standing in the street, watching as the men slid the stretcher into the ambulance and closed the doors. They said something to him, he nodded, then the men got in the ambulance and drove away.

"*Oh, hell,*" Moms whispered.

My heart suddenly leaped because I remembered the last word Gramma had ever said—Hell.

"It's all right for you to cry," Moms said.

"I'm not going to," I said.

And I didn't. I was thinking about Gramma dying in the night while I'd been dreaming. I hoped that she had been dreaming too. Dreaming and dying.

Not just dying.

On the day of the funeral, the sky was a lead slice, and cold wind ripped across Alameda. Pops drove us in the Impala down Central to Keyes Memorial Services. Moms talked about people at work like it was any normal day. But when we got out of the car, and the wind blew us toward a door with two white lions on either side, Moms burst out crying. Me and Pops led her to one of the lions so she could sit down.

"I have *no* one now," she cried. "*No one!*"

Moose came out and we all helped her inside. Lin was waiting on one of the benches, holding Freddy. There was nobody else in the place.

A minister showed up and gave a short speech about Gramma, telling us where she'd spent her childhood and how different life had been for her back in Missouri during the Great Depression. He talked about what a kindhearted person she had been, and how she was a dedicated wife, mother, and grandmother. I couldn't understand it. He'd never even met her.

Afterwards, I waited while everyone else went up to look at Gramma. She was laid out for people to cry on. When they were finished, I walked up to the casket. It hardly looked like her. Her face was white and flat, her mouth a thin line.

"Hi, Gramma," I said. "I sure miss you."

I checked to make sure no one was watching, then reached into my jacket and pulled out the TV channel changer from home. I slipped it into her casket. "Now you'll last the longest without yawning," I said.

I leaned over her face, until I was right up close, and took a big sniff. She smelled flowery, just like she'd told me the saints smelled. She had the Odors. I smiled wide.

Moms, who'd been speaking with the minister, caught me with the smile on my face. She said something to the minister, then walked over. Her expression looked nuclear.

"Why are you so happy, Con?"

I felt my throat tightening.

"Huh?" she said. She pointed at Gramma's white face. "Look at that. Your grandmother's dead. You're supposed to be sad."

She grabbed my arm and pulled me away from the casket, past Pops and the minister and out the door, until we were on the sidewalk where pigeons rushed to get out of our way. She dug her fingers into my arm and smacked me on the face.

"You're a shit," she said, tears in her eyes. She walked back inside.

I lowered my head. One-Eye the Pigeon was near my feet, staring up at me hungrily with his eye. Beat it, I said, I ain't got jack for you— my Gramma is dead in there laid out. *Give it a name,* he said, and he held his ground, keeping his eye on me.

I turned to face the building. When I saw the two long lion faces, my eyes started burning and I cried. Not over the ache in my arm, or my stinging face, but for my Gramma. The sky was cold and silver like an abalone shell, and waves of whipping gray wind tried to lift me up to it. Then the wind let out a high lonely whistle and I felt something rise above me and I knew it was my Gramma leaving. Even One-Eye the Pigeon looked away and I knew my Gramma was dead and gone.

21

On Sunday morning Moms woke me up and told me I was evil. What kind of son had she raised, who would smile at his own grandmother's funeral? For that, she said, I was gonna have to go to church. Then she left my room, slamming the door.

I went out to the living room where she sat on the couch. Pops was up and watching the Raiders pre-game show. "But you and Pops don't go to church," I said.

She glared at me, raising an eyebrow. "I had to go to church when I was *little*," she said, "and now so do you."

I didn't know much about church. I only knew it happened during Raiders games. So I hated it automatic.

"What church am I supposed to go to?" I asked, for the sake of purposes.

Moms looked at Pops, who shrugged his shoulders, then she turned to me. "Don't be a smartass, Con." She went into the dining room and got out the yellow pages and looked up a church for me. When she called the church, they said that if she'd just bring me in that morning, they'd be really glad to pick me up each Sunday morning from then on. *Tuh.*

Pops ended up taking me. We drove all over Alameda and he smoked three cigarettes just trying to find the place. He had it written down on his matchbook: *Alameda Southern Baptist Church of God in Christ.*

At least it had a good name. Any church with a name like that had to have some flow. I brought my mirrored sunglasses just in case.

We finally pulled to a stop in front of a church with brown cottage-cheese walls and stains dripping under every window. The building was small and sat alone in an old, bleached-gray parking lot. No trees, no grass. A sign out front said: COMING ATTRACTION: JESUS.

"Well, there it is," Pops said.

It was the most squid church I'd ever seen. Pops threw his cigarette in the street and walked me to the door. A blond man with bowl-cut hair came at us with a big smile. His chin was shaped like a foot heel. He smiled at my Raiders jacket and he smiled at Pops's jeans and work boots. He cocked his head and looked right at me with a smile, then did the same to Pops.

"Joining us in worship this morning?" he asked.

Pops pointed at me. "Just him."

The man looked confused for a second, then cocked his head and smiled at me again. "Just in time for Sunday School." He held out his hand and I shook it, but he wouldn't let it go and put his other hand on top of mine for a hand sandwich. "I'm Jim. What's your name?"

"Conrad."

Pops looked at Jim. "On the phone they said you could take him home."

"No problem! The van should have him home by one. We can pick him up for the evening service too, if you like."

I turned to Pops, hoping he would say no. "What time is that?" he asked Jim.

"Five to seven. We've got Oakland Tabernacle joining our service tonight. Should be real good."

"All right," Pops said. He came in with us and filled out a form with my name and address, then he gave me a look and went back out to his truck. Jim put his hand on my shoulder and led me down a brown carpet hallway, and I knew straight out I was Sir Conrad, Prisoner of Church.

We went to a room filled with squids my age, who were sitting around a table with a guy Jim called Morgan. "Everybody," Jim said, "this is Conrad." The squids all stared at me.

When Jim left, Morgan stood up. His hair was buzzed on top but long in the back, and he was thin as a fishing pole. He surprised me with a high hand slap. "Welcome Conrad," he said. "Cool. Why don't you sit down next to Eddie here? We were just sharing stories of how we got saved."

I found the empty chair next to Eddie, who wore a white button-shirt with a tie and seemed a few years older than me. "Who made you come here?" he whispered in my ear.

"My Moms," I said.

"My mom is dead," he said, then sat up straight.

I looked over at him. He was serious.

Morgan asked a girl with two brown ponytails to continue sharing how she came to take the Lord Jesus Christ as her personal savior. I had no idea what they were talking about. She told a story about how her dog Muffin got flattened by the movers' truck when her family first came to Alameda. She said she cried for three weeks straight, and needed help. That was when she asked God for help and was saved.

It was the boy next to her's turn. He hid his face by tilting his head down until his chin jammed into his chest. All you could see was the big flap of hair sticking out of the top of his head. He told us about his moms catching him stealing a Charleston Chew at Safeway and how she marched him down to the police station where the sergeant said they'd let him go but next time he'd be locked up. The boy went quiet and we all stared at the top of his head.

Morgan said, "And then you took Jesus as your personal Lord and savior?"

The boy's head nodded. Morgan said it was his *own* turn now and he was going to tell us about his wild past. Everyone looked at him, excited. His eyes lit up when he told us how he'd moved to Hollywood and spent three years following the band Guns 'n' Roses around.

"You *did?*" Eddie asked.

Morgan smiled proud. He said he grew his hair long and started his own rock band, and did drugs and was with a lot of women. All eyes were glued on him now, and his face became serious. "I hit the bottom then," he said, "and I needed help because I wanted to die. I looked around at the people I called friends, and I saw that they were too busy ruining their own lives to help me. I'd already cut myself off from my family because they hadn't understood my rock 'n' roll lifestyle. I realized I was totally alone. That's when I discovered Jesus. I asked Him for forgiveness and took Him as my personal savior." He smiled again, and told us he was married now and had devoted his life to the Lord and to keeping other young people from going down the bad path he had walked.

Judging by the jealous look in everyone's eyes around the table, it seemed like we all wanted to walk down the bad path too.

A girl across the table was staring at me. Her eyeballs swam around in her thick glasses, like they weren't tied into her head, and her shoulders and arms were covered with freckles. "That's Jeannie," Eddie whispered to me, "but everyone calls her Big Freckle. She's the choir leader."

Morgan finished his story and started going around the table again. Soon I'd have to tell how I'd been saved. I didn't know if the Lord had ever saved me, but I was hell-bent on saving my own ass, and needed to come up with something quick or else I'd look like a squid. I had enough philosophy to figure out that each kid was telling a sob story, then claiming that was when they took the Lord Jesus Christ as their personal savior.

When Morgan finally called on me, I said I got saved when me and my best friend Loop pulled a Five Fingers down at SportMart.

"Five Fingers?" Morgan said.

"That's right. See, Loop's moms Mary bought him a new pair of Air Jordans at SportMart. The next day was 'set-up' day: I sleazed down to SportMart with a pair of wire cutters and found a pair of Air Jordans in my size. I cut the plastic security tie and laced up the shoes. After I tried them on for show, I put them back in the box. Then I came back the next day wearing my oldest pair of shoes that I didn't care about. I found the shoes I'd set up, put them on, put my old shoes in the box, and walked out."

The squids blinked at me with shocked faces.

"Good," said Morgan. "Is that when you looked for help from Jesus?"

"Not yet, because me and Loop weren't done with our operation. I headed straight for Loop's and put my new Air Jordans in the shoe box that Loop's Jordans had come in. Then I waited a couple days and returned the shoes with Loop's receipt to SportMart for a C-note and change. I flowed Loop the change for letting me use his receipt and box, so he got his new shoes plus cash. I walked away with a big fat C."

Eddie raised an eyebrow at me. Jeannie was beaming me a smile. Morgan looked confused.

"I rode it wide," I said, "until me and Pops took a fishing trip on the bay and a fish jumped out of the water and got lodged in Pops's throat in the middle of a long yawn. I looked down Pops's throat and saw the fish tail way down there and I stuck my hand in but couldn't reach it. Another boat came over and the fishermen tried to help Pops, but by the time we got him to a hospital it was too late and he was dead."

Everybody seemed frozen. They were all staring at me.

"Then I took the Lord Jesus Christ as my personal savior," I said.

Morgan gave me a long look. "Okay—" he said. "Okay . . . *Good.*"

Eddie leaned over and whispered in my ear: "That was the greatest save by Jesus yet."

But I didn't feel good about it. I'd been in church twenty minutes and I was already telling lies.

Besides, I suddenly remembered that Gramma was gone and it put a sharp pain right through the middle of me.

Morgan ended class with a talk about handling problems by turning to Christ for help. I didn't know how to turn to Christ yet, but I was willing to do it if he could help bring Gramma back.

After class, Jeannie volunteered to show me the way to chapel. The hall was packed with people talking, and I followed close behind her.

"How do you turn to Christ?" I said.

She stopped and looked at me. "What do you mean?"

"I wanna turn to him."

"You're really weird."

"*Tub,*" I said. I pulled out my sunglasses and put them on.

"What did you just say?" she asked.

"What?"

"That noise you just made."

"Puh," I said.

"You *are* weird."

She pushed me in front of Preacher Jordan, an old man with gold hair and loose lips. He held out his veiny hand and I shook it. It felt cold as a frozen chicken thigh. "You going to remove those for the sermon?" he said, pointing at my sunglasses. "Feel like I'd be preaching to a four-foot bug."

Before I could even take them off, Jeannie pulled me away. We wove in and out of people chatting in the hall. "What school do you go to?" she said.

"Jack London."

"That's a black school."

"So?"

She stopped and looked at me. "My mother says that's where all the poor people are."

I'd never heard anybody talk about where I lived like that. Were Moms and Pops *poor people?*

We took a seat in the chapel and Jeannie explained everything to me: the people were called the *congregation;* a bench was a *pew;* a song was a *hymn;* a talk was a *sermon;* and money you gave to church was *tithes and offerings.* It seemed they were trying to mix you up by changing the name of everything.

"What do they call the carpet?" I asked Jeannie.

"Carpet," she said.

Church was gonna be harder than I thought.

A man named Mr. Garcia came over and eyeballed my Raiders jacket. He looked around, pulled his mustache, then whispered to me, "Raiders fan?"

"Yeah," I said.

His eyes moved around the room. "They're playing right now," he mumbled out of the side of his mouth, making sure nobody was looking.

"I know."

"We'll talk after the service," he whispered. He patted my shoulder and turned to hug an old wilma. Then he came back and leaned down close to my face. "Favorite player?"

"Otis Sistrunk," I said.

His eyes lit up. "*Otis?* That's going way back to the old school." He gave my hand a good squeeze. "Just win, baby!" Then he lowered his voice: "After the service." He went and sat down in another pew with his family and turned and gave me a wink and nobody had to tell me that he was an undercover Raiders fan.

Jeannie slid closer to me. "Have you been baptized?" she said.

I'd never heard of being baptized, but it sounded pretty weak so I said, "No."

"Then why did you tell us you were saved?"

"Because I was."

"People get *baptized* after they're saved."

"Well, I didn't need it."

"You'll go to Hell if you don't get baptized."

"No I won't."

"Yes you will."

"Nope."

"Yep."

I slid a few inches away from her. Her eyes caught me.

"You're gonna go to Hell," she said. "You better go up during bene-diction and tell Preacher you want to be baptized." She got to her feet and looked down at me. "Besides, everything you said in Sunday School was a *lie*—I saw your father bringing you to church this morn-ing." She walked proudly up to the pulpit, where she joined the choir.

Puh!

Everyone flowed into the chapel now. The old wilma I'd seen hug-ging Mr. Garcia sat down next to me and said her name was Mrs. Hayes. At first I was glad she sat beside me because she reminded me a little of Gramma. But then she warned me that she was the oldest lady in the congregation, and she pointed a crooked finger at me like I'd better watch out! Her breath smelled like a dirty-clothes hamper. She wasn't my Gramma.

There were only four people in the choir, including Jeannie, and they began a song. It was the worst singing I'd ever heard. I couldn't understand why Jeannie was the leader because she couldn't sing for jack. Big Bird could've done it better. The other women were old and stooped and couldn't carry a tune either. They cracked it like broken kazoos. They were gravel-pits. When they opened their mouths, it sounded like a bunch of crickets beating themselves against their throats.

Mrs. Hayes jabbed my shoulder and pointed for me to stand up like everybody else. I did it just to get her blue eyeball off of me. Jeannie sent me a fat smile and I felt my face heat up like a porch light. I put on my sunglasses, but Preacher Jordan shook his head at me from the pulpit, and his loose lips quivered like an earthquake crack. I took the sunglasses off.

I looked around the pews. The men were standing up but they weren't singing. They were only moving their lips. They were proba-bly busy thinking about the Raiders game, just like me. It was back East, which meant it had started at ten and would be finished by the time church let out at twelve-thirty. We'd miss the whole thing. I was sure we were all very sorry about that.

Well, the preacher preached, the choir choired, and the organ cried. A big black fly woodpeckered the window next to me, trying to escape, then it died. The congregation shifted and yawned and coughed and creaked while a fan above blended our breath. Outside a siren screamed and traffic hissed like a steam iron. Jeannie microwaved my ears for the eight-thousandth time and the preacher looked out at the congregation with his hands open, asking people to come up and be saved. At first nobody made a move, and every time I was sure the hymn was over, Jeannie would start in on another chorus.

Come on Jeannie, you blind betty, stop that crowing please!

One of Mr. Garcia's little girls ran up crying. Then Mr. Garcia's wife started crying and walked up too. The preacher held their hands and the three of them prayed with their eyes closed. Afterwards, the preacher stood up and looked out at us. "These two brave people—mother and daughter—have had the courage today to declare Jesus as their personal Lord and Savior. *Who* will take that courageous step and join them?"

The preacher's eyes caught mine. My heart jumped and I dropped my eyes to the carpet. When I looked up again he was eyeing the other side of the room. I took a deep breath.

The service finally ended and everyone stood outside, hugging and talking. I didn't wait around for the church van or to talk to Mr. Garcia. I ran down the street until it hit Central, and then I ran as hard I could towards Webster.

Around the time I passed Safeway, I started worrying I was headed for Hell.

When I walked in all out of breath, Moms was on the couch, smoking and watching television. She still looked angry with me.

"What did you do with the channel changer, Con? We tore up the whole living room and couldn't find it."

"I didn't do anything with it," I said.

She studied my face for a moment, like she was unsure about whether or not to believe me. Then she turned back to the television.

"Moms?"

"Hm?"

"Am I going to Hell?"

She lifted the cigarette to her mouth and took a deep suck off of it, squinting at the television. She blew a cloud of smoke into the air.

"It wouldn't surprise me."

I was watching the 49ers game and Moms was taking a nap when Pops came home later with a small cardboard package. He set it on top of the television, then went into the kitchen.

I tried watching the game, but my eyes kept moving to the package. What *was* it? I finally got up and walked over to it. The box was taped shut. There wasn't a label or any writing to tell what was inside.

Maybe it was more bullets.

Pops was still in the kitchen, so I picked up the box. It was only a little heavier than a box of cereal. I heard Pops coming, and I set it down and went back to the couch.

Pops had a beer in one hand and a sandwich in the other. He took a seat next to me and started watching the game, taking bites from the sandwich between slugs of beer.

"What is that?" I asked.

"What?" Pops said, his eyes focused on the television.

"The box," I said. "What's in it?"

"Mm," he said as he took a long gulp of beer. He pointed his can of beer at the box. "Gramma."

Pops was passed out on the couch when Moms woke from her nap and saw the box of Gramma's ashes on the television. She walked over and picked it up and held it in her arms and cried. Then she took it back into her bedroom and closed the door.

A honk came from out front. The church van had come.

I didn't move. Another honk.

"Go to church," Pops said, without opening his eyes.

I went and knocked on Moms's door. "What?" came her weak voice. I heard her sniffling.

"I don't wanna go back to church," I said into the crack.

"Just *go*, Con."

That night, I was back in Southern Baptist Church of Boredom. There weren't as many people in the chapel as there had been for the morning service, and the visiting church from Oakland hadn't shown up yet. I sat in a side pew by myself, listening to Jeannie and our choir sing "Bringing in the Sheaves" like a bunch of sick birds.

The hymn was coming to a close when the rear door of the chapel burst open and a big sistah rushed up the aisle singing at the top of her lungs: *"Bringing in the Sheaves! Bringing in the Sheaves!"* She was followed by fifty bruthas and sistahs from Oakland Baptist Tabernacle, all of them singing out loud, mouths open wide, all tongues and teeth. One sistah shouted, "We're holy ghost filled!" and she wasn't lying: it flowed out from their dipping and diving heads, and heated my face and tingled the back of my neck. *"Bringing in the Sheaves!"* They sang so loud the building vibrated, and the old wilmas in our congregation looked frightened and put their hands over their hearts. I sat up and gripped the pew with both hands. We had a *situation!*

I was glad to see our lame-ass choir taken out by a real gospel joint. But after the Oaktown choir had showed us what time it was, they quieted down and took seats in the pews around me to listen to our choir sing for *them*. When Jeannie and the three old wilmas stood up, I slid deep down in my pew so no one could spot me. I wanted to warn the people from Oaktown that Jeannie's singing was a one-man Emergency Broadcast: SOS now you poor people, run for the border! *Damn*, people, quick—Jeannie's going in for a sing!

But it was too late. Jeannie and the wilmas had already started into "Green Pastures." I eyeballed the Oaktown faces around me, waiting for them to lose it and break out laughing, but they watched her with serious faces. Some were even swaying. Maybe they were used to going to honky churches and hearing half-price singing.

Jeannie finished the hymn, and it went dead quiet, except for the fan overhead. I could see her chest breathing hard as she looked out over the pews, waiting. Somebody from Oaktown gave a clap. Then another. Then the people from Oaktown all stood up and gave her a standing ovation. The building seemed to shake. Jeannie was smiling and crying and I was surprised to find my eyes getting wet too, but I dried them straight out.

After everyone quieted down, Preacher Jordan handed over the reins to the visiting preacher from Oaktown. He gave us a sermon about how important it was to talk to Jesus. He told us to write a letter to Jesus and mail it to Heaven. He raised his arms and said, "Whatchoo gonna do?"

His people in the pews said, "Write a letter!"

"Whatchoo gonna do?" he asked again.

"Write a letter!" said everyone louder. This time I said it too.

The preacher cupped his ear with his hand. "I can't hear you!"

"WRITE A LETTER!" we shouted.

"Where you gonna send it to?" asked the preacher.

"HEAVEN!" we shouted.

"Where you gonna *mail* it to?"

I yelled as loud as I could. "HEAVEN!"

The preacher asked, "Where you gonna *FedEx* it to?"

"HEAVEN!" I screamed.

"Where you gonna *U.P.S.* it to?"

"HEAVEN!"

"Who you gonna send it to?"

"JESUS!"

"Who?"

Jeannie was behind the pulpit. We caught each other's eyes, and smiled as we screamed "JESUS!"

"*Who?*"

"JE-SUS!"

Service ended and the people from Oakland Baptist Tabernacle filled the parking lot outside, laughing and talking with each other. I was happy being surrounded by so many bruthas and sistahs, but our small congregation moved through them with watchful eyes, like jack smelt caught in a school of striped bass.

When I got in the van to go home, three old wilmas in the backseat were staring out the window at the visitors from Oaktown. "Interesting people," one of the wilmas said.

We dropped church members off at a rest home and at three different houses outlined with strings of sparkling Christmas lights. Then we headed up Central and turned onto Webster Street.

"Who lives over *here?*" asked one of the old wilmas.

"I do," I said.

She looked at me with a surprised face. "Oh."

"Too bad about the Naval Station," said our driver.

The van stopped in front of my house, and I got out and stood on the sidewalk to watch as the van pulled away down the street. I turned to the house. It looked small and dark against the gray night sky. The Alaska tree that Pops and me had bought sat in the living room window, still undecorated, and flashes of light from the television flickered off its empty white branches.

In my room I started writing a letter to Heaven, but Moms walked in before I could finish: *Dear Gramma, I miss you. I wish you were still—*

Moms pointed her cigarette at my letter. "What is *that,* Con?"

I lowered my eyes to what I'd written. "The preacher said we could write a letter to Heaven."

"Let me see." She snatched the paper out of my hands and read it, then gave me a look like I was crazy. "You're writing a letter to *Gramma?*"

I blinked at her.

She put the cigarette between her lips and squinted at the letter.

"It's kind of *boring*, isn't it? Why don't you tell her what's going on with you? Don't you think she probably wants to hear how you are?"

I didn't answer her. She handed me the letter and left the room. I heard the couch hiss in the living room as she sat down. I stared at the words I had written. She was right—they were boring. I tore the letter up.

Then I ripped the blankets off my bed. And the sheets too. I pulled the mattress off and all the wood planks and didn't stop until my bed was gone. I sat on the carpet and stared at the mess around me until my chest stopped heaving.

I wanted to sleep in Gramma's bed, surrounded by her smell. I tiptoed down the hall and into her dark room, then shut the door behind me and flicked on the light.

Gramma's bed was gone. So was her dresser. Moms had cleaned out the room and filled it with two racks of her own clothes. In the wastebasket was Gramma's Sea of Galilee bottle.

22

The next morning, Pops found me sleeping on the carpet where Gramma's bed had been. He nudged me awake with the toe of his boot. "That shit in your room better be cleaned up before you leave for school," he said.

It took me a lot longer to put my bed together than it did to tear it down. When I finally got to class, Mr. Garabedian gave me a bunch of cancer about showing up late. By the time the buzzer rang for recess, I was steaming mad. I made B.L.T. meet me in secret behind the big pine tree at the back of the school.

"When can you bring me the instructions?" I asked him.

He puffed out his cheeks, then sucked them in again. "I don't know."

"Tomorrow?"

"All right." He poked the dirt with his shoe. "Are you glad I'm gonna bring them to you?"

"Yeah."

He stepped out from behind the tree.

"Where you goin?" I said.

"I gotta go to the bathroom."

"Just go here."

"I can't. It's number two."

"Then hold it." I was afraid the other gritties might see us together.

"But I gotta go bad."

"Tuh." I watched him shift from one foot to another. "Well, don't tell anybody."

"I won't."

He trudged across the field toward the bathrooms, his head down. I moved around the tree again, out of sight. For some reason, I felt like I was about to cry. I waited a couple minutes just to be safe, then walked out onto the field.

Loop was standing right there.

"W'sup?" he said.

"Nuffin."

"I seen B.L.T. come outta there."

"Where?" I said.

He pointed to the tree. "From behind there. Where you just came out at."

"*I* didn't see him."

We looked each other in the eye.

"B.L.T. is a squid," he said.

"Puh! *I* know that."

"Then let's go get him."

"All right," I said. "Let's go."

B.L.T. hadn't made it into the bathroom yet. Some boys were hanging inside at the sinks, and B.L.T. would never go in as long as they were there. He was one of those squids who always snuck into the bathroom when everyone else was playing. If anyone came in while he was in the stall, he'd walk out and wait until they were gone. When it came to going to the bathroom, B.L.T. could only ship it solo.

"He waiting to go to the bathroom," Loop said. "Let's block him." Loop took off running, and I followed.

Everyone at Jack London Primary knew Garabedian's Recess Relief Rule: you had to go to the bathroom during the breaks, no excuses. It didn't matter if you were leaky or if you had a belly bomb exploding—you had to suffer through class until recess or lunch. Garabedian said class time was valuable and we had to learn to be adults, and adults *held* it. The rule didn't *always* work: Yolanda Cruz peed her pants at her desk one time and claimed that Chocolate Chip, who was sitting next to her, had peed on her leg.

B.L.T. was just going into the bathroom when we ran in and blocked the stall. He stood there looking at me, surprised.

"I gotta go," he said.

Loop was watching me. "Too bad," I said.

"Yeah, too bad," Loop said, "'Cause the toilet's broke."

"No it's not," B.L.T. said. He tried to see past us into the stall.

"Yes it is," I said. "Somebody plogged it up."

"Yeah," Loop said. "A plumber gots to plumb it."

"No he doesn't."

"Yes he does," Loop said, folding his arms.

B.L.T. went quiet. I didn't like the way he was staring at me. "No he doesn't," he said softly.

Loop shoved him. I pushed him too. His chest felt soft and jiggly. He dropped his eyes to the sticky wet floor. "I gotta go bad," he said.

"*Tough*," said Loop. He crumpled a paper towel into a ball, wet it under the faucet, then whapped it up against the roof where it stuck. "Roof wart."

B.L.T. wouldn't leave. Even when the buzzer rang and we had to get back or Garabedian would send us to detention, B.L.T. stood there looking right at me. The blue from his big wet eyes poured straight into me and filled me up until I couldn't breathe.

"Go back to class!" Loop yelled at him.

B.L.T. gave me one last look, then slowly turned and walked out and I suddenly felt empty, like he'd gone in and sucked everything out of me.

Loop pulled two packs of Bubblicious out of his jacket and handed one to me. "Save it for after school," he said.

I squeezed the pack in my hand while he whapped another roof wart against the ceiling.

"We schooled his ass," Loop said.

"Yeah," I said, swallowing. "We schooled him good."

Garabedian handed out a sheet of division problems and said we had fifteen minutes to finish. He disappeared into the big closet behind his desk.

I turned to check on B.L.T. He wasn't doing his math. He was bent over his desk, rocking back and forth. His hands grabbed at his stomach and his face was in a squeeze. It was clear he was a clog.

I tried to focus on my math. A few minutes went by and I looked back at B.L.T. again. He was crunched up and crying without making any sound. I didn't let it get to me. I was two thousand miles away from it.

B.L.T. finally stood up and walked quietly to the back corner where Garabedian kept the human skeleton on a stand. He slipped behind the hanging curtains into the space between the curtains and the back windows. I saw his pants drop to his sneakers. He was going to do it, right there in the room. I couldn't watch.

After a minute I looked back and saw B.L.T. creeping back to his seat. People were just finishing their problems.

Then the smell hit.

It was a different smell than what you got in the bathroom—that smell came at you from high up with metal and cleaner and pee mixed in. That smell stayed in one place. This smell *moved*. It was warm and started low and crept forward through the air, sinking deep into my nose. It stunk out the whole room.

Garabedian was still in the front closet. Loop, Douglas, and Clarence went in for nose pinches and kept saying "*Dang*."

B.L.T. ignored them and worked on his math.

"Someone cut it," Loop said.

"Someone laid it *out!*" said Clarence.

Everyone giggled. Clarence stood up and pointed to the back corner. "It's comin from back there!"

People got out of their seats. Clarence arched his head high and stepped toward the corner slow, like there was an alien hid out back there. B.L.T. was the only one not looking up.

"It smell *snacky* back here!" Clarence said. He went up to the skeleton and took a sniff of it. Then he looked down. "OOOOH!" he yelled, jumping up and down, pointing at the floor behind the curtain. He ran to the front of the room.

Garabedian came out of the front closet holding some folders and saw Clarence running toward him. "What the heck is going on?"

"Someone went to the bathroom back there!" Clarence said.

LaTonya screamed, Rashelle screamed, then everyone screamed.

"B.L.T. did it!" yelled Douglas.

Garabedian ran to the back corner and so did me and Loop and everybody else.

It lay on the floor, right under the curtain.

LaTonya and Rashelle yelled "Let us see!" and pushed through the crowd. Soon as they saw it, they screamed and jumped back.

Mr. Garabedian's eyes searched the room until they found B.L.T. He was standing at the front door, facing it, staring out through the tiny window. Garabedian went to talk with him for a second, then he turned and looked right at me. "Mr. Clay!" he called.

"What?" I said.

"Come–here–now."

Loop whispered in my ear that I'd been ratted out and told me to meet him after my detention in the alley behind the cafeteria. He wanted to show me a secret. He said to hide my pack of Bubblicious or else the gritties in detention would all hit me up for it.

When I got to the front of the room, Garabedian pointed at B.L.T. "I asked this young man why he didn't use the rest room during recess. He claims you prevented him from doing so. Is this true?"

B.L.T. was staring at me.

"Yeah," I said.

"That makes me very disappointed, Mr. Clay. You wait right here." He left me and B.L.T. standing there facing each other while he went to the back corner and ordered everyone to the front of the room.

"I thought we were friends," B.L.T. whispered to me.

I lowered my eyes. He walked past me and I turned to see him disappear into Garabedian's closet and pull the door halfway shut behind him. What was he doing?

Garabedian was still opening the back windows to air out the room. I pulled the pack of Bubblicious out of my pocket and slid it down into my sock like Loop had said to. Garabedian came over to me and told the class to get back in their seats and stay quiet until he returned from the principal's office. Then he took my arm and pulled me to the door. On our way out I looked for B.L.T. in the closet. He was squatting in there, his pants down, wiping himself with some papers from Garabedian's file cabinet.

• • •

Garabedian brought me to the principal's office, where four other grit-ties were already waiting. They were all sixth-graders and a lot bigger than me. Some were stuck in the sixth grade for their second time, like Hector Arleano, who had a tattoo on his shoulder that said *Tres* for the three times he'd been to jail.

The only open seat was next to Jerome Williams, who was six feet five and famous for being gold-plated at shooting hoop. His long legs spread wide and his knees pointed high. A toothpick hung from his mouth just below the thin line of his mustache. He wore a net over his black hair, and a huge white T-shirt that hung almost to his knees. I could tell the T-shirt was brand new because it still had the folds from being in a package. What scared me the most about Jerome was the way his dark eyes never blinked and never focused on anything.

I knew that Jerome and the others were in the principal's office for pulling badass shit like knifing people, and I was embarrassed about how wimpy my own havocs were. I just hoped nobody asked me what I had done.

We all looked up when our principal, Mr. Jorgensen, walked in. He was seven feet tall and whenever he said anything important he reminded you he'd played pro basketball back when it was a real sport and not a business, and that meant something. I couldn't figure out what that meant exactly, except that he had to sleaze around Jack London Primary giving us all a bunch of cancer instead of opening his own restaurant like a lot of pros did. He always pointed to the white scar over his left eye given to him by Walt Frazier in nineteen seventy-two—he said it was part of his permanent collection of origi-nal artwork by Clyde. We called him "Mr. Sickantired," because he was always "sick-an-tired" of everything, like how our parents weren't doing a good enough job disciplining us. He said he believed the bedrock of learning was lying asleep in the floorboards of home.

"You men are an embarrassment," he said, walking back and forth in front of us. "I've worked *too* hard to have a pack of lowlifes in this school and I'm sickantired of seeing your faces in here. You're ugly to me. You're nothing but a bunch of mixed-breed dogs, and I've ordered shots for all of you."

"Dang, why'd you do that?" said Jerome.

"Because I'm convinced you have rabies." He stuck his face in Jerome's to see if he had anything else to say. Jerome did not. "Now, I have work to do," Mr. Jorgensen said.

After he left the room, everyone complained and moved in their chairs and bragged about how they were gonna get ignorant on Mr. Jorgensen when he wasn't looking. Some were gonna use a lead pipe, some a two-by-four. Jerome talked about the hard end of a pistol butt. I got all excited and said that Mr. Jorgensen's Infiniti was first on the list for the Loop and Conrad Spray-Painting Show.

Everybody stopped talking.

Jerome took a chew off his toothpick and turned his slow black eyes on me. "Whatchoo in here for, holmes?"

I almost had a heart attack right there. I had to crack it tough, or else I was dead. "B.L.T. was giving me cancer," I told him, "so his ass was *toast,* and me and Loop—we schooled his ass! We took him into the bathroom and beat him down and his face was all *blood,* noamsayin? It was blood everywhere and we packed him into the toilet until he said my name, Big Poppa. Then we asked him if he was gonna act all French anymore and he said, 'No! No! Don't let me die!' and we said, 'Okay, go back to class and don't tell Garabedian.' But he was so afraid of me in class he went to the bathroom and ratted on me and that's why I'm in here."

Jerome's eyes didn't blink. *"Yeah?"*

"Yeah."

"Cool," said Jerome. "Now flow me some of that Bubblicious you got hid in your sock."

23

When I got out of detention I went straight to the alley where Loop said he'd meet me. He wasn't there. The alley was asleep—even a cricket didn't crick it. I got quick into feeling lonely and the day was dead.

"Hi," came a quiet voice behind me.

I turned around. LaTonya was leaning against the wall, wearing a black coat, carrying a purse. "What are you doin?" she asked.

"Nuffin. Waiting for Loop."

She nodded. She seemed to be watching for something down the alley, and her face looked worried. She pulled out a cigarette and lit it, blowing a stream of smoke out the side of her mouth. We stood there like that without saying anything, her smoking and me watching.

"You ever smoked before?" she said.

"Yeah, I smoked before. *So?*" I said it without swallowing first and I almost choked on my own spit but she didn't seem to notice. I'd never smoked anything in my whole life.

She held out the cigarette for me and my chest started thumping. I put it in my mouth. Her lipstick was on the butt and it got all over my tongue. I sucked in some smoke, but it tasted terrible and I blew it straight back out like I'd seen Moms and Pops do. She watched me, then took back the cigarette and put it in her mouth and puffed on it while looking at me. "You're cute," she said.

Her eyes turned to the alley again.

I was vibrating with the muddy taste of her lipstick in my mouth. We'd put the same cigarette between our lips and as far as I could tell that was as good as a kiss or better. I suddenly got all embarrassed thinking about it and lowered my eyes.

"Well," she said, flicking the cigarette at the wall, "later."

"Later," I said.

Her heels echoed the alley as she walked away and moved out into the wide-open light of the blacktop before turning out of sight. The cigarette was burning at my feet and I picked it up. There was still lipstick on the butt. I scraped the lipstick into a small mound on my finger and sniffed its sharp smell. Then I wiped it on the wall and chucked the cigarette.

After a while, Loop came running down the alley.

"Did you rat me out?" he said.

"No way."

"Where your pack of Bubblicious?"

"Jerome jacked it in detention."

"Why you didn't hide it in your sock?"

"I *did*. He X-rayed it through my pants."

Loop didn't look happy about that.

"I kissed a betty, though," I said.

"*Who?*"

"LaTonya."

"No you didn't."

"Yes I did. Right here before you came."

"Then you dead," he said.

"*Why?*"

"I'll show you."

We left the alley and sidestepped like crabs across the blacktop all the way to the cyclone fence backstop, where Loop told me to duck down behind the wood base. We raised our heads and peered out.

Across the baseball field, on a bench at the far end of the school, LaTonya was on her back. Her naked knees were up in the air and Jerome had his head between them. Every once in a while he popped his head up to look around.

I reached for the cyclone fence to hold on. "What's he doing to her?"

"He diggin her out."

I'd never heard of digging anybody out, but I didn't wanna look like a squid so I didn't say nothing. I could still taste her lipstick in my mouth and I felt stupid now.

"Dang," Loop said. "He got her underwear off."

"He touching her?" I asked.

"Yeah."

"With his mouth?"

"Yep. He lickin her."

"Why?"

"He tasting her." Loop pointed to his crotch. "Down there."

"Dang," I said.

"I know." Loop picked a wood splinter off the backstop with his fingers.

"Does it taste good?" I said.

"Naw. It's snacky."

"Like squash?"

"Yeah, like rotten onions and radishes."

"Dang."

"And coleslaw and some Swiss cheese and shit."

"*Dang.*"

"That's right."

"You tasted it?" I asked.

He let me have a slug. *"No!"*

Loop said we had to get out of there before Jerome spotted us. We snuck away from the backstop and left through the front of the school. Outside the gate, Rashelle leaned against a tree, waiting to walk home with LaTonya like she always did. She pretended she didn't see us and I could tell she knew what her twin sister was doing with Jerome. Loop wanted to talk to her and I tried pulling him away, but he turned and yelled: "Hey Rashelle, where your sister at, huh?"

"Shut up," she said.

"Why you got a dumb name like Rashelle?" Loop said.

"Ain't dumb. You just never heard of no French."

"*I* heard of French," he said to her.

"Say something then."

"Jack Cousteau," said Loop.

"Who *that?*" she said. "He ain't French."

"Neither are you."

"Am too," said Rashelle. "My grandma came from Louisiana and she said we French."

"No you ain't," Loop said. "You *black.*"

Loop turned and walked past me down the sidewalk like he was making a point, leaving me alone with Rashelle. She was staring at me. All I could think of was her sister's naked knees with Jerome's head between. I was sure Rashelle could see what was in my brain like it was a Polaroid on my forehead. I lowered my eyes and walked away slow. Then I broke into a run and didn't stop until I caught up with Loop.

We didn't say anything for a while.

"How come LaTonya let Jerome dig her out?" I said finally.

"She ain't the only one," said Loop. "*Lots* a hos be wantin to throw down wid Jerome."

I'd always thought LaTonya was just a girl.

"Is LaTonya a ho now?" I asked Loop.

"Yep."

We walked all the way out to an old empty warehouse near the Ferry Terminal, then went around the back and sat down next to a rusty Dumpster to chew Bubblicious. After a while Loop pulled a jar of Vaseline out of his jacket.

"Where did you get that?" I asked.

"My moms's dresser drawer."

He started to unbuckle his pants.

"What are you doin?" I said, looking away.

"Showin you my secret."

I heard him pop open the jar.

"Don't you wanna see it?" he said.

I turned to look. A sharp tongue of Vaseline curled up out of the jar where Loop's finger had taken a scoop.

He had his penis out.

I watched his fingers rub Vaseline up and down on it. I wasn't breathing.

"You can't tell *no one,*" he said.

"I won't."

"You know what I'm doing?"

"*Tuh!* Yeah."

I had no idea what he was doing. He closed his eyes. I felt weird watching.

"I'm pretending LaTonya is sitting on me," he said.

I didn't know about that. I didn't say anything.

His hand stopped rubbing and his eyes suddenly opened on me. "You gonna tell anybody?"

"No."

He held the jar of Vaseline out to me. "*You* try it."

"Nah."

"Don't be a chicken," he said. "I got a idea. You pretend you're LaTonya."

"I ain't no betty."

"Just *pretend* you are," he said. He held his penis out. "Touch it."

"Nah."

He glared at me. "Come on, don't be a squid."

I looked around to make sure nobody was coming, then I reached out and touched it. It was hard and slimy. It didn't seem like anything much. Loop closed his eyes and stopped chewing his gum. *He* wasn't having trouble pretending I was LaTonya.

I wiped my hands on my pants and stood up. Loop buttoned his jeans and put the lid back on the Vaseline. He started chewing again. "Malik showed me how to do it," he said, all proud.

"Oh," I said. I wanted to leave.

"You tell anyone," he said, "then I'll tell Jerome you kissed LaTonya."

I looked at him. He was serious.

"I won't," I said.

That night I searched the cabinet and drawers under the bathroom sink. There was no Vaseline anywhere. In the kitchen I opened the refrigerator and stared at the carton of margarine. I took it to my room and turned off the lights, then I got undressed and sat on the edge of my bed and opened the carton. I did exactly what Loop had shown me, using the margarine instead of Vaseline. It was freezing at first, but then it went warm and oozy. I tried to imagine LaTonya naked, but the margarine melted all over my hands and smelled like breakfast, and I kept thinking of buttered toast.

24

LaTonya stopped me the next day near the tether balls. I was on my way out to the big lunchtime baseball game.

"I think I did something," she said. "I told Jerome you were cute."

"*What?*"

She looked at me with her big sad eyes. "I told him not to be mad. I was just tellin him about smoking a cigarette with you, that's all. I'm sorry, Conrad."

She left and I turned to face the field. Jerome was out on the diamond with the other gritties. Everyone was waving for me to hurry up, and I walked over.

Jerome and Hector were the captains and they were picking teams, and we all had to get in a lineup. I was the first one Jerome picked. He didn't say anything, he just pointed at me. I slowly walked over and stood a few feet from him. I didn't dare look him in the eye.

I was glad when Jerome picked Loop. But instead of coming over to me, Loop went and stood right next to Jerome, looking all proud about it.

B.L.T. was the last player in the lineup. Nobody wanted him because he couldn't run and wasn't any good with a glove either. Even tiny Chocolate Chip was a better player than him. I caught B.L.T. hawking me a few times with his narrowed eyes. It didn't look like he was gonna be bringing me any pipe bomb plans now.

"Who gettin B.L.T.?" asked Douglas.

Hector looked at his feet, Jerome just chewed on his toothpick.

"Flip for it," someone said.

"Yeah!" shouted Loop. "Flip for it!"

"Who got a quarter?" Douglas said.

"Not me," I said.

"Not me," Loop said.

"I left mines back in my pack," said Hector.

"Dang," Douglas said. "Everybody all broke an' shit."

"I got a nickel," B.L.T. said.

We all turned and stared at him. He held out his chubby right palm, and a small shiny nickel.

"A'iight," Douglas said. He took the nickel from B.L.T. and turned to Jerome and Hector. "Who callin it?"

"I'll let Jerome do it," Hector said.

Douglas put the nickel on his thumb while Jerome and Hector crowded around him. The nickel flicked into the air.

"Heads," Jerome said.

"It's tails!" Douglas shouted.

Hector's team cheered as B.L.T. slowly walked over to our team. Jerome rolled the toothpick between his teeth and followed B.L.T.'s head with his eyes.

"Let's tear it up!" Douglas yelled.

Hector's team went to bat first. We yelled *"Hey BatterBatterBatterBatter!"* but B.L.T. missed catching a pop fly, which loaded the bases, and Hector hit a grand slam home run right over the pine trees. We finally got three outs on them and ran to the bench. B.L.T. was last getting in and when he sat down next to Jerome, there was a popping sound. B.L.T. stood up, and we could all see a long smear of ketchup on his pants. He picked up an exploded ketchup packet from the bench and everyone laughed except for Jerome.

Jerome went to bat first. "Sky that thing," Loop told him. We yelled at Hector on the mound:

> *Pitcher's in the hole,*
> *Ten feet deep.*
> *Can't get out,*
> *Cuz he got no heat.*

But Hector had lots of heat and he struck out Jerome in three pitches. Jerome was quiet coming back to the bench. I was up. Hector fired three pitches and I swung three times—the balls hissed past me. I walked back to the bench and took my seat.

Something popped under me.

I stood up. There were mustard and ketchup splats up and down my pants. No one was laughing this time. I tried to wipe them off with my fingers but it didn't help. When Jerome wasn't looking, Loop whispered to me to try rubbing dirt on the stains and dry them up. The dirt just stuck to my pants and made them look worse.

It was our turn to take the field. I found my glove and put it on, but my fingers slipped into cold ooze inside, and when I pulled them out, they were covered in more ketchup. I looked up and caught Jerome's eyes staring me down.

After school, Pops was home watching bass fishing on television.

"What happened to your pants?" he said when I passed between him and the television.

"Nothing."

He leaned to one side and stared at the stains. "What *is* that?"

"Ketchup and mustard."

"How did that happen?"

"Jerome did it."

"Jerome? Who the fuck is *Jerome?*"

"He's in sixth grade. He's big."

"How big? Bigger than me?"

I looked at Pops's arms. They were thicker than Jerome's. But Jerome was taller. "I don't know," I said.

Pops's eyes covered me up and down. "What do you mean you don't *know?* What does he look like?"

"He's got a mustache. And a hairnet."

"A *hairnet?* Like a woman?"

"No."

He turned his attention for a second to the television. A bearded man in a baseball hat was pulling a shiny brown bass from the water. Pops narrowed his eyes on me again.

"Don't tell me you're afraid of a guy who wears a hairnet," he said.

I blinked at him. I was very afraid of a guy who wore a hairnet.

At lunch the next day we had another game going. This time I wasn't on Jerome's team. I was on the bench next to Chocolate Chip when I spotted Pops walking onto the playground from the far side of school.

He was heading toward our game.

I stood up and grabbed the cyclone fence. He crossed the tan bark and passed through the tether balls and stopped at the fence by the other team's dugout. His eyes were on Jerome, who was on the mound, wearing a hairnet beneath his A's cap. Jerome was just about to throw a pitch.

"Hey!" Pops called out to him.

Jerome spun around immediately, as if he was always expecting someone to bother him. "*Me?*" he said.

"Are you Jerome?"

Jerome's voice went tough. "Yeah. W'sup?"

"Come over here. I want to talk to you."

Jerome threw down his glove and walked toward him slow, his shoulders swinging side-to-side, his eyes glued to Pops's.

The second baseman said, "Who's *that?*"

Loop, who was at first, said, "Con's pops."

"It's gonna be a fight," someone said.

Everybody on the bench stood up. The outfielders ran in and joined the infielders in an arc around the edge of the diamond. I held onto the fence, my heart pounding.

It took Jerome forever to get to Pops. When he did, Pops hopped up onto the fence. He reached over and grabbed Jerome by his shirt collar, then lifted him off the ground until his face was inches from his own. Then he said, "If you ever fuck with Conrad again, I'll come back and kill you. Understand?"

Jerome looked straight into his eyes. "Yeah."

Pops let Jerome back down, hopped off the fence, and walked back the way he came.

Jerome pulled at his shirt and tried to get the stretch out of it. Then he walked to the mound. As he bent down to pick up his glove, he gave me a quick look. When he straightened up, his eyes were already focused on Douglas, the catcher, who was waiting for his pitch. Jerome flung a fastball. It made a sharp smacking sound in Douglas's glove.

Chocolate Chip whispered to me, "You dead."

Loop disappeared when class was over and I went looking for him everywhere. I wanted to talk about Jerome.

I ended up in front of Loop's house. Out on the sidewalk was a crowd of neighbors staring at the wrestlers' house next door. They were watching Mary and Moon Dog and Cinci, who were busy scrubbing the front wall, trying to remove graffiti someone had painted overnight in giant, dripping black letters:

GO HOME FAGGOTS

Moon Dog was up on a ladder, getting at the high spots with a scraper. Mary and Cinci were leaning over bushes to reach the wall with rags and mops and sponges.

I stood there and stared at the words. At first I wondered who was stupid enough to write that. Whoever it was, they were asking for trouble messing with the wrestlers. Then suddenly my eyes moved to the wrestlers—to the jiggling fat of Moon Dog's arm as it scraped the wall, to the crack of Cinci's butt cheeks peering out above his belt. I tried to think. They'd been tag team partners in the ring. They lived together. They argued all the time, like Moms and Pops did. They called grown men "girls."

"Con!" Mary called to me. She rubbed her cheek with the back of her hand. "Where's Loop?"

I shrugged, my brain buzzing and confused.

"Well get on over here and help us clean this off."

She handed me some steel wool. "Here," she said, pointing, "dip that in the bucket of Ajax water there and scrub firmly but not so hard you take the white paint off underneath."

I went to work. I didn't know what else to do.

The wrestlers were gay.

The more I scrubbed at the black paint, the more I got used to the idea. Mary rubbed at the graffiti with a soapy rag, leaning her whole body into it. "It isn't right," she said under her breath. "It just isn't right."

It took us a while, but we scraped off half a word so that it just said FAG.

"Why would anyone want to do this to us?" Moon Dog said.

"Drop it!" Cinci said to the wall, like he was telling it to drop the paint to the ground. He caught me looking at him. I stopped breathing. He wiped his head, shiny with sweat, and turned back to the wall.

After a while, a beat-up Plymouth pulled up in front and Loop climbed out of the back. The driver was some older guy I'd never seen before. In the passenger seat was Jerome. He waved good-bye to Loop as the car pulled away, and I felt the skin on my neck go hot.

Jerome was jacking Loop away from me.

Mary yelled at Loop to come over, but when Loop saw the words GO HOME FAG on the wrestlers' house, he froze in his tracks. He stood there for a second, just staring at us. He seemed afraid. Suddenly, he dropped his backpack and ran down the street after the Plymouth.

"Loop!" Mary shouted, but Loop didn't stop and soon he was out of sight.

We all looked at each other. Mary let out a sigh. "Well, come on then," she said. "Let's get this wall clean."

We worked hard, and every once in a while I caught the wrestlers eyeing me with worried faces. By the time it was getting dark, we'd scraped off the rest of the word FAG. All that was left was GO HOME. Moon Dog stood there, staring up at the words.

"We *are* home," he said.

The next morning was the last day of school before Christmas vacation. I was on my way to class when I spotted Loop and Jerome and the other gritties outside the bathrooms. They all stopped talking and stared at me. I pretended I didn't see them and looked around the blacktop like I was trying to find somebody. My eyes caught B.L.T. standing near the tether poles, hands in his pockets, watching me too.

"Con!" Loop called out. He was waving me over.

I didn't want to go, but the way they were hawking me with their eyes—it was like they were remote-controlling me over. My feet were already moving, so I tried playing it wide like I was taking my time. "W'sup?" I said.

Loop's eyes looked big and scared. His chest was breathing fast.

"Tell 'em, Loop!" Jerome said to him. "Tell everybody about what you told me—how he cleaned them fags' house."

Loop's nostrils flared. His jaw muscle tensed. "He a *fag*," said Loop, turning his eyes on me. The word hung in his mouth like a bad taste, and his lips snarled at one end.

"He a faggot whiteboy."

It was a good thing Mr. Garabedian didn't call on me in class. I wouldn't have been able to talk. My throat felt like it had a golf ball stuck in it. I just sat there, staring at the cuss words and names scratched into my desk. It was only a half day, and finally Garabedian wished us all a happy holiday. There was a roar of talking and squeaking shoes as everyone got up to leave. I didn't move. I didn't look up. I was waiting until they were gone.

A hand slipped an envelope onto my desk and I looked up to see the back of B.L.T.'s puffy jacket as he shuffled out. I turned my eyes to the thick envelope. It was sealed and covered with smudge marks and it said: FOR CONRAD. I ripped it open at one end and a small piece of paper fell out—a note from B.L.T. telling me to come see him over the break. He'd written down an apartment number in Naval Housing where he lived. I pulled out the rest: four folded and wrinkled pages torn from a book. Each page was filled with diagrams and instructions. At the top of the first page, in dark letters, it said: BUILDING A PIPE BOMB IN TEN EASY STEPS.

I stuck the pages back in the envelope and headed to the door. Mr. Garabedian was cleaning his desk, and he looked up at me. "Have a great Christmas, Conrad!"

I accidentally waved the envelope at him.

"I will," I said.

25

They said I couldn't see colors. Maybe. But I could make everyone else see them. Yellow. Orange. Red. Even blue. The color of fire. The color of a bomb exploding. The color of Conrad Clay.

First I had to find eight inches of steel pipe.

I rolled into a small, cramped shop on Webster called Aram's Plumbing Supply, holding the pipe bomb instructions in my hand. A Chihuahua that had been asleep on the counter jumped to its feet and growled at me. The dog had a strange black stripe running down his back. Behind the counter sat a gray-haired man with angry lines carved into his face and a tired eyelid which drooped over one eye. He got up from his chair and shook a finger at me. "No skating in Aram's shop!"

I stepped off my board and blinked at the man. He had to be Aram. He ran a greasy hand down the dog's shivering back and pushed the dog's tiny arched body down. "It's okay, Ronald Reagan," he said to the dog, "It's all right." The dog stopped growling and curled up again, staring happily into Aram's eyes. It didn't seem to notice that Aram had one of the meanest-looking faces in Alameda, or that his stained hands were spreading grease on his fur. Aram was a black grease rag, and everything he touched seemed to be stained with it: his shirt, his pants, even the arms of his chair, which were oiled down dark like the elbows of a hippo's hide.

I went up to the counter and patted the dog's head. "Why is his name Ronald Reagan?"

Aram slapped the counter. The dog jumped to his feet again, but Aram pushed his trembly butt back down to the counter. "Ronald Reagan was greatest president America ever has!" said Aram. "Did not lie like Clinton! Ronald Reagan would not shut down Naval Station! Ronald Reagan recognize Armenia too!" Aram eyed the instructions in my hand. "What you have there?"

I immediately stuffed my hand into my jacket pocket. "I need some steel pipe," I said.

"Steel pipe steel pipe."

"If you could cut me eight inches—"

"If I could cut *nothing!*" He sliced the air with his hand. "Nothing. I cut *nothing.*"

"But—"

"No. I say, *No* more!"

"Why not?"

He waved a hand around the room. Against every wall, in every corner, were stacks of all different kinds of pipes—plastic, metal, thick, thin, straight and bent. "Too many pipes," Aram said. "I am tired of pipes. Pipes! Pipes! Pipes! *No more!*" He pointed a black finger at me. "No more—I am not nice!"

"I know," I said.

He looked at me, surprised, and was about to say something but the door swung open and a man in a sweatsuit came into the shop carrying an old section of piping. The pipe had two right-angle elbows in it and was caked in brown muck. It also smelled like rotting sewage. The man held the smelly thing away from his own body, and motioned for Aram to take it, but Aram refused to touch it, and didn't look happy about the drops of brown water falling onto his counter either.

"Please!" the man said. "My wife is gonna kill me. I took apart our bathroom. I got overambitious. Our whole house reeks." He shook the piece of pipe in his hands. "I need a replacement for this."

He plopped the thing down on the counter, sending Ronald Reagan to his feet again. Aram's eyes narrowed on the leaky pipe as

his hand automatically reached out and pressed Ronald Reagan's
behind back down. The dog tried to stick his nose in one opening of
the pipe, but Aram pushed him back.

"Lead pipe!" Aram said.

"Yeah, I know but—"

"Terrible pipe!"

The man stared at Aram. He looked shocked. *"Well,"* the man said,
starting to sound angry, "I would like to replace it with something better, *obviously."* The man's eyes searched the shop. "You must have
another part like this—"

"Maybe. But bad pipe!" Aram disappeared into the back. We could
hear boxes being tossed, pipes clanging. "Bad! Bad! Bad!"

The man turned and gave me a look, shaking his head. "What are
you in here for?"

"I need some pipe."

"You too, huh? I'm telling you, trying to fix things yourself is a bitch
and half."

I nodded.

"You helping your dad or something? What kinda problem you
got?"

I didn't know how to answer that. I just stared at him.

"Shit. That big, huh?" he said.

I nodded again, and reached out to pet the dog.

"What a pathetic-looking dog," the man said.

"His name is Ronald Reagan," I said.

"Yeah, right."

"Because Ronald Reagan was America's greatest president."

"Don't make me laugh, kid."

Aram came back out to the counter. "I don't have."

The man's eyebrows flew up. "Well, where else am I supposed to
go? This *is* a plumbing supply place, isn't it?"

Aram pointed at the broken piece. "I can make."

The man shrugged. "Okay. So *make* it."

Aram grabbed a pen and an order pad from near the register and
started writing up an order. "Name?" Aram said.

"Phil—It's Phil. Do you need my last name?"

Aram began to write. He said, "F—E . . ." He stopped and looked up at the man. "Is that one 'L' or two?"

The man cracked a smile at me, then held up two fingers for Aram. "*Two*," he said. "What the heck."

Aram finished writing the man's name. "F - E - L - L," he said. "Fell!" He tore the receipt from the pad and handed a copy to the man. "Come back in three days."

"*Three days?*"

"Three days," Aram said.

The man shook his head, reading his receipt as he walked out of the shop. I heard him tell someone out on the sidewalk that his name was *Fell*.

"I could have his order done in one hour!" Aram said to me. He tossed the old lead piece onto a pile behind the counter.

"You spelled his name wrong," I said.

"I change his name on purpose! I don't like his pipe!"

Aram turned his eyes on me now. "Don't give me any more broken pipes to fix today!"

"I don't have any," I said.

"You *don't?*" He suddenly looked so sad that I almost wished I *did* have a broken pipe to give him, because he seemed happier when he was mad. I got him mad quick enough, though, when I asked him about my pipe.

"What kind pipe?" he said. "How thick?"

I had to pull the instructions out and look. Aram pointed at them. "Show me show me!" I turned my back to him and searched the pages for the thickness. When I looked back, he was leaning over the counter trying to see. "What you are making there?"

"Nothing."

I found it. The instructions recommended three quarters of an inch diameter, with threads at both ends so they could be capped. I put the pages back in my pocket and told Aram. He complained about the threads, then took me into the back of the shop, where the air was sour with the smell of metal and grease and dog pee. The place was crammed with boxes and shelves filled with pipes and fittings and faucets. Along the back wall were power saws and greasy drilling machines. Aram went digging through the boxes, picking up one piece of pipe after another, putting his nose up inside each one and mumbling in another language as his eyeball moved all around. He stole looks at me every now and then, and at my jacket pocket, which had the instructions. He finally found a short piece of pipe he was satisfied with—it already had threads on both ends. He picked out two caps from a box and we went back to the counter where he rang me up. The whole thing was only twelve dollars, and I paid him with the money I'd gotten from Sandra. Then I grabbed my deck and headed to the door.

"Stop!" came Aram's voice. I spun around. He walked out from behind the counter and I was sure he was gonna ask me what I using the pipe for, but he surprised me and opened a small refrigerator sitting in the corner. From a brown paper sack he pulled out a thin slice of meat and handed it to me. It was dry and so thin that I could see right through it. It seemed raw. "Eat!" he said.

"But it isn't cooked," I said.

"No cook. Smoke! This is basturma. Smoke is better! Taste!"

I sniffed it. "Beef jerky!" I said.

"Basturma!" Aram said.

I was so happy he wasn't bothering me about the pipe that I bit into the meat. It was soft as butter and not as salty as beef jerky. It was really good. I stuffed the rest in my mouth, and Aram nodded in approval, then handed me a glass bottle from the fridge, which was filled with dark liquid.

"What is this?" I asked.

"Apple juice. I make!" He pushed me toward the door. "Out! Out!"

And I was out. So was the sun, and I stood on the sidewalk squinting in the bright light. People passing by stared at the pipe in my hand. I slipped it into my backpack, then opened the bottle of juice and took a sip, closing my eyes. The apple juice eased into my mouth, cold and sweet and thick. I could taste trees. I could see roots rooting. It was the best juice I had ever tasted.

I took another sip, then tilted my face to the sun and opened my eyes. I let the sunlight fill me up. I let it bake my eyes blind. Then I looked away, and the street was filled with a burning ball of fire. I knew right then it was the sun sending me a picture of the future. A vision of my bomb exploding.

26

Moms didn't care that Sunday happened to be the Raiders' last game of the season—it was Christmas Eve, she said, and I still had to go to church. Just before the service, Mr. Garcia pulled me aside. It turned out I'd been right: there was a whole posse of men in the congregation who'd been dying every Sunday from missing the Raiders games. Mr. Garcia slipped me the keys to his Toyota truck. He had a plan.

Later during the sermon, I got up to go to the bathroom a couple times, only I made a right turn at the men's room and bolted for Mr. Garcia's truck in the parking lot. I listened for the Raiders score on the radio, wrote it down on a Tithes and Offerings envelope, then ran back into the church. It took about as much time as a long-ass leak. The envelope got passed around to all the men during the commotion when the congregation stood up to sing a hymn.

On my final trip out to the parking lot to get the scores, I clicked on the radio and heard the announcer speaking like someone had just died. The Raiders had lost. Probably because we weren't watching them. I sat there in Mr. Garcia's truck, picturing the players standing around the frozen Denver field. They held their helmets low, and I hung up the towel on their asses.

Back inside the chapel, I passed the envelope with the final score to Mr. Garcia, but it was intercepted by old Mrs. Hayes, who plopped the envelope into the money-basket. Mr. Garcia shook his head as he watched the basket with the news of the Raiders' loss get sent to the front.

A sad offering to the church.

Me and Moms waited all afternoon in the living room for Pops to come home and open presents. The sun poked through the window curtains for a few minutes before sinking behind the house across the street, then the room went dark. Moms said the undecorated tree was depressing and she got out Gramma's old hat box filled with ornaments and began to hang them on the branches. We hung two of Gramma's hand-knitted birds, then Moms burst into tears and sat back down on the couch.

"Just put them away," she said, waving a hand at the box.

By eight o'clock Pops still hadn't shown up. Moms opened a bottle of wine and turned on the television. We still didn't have a channel changer, and I had to get up and go to the TV each time she wanted a new show. She finished half the bottle of wine, then turned to me with a blurry-eyed stare and told me she should have married her old boyfriend, Victor. "At least I'd be living over in France right now," she said.

She asked me to get her a Pepsi out of the fridge. I was about to leave the kitchen with a cold can when my eye caught the cabinet door beneath the counter. I set the Pepsi on the counter and opened the cabinet.

The fungus from Pops's bowl of tea had grown out of control. It spilled out from under the tinfoil and sank to the cabinet shelf where it piled up in foamy blobs. The tea hadn't been touched in days, maybe weeks. I had the sudden cold feeling that Pops wasn't hooked into our house anymore.

Moms didn't touch the Pepsi I brought her. Instead she drank the rest of the bottle of wine and said "Victor, Victor, Victor," and I had to hold her arm to keep her from falling off the couch.

"Let's open the presents," she said, finally.

"What about Pops?" I said. I'd wrapped a present for Pops, a key-chain that said DAD, which I bought at the 99-cent store on Central.

"Screw him." She handed me a large wrapped box. "This is for you."

I stared at it for a second, then slowly undid the wrapping and opened the box. Inside was a Raiders helmet. A real one. "Man," I said, holding it up. Its surface stuck to my fingertips and felt tacky, the way new plastic always did. I looked up at Moms. "Did you get me this?"

She seemed to be deciding what to tell me. "Your father went and got it," she said. I lowered my eyes to the helmet. "Aren't you going to try it on?"

I pulled the helmet over my head. The cushioned lining hugged my ears and suddenly I was surrounded by the strong, sharp odor of foam and fresh plastic. It was a good smell, the smell of something new.

I snapped the chinstrap and looked out at Moms through the bars of my facemask. From inside my helmet, the words coming from the television were distant and windy, like I was hearing them from inside a seashell. It felt safe in there.

"Well?" she asked.

"Perfect," I said.

I handed her the present I'd bought her, also at the 99-cent store. She struggled with the ribbon, then tore the paper away and held up my gift: a cooking apron which said WORLD'S GREATEST CHEF. "Wow," she said, staring at it.

"It's for your work," I said.

Her eyes filled with water.

"Don't you like it?"

She nodded and began to cry. The apron slipped out of her fingers and landed on the carpet. She fell on her side and curled up on the couch, shaking.

"What is it?" I said. "What's wrong, Moms?"

Her mouth opened and her lips were saying something, but no sound come out.

"*What?*" I said.

Her chest heaved and her breath stuttered. She snuffled and I could see her lips struggle to stop trembling. Finally they mouthed three words:

Where. Is. He.

I swallowed. "I'll find him," I said.

I thought I saw her head nod a little, then she began to sob all over again. I grabbed the apron off the carpet and spread it over her. With my helmet still on, I stood up and went to the door. Before I walked out, I looked back at her. She lay there on the couch, the words WORLD'S GREATEST CHEF rising and falling with her breaths.

Pops wasn't at Patti's Bar. I decked hard and fast through the cold empty Christmas streets to a place on Central I knew he liked. I still had my new Raiders helmet on. I wanted Pops to see me wearing the present he'd gotten me.

An electric palm tree glowed blue against the sparkly rock wall outside the Island Club. The entrance was so black it looked like the opening to the end of the world. Maybe that was why Pops liked going in there. A man sleazed out wearing a Santa's hat. "You know who's sleeping with my wife?" he said, bending over me with sour breath. I shook my head, and he stared out at the street for a moment. Then he tapped my helmet: "*You* ain't sleeping with my wife, are you?"

"No."

His glassy eyes looked confused. "Oh," he said. He took a couple steps down the sidewalk, then came back and held out his hand to shake with me. "Have yourself a good evening," he said, then he walked away.

I entered the bar with my deck under my arm. Silver tinsel hung from lamps at every table, and was strung along the bar too. A jukebox sang "Peace on Earth." The place was dark and mostly empty and I didn't see Pops anywhere. Near the jukebox a big wide woman had her arms around a scrawny man at least a foot shorter than her. She pointed her drink at my helmet. "You should be home, little spaceman." She and the scrawny man started laughing at me, and I headed for the door.

Outside, I started walking against a cold wind. Soon I saw the Impala racing up the street toward me. It pulled over with a long screech, and the front tire jumped up onto the curb before falling back down. In the windshield, I could see Moms. Her hair looked whipped and wild, like it was alive. She unlocked the passenger door and waved for me to get in, and I did. The wind pushed my door shut with a heavy *whoosh*, packing the air inside the car, which reeked of Moms's wine breath.

"Was he in there?" Moms said, eyeing the Island Club.

"No."

She revved the engine and pulled out into the street. In the gold dashboard glow her face looked tired. Her eyes were baggy and lines ran from the sides of her nose down to the edges of her mouth, cutting a triangle into her face to match the smaller one between her eyebrows.

She caught me staring at her. "What are you looking at?"

"Nothing." I looked away.

"Tell me what you were staring at, Con. I want to know."

"*Nothing.*"

She slammed the brakes. My hands shot out and caught the dashboard just before the facemask of my helmet rammed into it. She flicked on the overhead light and adjusted the rearview mirror in order to look at her face. We were in the middle of Central Avenue. "What did you see, Con?" She put her fingertips on her cheekbones and pulled her skin back. "My crow's feet?"

"No."

"Huh? Was it my bags?" She pushed the skin under her eyes toward her nose so it bunched up. "Con? Was *that* what you were staring at?"

"No."

"Then what was it? I want to know. Was it my nose?"

"No."

"My cheeks? They're too fat, right? You think my cheeks are fat, don't you?"

"*No.*"

She grabbed my mask and pulled me to face her. "Your mother wants to know what you were staring at. Tell me what you were thinking. You think I look like shit, don't you?"

"No."

"Well then, what?" She turned back to the mirror and ran her fingers down the sides of her face. "I can't see anything in this light."

A car came up behind us and its headlights filled our car with white light. It blasted its horn, but Moms didn't seem to hear it—she just used the light to get a better look at her face in the rearview mirror. "My pores are too big," she said.

The car honked again.

"Was *that* it, Conrad? My *pores?*"

"Moms—"

The car blasted one long honk. Moms was yelling over it: "TELL—ME—WHAT—YOU—WERE—LOOK–ING—AT!"

The other car revved its engine and flashed its high beams.

"Oh all right!" Moms said, throwing the Impala into Drive. We tore off down the street with the other car riding our behind. She straightened the rearview mirror, and the other car's headlights laser-beamed off of it, catching her blinking eyes by surprise. At the red light Moms pulled to a stop and the car behind us squealed around to her side. It was a brand new silver Toyota, driven by a lumpy-faced man. His eyes stuck out of his head like a crab, his chin and mouth were swallowed in a sea of fat, and his tie hung loose around his neck flab. He looked like meat. He was already rolling down his passenger window and pointing for Moms to do the same.

"What does he want?" Moms said. She rolled down her window, and I could hear the man's radio blasting the news. He lowered the volume and leaned all the way over his passenger seat toward us, keeping his big white eyes on Moms.

"ARE YOU *CRAZY* YOU FUCKING BITCH?" he yelled. Then, nodding his head at both words, he said: "FUCK—*YOU!*"

He rolled up his window and peeled out into the intersection, making a right turn in front of us and screeching down a side street.

Moms rolled her window back up slow, then gripped the steering wheel with both hands. I could hear her wet breathing. The light turned green. We didn't move. The signal turned yellow, then red again. Moms stared at the light, streaks running down her face. The light went green, then just as it blinked yellow she pulled us forward through the intersection, wiping her eyes.

"I'll watch out for Pops," I said.

She nodded, sniffling, and I turned my attention to the street as the fluorescent lights of the stores snaked across our windshield. No one was out. The sidewalks were empty. Moms drove us all over Alameda, to bars I hadn't seen before. The Shamrock. The Black Sheep. The

Foxtail. 1902. Flint's Forty. We slowed down in front each place, searching for Pops's truck, but found nothing.

Moms said there was one more bar she had forgotten about. We turned onto Park, and I could already see a sign glowing halfway down the block. The bar was called The Fireside, and over the door was a neon fire burning in a neon brick fireplace. Moms slowed down at the curb in front.

Pops's truck was in the lot.

"He's there!" I said to Moms all excited, but then I saw the serious look on her face.

We got out, and Moms pointed at my helmet. "Why don't you take that off, Con?"

"I don't want to," I said.

She pressed her lips together and sighed. "Okay." She took my hand and half-pulled me under the sign of burning fire, through the dark open door and into the crowded bar. The air was smoky from flames blazing in a round stone fireplace in the middle of the room. A metal vent hung over the fireplace, but the wind outside was causing smoke to spiral over the crowd of people sitting in leather seats around the fire. The bar was so dark that you could barely see faces, but fingers and rings and watches flickered bright under low lamps that dropped down on cords out of the smoky dark above. The sounds of music and talking and laughing echoed inside my helmet, and a dizzy parade of black shoes and high heels stepped out of our way as Moms pulled me through the crowd. People pointed at me and at my helmet and whispered "Look!" and "Check this out!" One woman saw me with Moms and said, "Oh, no." Moms's grip tightened and pulled me around two men wearing cowboy boots until we stood in a clearing. I saw Pops and froze.

He sat at a table, leaning over a candle that lit his face from underneath. Seated across from him was Ms. Van Pelt. She was laughing at something he was telling her.

Moms tried pulling me toward them, but I fought against her. She jerked at me and I hit her arm with my free hand. "Dammit!" she said. She dug her nails into my wrist and I had no choice but to follow. She yanked me right up to the edge of the table, and in that one moment I felt all the blood bleed out of me until my heart rang hollow and alone in my chest.

Pops was still hunkered down over the candle. He was in the middle of saying something to Ms. Van Pelt, when his eyes caught mine staring back at him from inside the helmet he'd bought me. His eyes raised to meet Moms's, his mouth frozen open.

"Hello, Ray," Moms said.

He straightened. "What are you doing here?"

Ms. Van Pelt sat back and smiled at Moms. "Hi, Jan."

Moms ignored her. "Con wanted to see where his father was taking his girlfriend," she said, "instead of coming home and opening presents with him on Christmas Eve."

I looked up at Moms. Girlfriend? What was she talking about?

Ms. Van Pelt let out a laugh, pulling a strand of hair back over her ear. "We were only talking," she said, nodding toward Pops. "And I'm not his *girlfriend.*"

I was glad to hear that.

"Then why are you sleeping with him?" Moms said.

"Jan—" Pops said.

"*What?*" Moms said, eyeing him. "That's what you've been doing every day for the past month while I'm at work, isn't it?" She looked at Ms. Van Pelt. "Neither of you has a job, so why not have a little midday fuck while I'm slaving away."

I stood there, confused and blinking at Pops through my facemask. I still wasn't sure exactly what was going on. All around the bar, firelit eyes were turned on us. A man in a 49ers cap tried to stop his wife from staring, but she kept turning to watch. I tried to clear my mentals and get a grip on what Moms was saying. Pops *had* been home alone while she was at work and I was at school. And I'd seen his fungus tea in Ms. Van Pelt's kitchen.

Ms. Van Pelt smiled at Moms. "Why don't you join us, Jan?" she said. "Have a drink and let's talk about this." She pointed at me. "We can get Conrad a soda."

Moms jerked me until my back was up against her stomach. She lowered her voice: "I'm not talking to you about your little romantic affair with my husband."

Pops stood up and grabbed Moms's arm, but she shook it free. Ms. Van Pelt had an angry look on her face now. "It's not an *affair*," she said.

"Oh, it's *not*?" Moms squinted at her. "Then what is it? *Love*?"

Pops said, "Jan, stop—"

Moms looked at him. "Is that it? You're in love with each other?"

Ms. Van Pelt lowered her eyes. Pops took Moms's arm again and tried pulling her away, but she held her ground. "Come *on*, Jan," he said.

"You shit," Moms said to him. She turned to Ms. Van Pelt. "Fuck you."

Moms took my arm and pulled me away toward the door. People stepped back and made room for us. Suddenly we were out on the sidewalk, in the cold quiet night. Moms let go of me and walked to the Impala and got in. I followed her and did the same. She was quiet, and I was afraid to say anything. I didn't dare take off my helmet.

Pops suddenly burst out onto the sidewalk. "Jan, stop!" he yelled at us.

Moms pressed her door lock down. "Lock your door, Con!" she said.

He was running toward us.

"Con, lock your door!"

Pops's eyes were on me. Moms was yelling. My ears were ringing inside my helmet. I reached out and held my finger over the knob.

"Don't!" I heard Pops shout. "You promised you were on my side!"

I felt like a bending bone. I looked at Moms. Her face was screaming at me. I turned back to Pops. He was almost to my door. I banged the lock down. His mouth opened into a big black O—"Open it!" His teeth flashed angry. "Open it! Open it! *Open* it, Con!" He slammed my window with his hand. His palm pressed flat and dark against the glass. I jerked back. Moms revved the engine. His fingers slid down my window, leaving oil streaks. He ran around the front, squinted in the headlights, then moved to Moms's side. She began to drive and he pounded the windshield. He grabbed the antenna and bent it. Moms stared at the road ahead and drove. "Jan! Stop! *Stop!*" He was running with us, holding onto the door handle. Moms sped up and he ran faster, holding on. Then he wasn't yelling anymore. Just running and breathing and holding on. We were almost to Central when his hand let go and I looked back. I could see him in between the bars of my facemask. He was hunched over in the middle of the street, hands on his knees, trying to catch his breath, staring at the cement.

At home, Moms went to her room, crying. I took the present I'd bought Pops and chucked it at the wall. Out the window I could see Ms. Van Pelt pulling into her driveway. She got out of her car and went into her house.

Pops's truck pulled up a few seconds later. I ran to my bedroom and shut the door. I still had on my helmet.

I heard Pops push the front door open so hard it slammed against the wall. From the kitchen came the hissing sound of a can of beer popping open, then the toaster being pushed in. Soon I could hear a knife scraping over toast. It was quiet for a moment, then Pops clomped into the hallway. From the bathroom, there was a loud racket of drawers sliding open and slamming shut.

I snapped the chin strap of my helmet and went out. He was in the bathroom, throwing things into his Navy bag: a comb, shaving cream, a box of borax. His eyes were wild and roaming. He stormed out of the bathroom, right at me, but he didn't seem to see me standing there and I had to step back or be run over. He was in his closet now, banging things around. He came out with his rifle, a pair of boots, and his old camouflage sleeping bag. When he saw me watching him he pointed a finger at my eyes, right through my facemask. His mouth was snarling and I could smell his sour breath. "You can tell your mother I'm not coming back," he said.

He threw what he could into the Navy bag and carried it all out to the couch. Then he disappeared into the kitchen again and I could hear him pulling out drawers.

I was in the hallway, shaking. Moms's door flung open and she stood there in her pajamas, squinting at me. "Where is he?"

"The kitchen."

She left me standing there. Soon there was a loud crash and the sound of silverware clanging to the floor. Moms was yelling that she was gonna kill him. I ran for the kitchen.

Pops was up against the counter. Moms was pointing Gramma's old silver turkey knife at him and screaming she was going to kill him and kill that slut Ms. Van Pelt too and how would he like that? She lunged at him with the knife but he grabbed her wrist and squeezed it tight until the knife shook and dropped to the linoleum. She screamed and slapped him with her other hand. Then he clocked her on the cheek with his fist.

It sounded like the crack of a baseball bat.

I ran and jumped on him but he threw me to the floor and the back of my helmet smacked linoleum. He pointed his finger down at me and said he'd rip off my head if I moved an inch. Moms was screaming at him. He grabbed both her hands and pinned them against the cupboard, then he took her jaw and pushed it up so she couldn't yell at him anymore. He looked like he was going to say something to her, but nothing came out of his mouth. He just held her there against the cupboard, her jaw trembling in his hand, her eyes wide and afraid and staring.

There was a sound from next door. A door slamming. Ms. Van Pelt was leaving her house. Her car engine started.

Pops let Moms go and took a giant step right over me.

"No!" yelled Moms.

I threw my arms around his leg to stop him, but he reached down and peeled my fingers off his jeans, one by one. In the living room he grabbed his Navy bag and rifle and headed out the front door. The screen slammed.

Moms ran past me and I got up and followed her outside. Ms. Van Pelt's car was leaving down the street and Pops was already in his truck.

"Ray!" Moms shouted. "Ray!"

He started the engine and began to pull forward. Moms ran in front of his truck and lay down on the asphalt, flat on her back. A car was parked behind him. If he wanted to leave, he was going to have to run her over.

She lay there, chest heaving, waiting. Pieces of broken glass flashed all around her in the streetlight glow.

I ran between her and the truck and turned to face Pops behind the wheel, then I pushed on the hood with both hands and glared at him through my facemask. The windshield was covered with water spots and he seemed afraid and alone in there, like a fish lost in a dirty tank.

I felt the engine go dead. He got out and ran around to Moms and knelt beside her on the pavement. She was sobbing and her eyes were rolling around, not focusing on anything. He put his arms under her and picked her up off the asphalt. Pebbles and bits of glass fell from her back and bounced to the ground. He carried her into the house and I was right behind him.

He set her down across the couch and eyed her for a moment, like he was making a decision. Then he turned and walked past me to the door, kicking the screen wide open. For a second the back of his camouflage jacket filled the doorway. Then he was gone.

27

Something shook me awake the next morning and I opened my eyes to the stare of a monster. I sat up with a jerk. It was only the facemask of my Raiders helmet lying on the pillow.

Moms stood over me in her robe. She was trying to get my attention, waving a piece of toast in the air. There was a bite taken out of it. "Con, *whose* toast is this?" she was saying.

I remembered the sound of a knife scraping toast the night before. "Pops's, I guess."

She looked at the piece of toast, then carried it out of my room. I heard the front door open and I went to my window. She was on the lawn, holding the toast out in front of her like it was poisonous. She crossed the grass and went around the side of the house. I lifted the shade of my other window in time to see her dump the toast in Ms. Van Pelt's trash can.

I let the shade drop. I'd slept in my clothes and they were soaked with sweat—the heater had been going full blast all night. My head hurt too. I went over to my bed and picked up the Raiders helmet. It was Christmas Day. Pops was gone.

The bathroom was a mess. Drawers were pulled out. Hairpins and cottonballs and Q-tips lay all over the floor. Pops's Speedstick was gone from the top drawer. His Listerine was gone from the medicine cabinet. So was his yellow throat medicine. My eyes stopped on the shower curtain. I pulled it back. On the soap dish, stuck in old white crud, was Pops's razor. To me, that proved he was coming back.

Later that morning, I heard Moms's screams coming from the bathroom. "Shit!" she cried.

I ran to find her being dive-bombed by a giant moth. She was swiping wildly at it with her *Vogue* magazine. She slammed the wall three times, then sank to the floor, the magazine in her arms. She started to cry.

"I'll help you, Moms," I said, going to her.

She tried to hold the magazine out to me, but the more her tears fell on it, the heavier it seemed in her hands. I knelt down and took it from her, then climbed onto the creaking bathroom counter, eyeballing the moth up in the corner of the wall.

It rose a little and bumped into the ceiling, falling then shooting up over and over. I gripped the magazine and looked back at Moms crumpled on the floor. Then I turned to the moth and smacked it against the wall so hard it made a hollow booming sound. The moth's body popped and guts squirted out, but I didn't stop. I smacked it until it was part of the paint. I smacked it until the whole house seemed to rattle.

"I killed him," I said when I was done.

Moms nodded, wiping her cheeks. "I know," she said. "Thank you."

I sat with her and held her hand until she slipped her fingers away. "Give me a second, Con. I have to use the bathroom."

I stood on the heater vent in the hall, and she closed the door. Something about the sound of her peeing made me sad. Her leak was lonely. "Do you want me to find Pops?" I said to the door.

"I don't know, Con. Please—leave me alone, okay?"

"I'm gonna find him."

"Go away. *Please.*"

I went to my room and sat on my bed. I was worried about leaving her alone. Then my eyes fell on my Raiders helmet.

It took me a couple minutes to remove the shade from the stand-up lamp in the living room, drag the lamp into the hallway, plant it in front of the bathroom door, and dress it in my clothes. I hung the

Raiders helmet over the light bulb in place of the shade, and turned the facemask to the bathroom door. "Bye, Moms," I called out.

No sound from her.

So I left my scarecrow to keep her company.

Alameda was empty. Even the big streets like Webster and Park and Central had no traffic, and I decked straight down the middle of them. There were no people on the sidewalks, except in front of Mission for the Homeless where the cement-sleepers sat, begging and bent. On the smaller streets, the ones with houses and apartments, squids were walking out of their houses looking stuffed with Christmas turkey and throwing new footballs with their dads.

Pops was nowhere to be seen. I kept going.

I took Atlantic for almost a mile, past Pete's Bait 'n' Tackle, to a part of Alameda I'd never been to. The air was thick and fishy, the buildings old and worn-down. Fenced-in yards were crammed with boats on stilts, boats on trailers, and boats just on the ground, some of them upside down, others on their sides. Dried salt was caked over most of them. A few boats had brown seaweed muck clinging to their sides. Everything—the boats, the yards, the buildings—had the look of being stained.

One shipyard had no fences. In the center was an old cement boat with a ladder leaning against it. No one seemed to be around, so I left my deck on the ground and climbed the ladder. At the top I saw that there wasn't anything left of the boat except the shell. I crawled down into it. The day was cold and clear and the sun was a small yellow seep, but it still heated up the polished cement shell and I leaned my back into the smooth curve. The cement smelled like a rusty iron pot. You couldn't hear anything except the air whispering overhead. I didn't feel like looking for Pops anymore. Who wanted him back, anyway?

I spread my arms and legs outward like wings. I could almost feel myself rising up into the blue sky, riding a slow turn on the whistling air. If he did come back, I'd be waiting for him. I'd be waiting with a steel-pipe present.

•   •   •

It was dark by the time I got home. Moms wasn't there, but she'd left all the lights on. A candle on the television had melted down to the base, and wax drips had hardened over the screen like yellow icicles. On the coffee table sat another empty bottle of wine, and cigarette butts filled an empty glass. I was starving.

The kitchen was a wreck. Dirty dishes in the sink. Jars of pennies on the counter. Potato peels in the trash. Pepsi bottles on the floor. Everywhere were syrup circles, milk marks, wax drips, pliers and papers and pens. There was nowhere to spread jelly, nowhere to pour Pepsi, nothing to drink with, nothing to eat or to clean with. Pops's fungus tea bowl lay smashed in the sink where Moms must have thrown it. I gave up.

My scarecrow still stood in the hallway, pushed against the wall, the Raiders helmet drooping to one side. In Moms's room, shoes and underwear and bras were sprayed all over her bed and carpet, and a Hershey's chocolate wrapper lay on the pillow. I went to her dresser and stared at a row of her perfume bottles. I picked up a blue one and unscrewed the tiny silver top. There wasn't any perfume left but I could smell a whiff of rose. It was a smell I'd known my whole life, the smell of Moms's skin. The more my nose filled up with its flowery odor, the more beautiful Moms became in my head.

I picked up a framed photo of her and Pops cutting a cake together at their wedding. Moms looked so young in the picture, but Pops was pretty much the same as he was now, except his hair was a little shorter. His face was serious, his eyes focused on the knife and the cake, like he was concentrating on cutting it right. Moms wasn't even looking at the cake. Her eyes were on Pops.

I set the photo down and flicked off the light. Then I lay in her bed in the dark, surrounded by the smell of her sheets and shoes. . . .

Moms woke me up around two-thirty in the morning—she'd been out looking for Pops all night. It took me a second to remember why I was in her bed. She had already undressed, except for her bra and underwear, and got in bed with her back to me. She smelled of cigarettes.

I started to get out of the bed. "You can stay if you want," she said.

I stopped. "Stay—*where?*"

"In my bed."

Did she think I was Pops? I didn't move.

"Get in, Con—it's cold."

I slid back under the covers, confused. I couldn't remember ever sleeping next to her. I felt the heat from her back on my face and chest, and I liked her smoky deep smell of cigarettes and skin and perfume. Now that Pops was gone, maybe I could sleep next to her *every* night. Pops could have Ms. Van Pelt. *I* had Moms.

She cleared her throat. For some reason it sent a shiver down through me and I started thinking Pops was going to bust in any moment and find me in there. Who knew what he'd do to me then. I turned away from her and moved to the far edge of the bed.

It was hard sleeping after that. I kept seeing Pops's angry face. I'd start to fall asleep, then roll side-to-side, come half-awake with fear, then fall back into a dizzy dream. It was seasick sleep.

"Stop moving," came Moms's voice. "You keep waking me up."

I froze. In a while, her breaths slowed and she was asleep. That got me breathing slow too, and finally I was too tired to worry about Pops or anything else.

"Wait here and lock the doors," Moms said.

We were somewhere up in the Oakland hills, in the steep parking lot of a place called Skyline Market. We'd been looking for Pops, and had already covered Alameda and most of Oakland. Now we were thirsty and Moms was getting us some Pepsis.

After ten minutes she hadn't come out of the market. I decided to go find her, but when I undid my seat belt, I felt the car start to move. It was rolling backwards out of the parking space, picking up speed as it rushed toward the sidewalk and the busy street where cars blew past in both directions.

I looked back at the store. No sign of Moms.

I took hold of the wheel and turned it, but the car swerved toward a row of parked cars. I pulled the wheel the other way and the Impala straightened and jumped the sidewalk and shot out into the street. I let out a scream as cars honked and screeched around me. The Impala came to a stop, halfway into both lanes.

A lowered Honda with tinted windows pulled to the side and three older gritties with shaved heads and baggy pants got out, eyeing the Impala. They ran in front of traffic like they didn't care, and cars swerved and skidded in order to miss hitting them. The gritties laughed. Now they were circling the Impala, checking it out like it was for sale. I could hear them comparing notes about its year and engine, even the tires. Then they came over to the driver's-side window. One of them had a scar on his eyelid. "Yo holmes," he said to me. "Where's Mommy, huh?"

"Check this kid out," said his friend, who had a beanie pulled over his head. "He's all driving by himself and shit." He started laughing, and there were more gums in his mouth than teeth. "Open the door, ese," he said.

The third gritty wasn't talking. He pulled his bandanna farther over his eyes and looked both ways down the street, then stepped back and karate-kicked my window with his shoe, splintering it with a big crack. I screamed and slid away.

"Dang, holmes!" said the one with the scar.

"Do it again," the gummy-mouthed one said.

The gritty with the bandanna watched for cars coming behind him, stepped back, then gave the window another kick, and the crack spidered to the edges of the window.

"Shit!" said one of them, and suddenly they were gone, running back across the street to their car. They jumped into the Honda and peeled out.

A face appeared in my window. It was a man with small dark eyes, pressing his body against the door as cars roared past. He rapped his knuckles on the glass and shouted for me to unlock the door. Steamy breath floated out of his mouth.

I didn't move. He pounded on the glass. "Open it! Come on, kid!" I sat up and saw that he'd parked his car in front of the Impala. It was an old yellow Nissan; the emergency blinkers were flashing. I looked at the man again. His forehead was creased. He seemed like he wanted to help. I pulled the lock up.

He opened my door and let in a rush of cold air. "Where's your father?" he yelled.

"My Moms," I said.

"Your *mom?*" The lines in his face doubled. "Where *is* she?"

I pointed at the market. The man eyed it, then turned back to me.

"What does she look like?"

"Yellow."

"What d'ya mean, *yellow?*"

"Her hair."

He slammed my door shut and bolted out into the street, his face filled with worry as he eyed honking cars rushing at him. He made it across and ran up the parking lot and disappeared into the market. A minute later he came back out with Moms and pointed at me in the Impala. She put her hand over her mouth.

The man helped her across the street and I heard him tell her to pay more attention and put the emergency brake on next time. He gave her an angry look and got back in his yellow car. A cloud of smoke shot out of his exhaust pipe, his small car trembled, then it peeled away on its thin tires with the blinkers still flashing.

Moms came around and got in. "Shit," she said, putting her key in the ignition and eyeing the cracked window. "How did *that* happen?"

"Some gritties did it."

"They tried to break in?" I nodded and she lit a cigarette and blew smoke at the windshield. "I hate Oakland."

A car roared past with one long honk. "I'm going!" she yelled.

"Why did you leave without putting on the brake?" I said.

"I'm *sorry,* all right?" She turned on the engine. "You're okay, aren't you?" She looked over her shoulder, and pulled out into the lane. "Fuck, that was embarrassing. That man yelled at me in the middle of the line with all those people staring." She pushed a paper bag toward me. "Here's your Pepsi."

"Can you teach me how to stop the car?" I said.

"What?"

"So if it happens again—"

"Look, just leave me alone, okay?" She put the cigarette to her lips and sucked on it, squinting at the road. I didn't say anything else. On the way home rain began tapping the roof and drops swelled on the windshield and flattened the world outside.

I couldn't take my eyes away from the crack across the window.

We'd promised Chuck, the man who'd sold us the Impala, that we'd do the car justice. Now the crack was like a big scar on us.

When we got home, Moms told me to check the mailbox while she opened the front door. I pulled the metal latch. One envelope lay inside.

"Anything?" she said, jiggling the key.

"Yeah, one." I turned the letter over.

It was from Eye Master of the Universe, addressed to *The Parents of Conrad Clay*. My heart almost stopped.

"Who's it from?" Moms called from the living room.

I opened the envelope and unfolded the letter. It was a reminder to Moms and Pops that I was partly colorblind, and that colorblindness was something to be taken seriously, since it could affect certain choices for me down the road. I swallowed. What did he mean by *that?* He wanted Moms and Pops to bring me into his office for an appointment and more testing. The man just didn't give up.

I read the letter over again. Moms was gonna give me a ton of cancer when she saw it. Already, Pops was gone and we didn't have much money, and now she'd have to spend more money on my lousy eyes.

"Bring it in, Con," came her voice.

I went inside. She was watching television on the couch, smoking a cigarette, a Pepsi between her legs. "Let me see it," she said, her eyes glued on the television. "God, I *hate* not having a channel changer. Change it to Channel Two for me."

I did.

"Who's the letter from?"

"No one."

"*No one?* Then why'd you open it? Bring it here."

She took the envelope from me, and finished watching a commercial before looking at it. "*Dr. Theodore Chow?*" She pulled the letter out and began to read, wrinkling her forehead. "What *is* this?" she said, her eyes sweeping back and forth across the page.

Then suddenly her face seemed to lose interest. It just went flat, like a plate.

"Oh," she said, turning back to the television. She handed me the letter like it was a piece of junk mail. "It's for you."

28

On Sunday, Moms made me take the Christmas tree outside and lay it next to the trash can before I left to go to church. I stood there staring down at the tree. The needles were hard and dry. We'd bought the tree when Gramma was still alive and now she was dead and we were throwing it away. It never did get decorated.

Later, when the church service started, Preacher Jordan stepped up to the pulpit, took a good long look at me, and began: "Your relationship with God is like a football game."

I sank into the pew. Mr. Garcia hacked a loud cough and raised an eyebrow at me. Clearly, the preacher had gotten hold of the Tithes and Offerings envelope—the one with the Raiders' final score scrawled all over it in my handwriting.

I caught Jeannie staring at me from the choir like I was a sinner. Then I realized she just wanted to look at my face, *period*. She couldn't seem to *stop* looking at me. All through the first hymn, she stared at me from behind her thick glasses, waiting to catch my eyes. I tried not to look at her but I couldn't help it. Her hair was clean and glowing and she was wearing a puffy white dress.

Something about Jeannie right then reminded me of the way Moms looked in her wedding day photo. Jeannie seemed alive and shiny and round. She was a bright bare bulb.

Each time our eyes met she smiled. I hung tough through four of

her smiles, but on the fifth one my cheeks gave out and I flashed her a
big smile back. Eddie, who was sitting in the row in front of me,
turned and thought I was aiming for him and he smiled at me too.

When the hymn ended, Preacher Jordan got down to business. He
said that if we were to get any message out of his sermon today, it was
that he wanted us to go with God. He repeated it: "Go with God!"

If God could get me in touch with Gramma, I was willing to go
with his ass straight out.

For the first part of the sermon, Preacher Jordan cracked Creation
into us, and for the second half, he showed us God's power by telling
the story of Moses and how he got put into a mud-caked basket and
sent down the river. I didn't pay much attention, except to the part
about how Moses got his name when the Pharaoh's daughter pulled
him out of the river. I couldn't stop wondering what would've happened if the Pharaoh's daughter *hadn't* snagged Moses. Would Moses
have been walking around without a name? I got all heated up about it
and my brain was buzzing with questions: Who was Moses before he
was named Moses? What if a person didn't have any name at all?

Then I had a horrible thought. If your parents gave you a name
when you're born, did that mean you lost your name when you died?
What if Gramma was floating around dead now with no name?

I must have lost myself in my mentals for the whole rest of the sermon, because by the time I focused on Preacher Jordan again, he was
giving the benediction and looking right at me. It took me a second to
realize he was also *talking* to me. "Come on up, son," he was saying, his
open hand reaching toward me. "Come on up."

Before I knew it, the whole congregation was eyeballing me, their
bodies swaying together to the organ's vibrations and pushing me to
go on up, like rolling bay waves. They were looking at me like I was a
sorry case and I was sure they knew everything: That I lived near Jack
London Primary. That my parents never came to church. That I didn't
even have a pops anymore. My cheeks were hot and my stomach hurt
and I looked around for help. Jeannie was swaying along with the
choir, smiling at me. She wanted me to go on up and finally get saved
by Jesus for reals. She probably was feeling sorry for me too, like
everybody else in the congregation. Even Eddie turned around and

motioned for me to go up. "Just *go*, Con," he whispered. "Go on up."

I was surrounded like a weak wolf. I stood up. Mr. Garcia's wife smiled and nodded like I was doing the right thing. Mr. Garcia gave me a wink, and I could see he'd given up on the Raiders after their bad season and had let church marinate his brain complete. I stepped out into the aisle. The preacher was waiting for me at the front, his crooked lips stretched into a wide smile.

My whole body was sweating. I didn't know how Jesus was gonna save my ass this late since I was already ten and I'd done a lot of lying. I'd pulled off lots of other havocs too, like smoking with LaTonya and touching Loop's penis and stealing and cheating and making B.L.T. lay a log in class. If anyone threw it all in the mix and put my record ver- sus any of the other kids in church, they'd have seen I was straight-up unsavable and headed for Hell just like Moms had said. Even if for the sake of purposes Jesus decided I had a fighting chance, he was gonna have to do some awful work on me just to get me in shape, and I got so scared now that my knees started to give out.

In order to make it to the front I had to trick myself that I wasn't sleazing up for a save by Jesus but instead to get married to Jeannie. I moved up the aisle slow, taking one step at a time like in a wedding. As I passed each pew, people turned and nodded with smiles on their faces, and I pretended they were happy for me and Jeannie, not me and Jesus. I beamed a smile up at Jeannie in the choir, and by the way she smiled back, her eyes gleaming, I thought maybe she was pretend- ing too.

I made it to the front and Preacher Jordan got down on his knees and told me to do the same. He put his arm around me and his armpit was full of sweat and smelled like matches. He pulled me toward him so we could hear each other over the organ, and our heads were bowed so close that we had to stare at the carpet below in order not to touch noses. We were a football huddle. "Son," he said, his breath filling me with the sour smell of eggs and coffee, "can you tell me why you've come up here today?"

"To get married," I said.

He let out a choking cough and our heads banged. "You mean, to Jesus?"

"No, to Jeannie Morrison."

I was too close to get a look at him, but I was sure he was laughing and trying not to. He held his fist to his lips until his chest stopped heaving.

"Take my hand, son," he said. "You've come here to declare your readiness in front of everyone to accept the Lord Jesus Christ as your personal savior. Do you have any questions to ask Jesus?"

"Yes," I said to the carpet. "How do I get to Heaven? I got some business there with Gramma."

"If you accept the Lord as your savior, he'll take you into Heaven when your time comes."

"But what if Gramma doesn't have a name anymore?"

"Huh?"

"When Moses was born, he didn't have a name, right?"

"Well, I suppose you could say that."

"Then if we don't get a name until our parents give us one, what if we lose the name when we die? How am I gonna reach Gramma? What's she called now?"

Preacher Jordan shifted on his knees and cleared his throat. "Let's talk about this later," he said.

He rose to his feet but kept me on my knees by pressing my head down with his palm. Then he told the congregation that I'd accepted Jesus' hand and tonight Jesus was going to save my soul so that it could be lifted up to Heaven on the day of judgment. I'd be baptized after the evening service and everyone was welcome to be witness.

I was so nervous about my baptism that I didn't hear a word of the preacher's evening sermon. After the service, he made me stand with him by the chapel door while Mrs. Connally played the organ and people lined up to shake my hand and congratulate me for deciding to turn to Christ.

I could feel my legs trembling as all kinds of ideas of baptism raced through my brain: Me getting whipped. Me being hung from the chapel rafters. Me being passed overhead from person to person, until every hand in the church had touched me. In each case, I was naked.

When Eddie came to shake my hand, I stepped aside and asked him to tell me what I was gonna have to go through. "You don't *know?*" he said. He looked at the preacher, then turned his back to him like what he had to say was top secret. "How old are you?"

His hushed voice already had me scared. "*Why?*" I whispered back.

"Because the older you are, the worse it is."

"I knew it," I said.

"Yeah," he said, nodding his head and looking at me like I was already dead. "A guy as old as you, they're probably gonna give you the lobotomy."

"The *lobotomy?*" I said. "What's that?"

He pointed past the pulpit where Jeannie and the rest of the choir were talking. "See where they're standing?"

"Yeah."

"Underneath the floor is a pool where Preacher Jordan and Morgan pee into. It's filled with their pee."

I looked at Preacher Jordan, who was giving old Mrs. Hayes a hug. "No it's not," I said.

Eddie glared at me and held out his hand. "I'll bet you." I turned to the choir and eyed the floor beneath them. "The lobotomy," Eddie continued, "is when they take you and dunk you in a pool of their pee. Everybody's watching. Then they bring out a silver bowl on a tray, and it's filled with Preacher Jordan's poo, which they make you take a bite of, and you have to swallow. Then they dunk you back into the pee and that's it—you're done."

I thought about it for second. "Naked?"

Eddie gave me a sad look. "Yep."

It was worse than I'd thought.

I searched the doors, looking to make an escape, but just then Preacher Jordan called me back over to the line. I couldn't stop thinking about his pee and I tried to keep space between us, but he put his arm around me and told people in the line how proud he was that I'd made the decision to walk with Jesus. I kept eyeing the choir area, wondering if Eddie was telling me the truth.

When it was Mr. Garcia's turn to shake my hand, I asked him if there was a pool under the choir. He looked up there, then smiled.

"Sure there is," he said. "Where else do you think they're going to dunk you?"

My heart pounded as he gave my head a pat.

"Make sure you hold this boy down good," he said to Preacher Jordan. "Make him hold his breath a little."

Preacher Jordan chuckled and said, "Oh, we will. We'll get him nice and wet."

I felt like I was already swimming in Preacher Jordan's pee, and I had to hold back a stomach heave.

"He looks frightened," Mr. Garcia said, winking at me. "Don't worry, we've all been through it."

He went to join his wife and left me standing there, wishing I'd never come to church. It was the weirdest place I'd ever been, where people laughed about getting dipped in pee.

Preacher Jordan told Morgan to prepare the baptismal tub and show me the changing room. Morgan led me up to the front and opened a side door. Right before going in, I saw Jeannie waving at me, but I didn't wave back. It was her fault I was heading for the lobotomy.

The changing room was really only the back part of the church. The walls weren't finished and you could see all the beams, like in a garage or an attic. The room was dark and dusty and filled with old beat-up pews and chairs and other junk. Morgan pulled down a folded robe from a shelf and handed it to me, telling me to put it on while he went out and got the tub ready. Then he left me alone.

I stared at the robe, listening to the moan of the organ and the squeal of wood as Morgan began to pull up the floor boards just outside the door. I tried to breathe. The organ shifted to a sad cry. Another floor board let out a squeal.

I threw down the robe.

There was an EXIT sign above a door at the very back. I ran for it and suddenly I was outside in the cold night air behind the church. Some people were standing around their cars in the lot. I froze flat against the wall, but one of them spotted me. He said something, then everyone turned to look.

I did a buck-fifty in the other direction, hopping down into the alley behind the church, then out onto the sidewalk and up the street.

I turned on Central and ran full blast all the way to Safeway, where I ran around the side and into the dark back alley. I hid beside a Dumpster filled with crates of rotten food. Nobody would find me here. I leaned back against the cold cinder-block wall and breathed in the stinky, wonderful air. It was quiet, except for the humming of a generator, and all around me the alley was pitch black. Scattered everywhere were pieces of broken glass that twinkled like stars fallen to the ground. I'd blown my chance to turn to Christ, and now my soul would stay on the ground too. But I'd already sleazed through ten whole years this way. I'd probably be okay cracking through a few more.

29

Lucky for me, Moms wasn't home when Preacher Jordan called our house. He said he wasn't happy about me escaping my own baptism, but mostly he just wanted to make sure I was okay. He'd see me in church next Sunday, he said.

For most of the rest of vacation, I was busy building a bomb. The instructions said that if you couldn't find gunpowder, it could be taken out of fireworks. It didn't say anything about bullets, but the gun shop on Webster wouldn't sell gunpowder to anybody under twenty-one, and bullets were all I had—Pops had left all eight boxes in his closet. I just hoped he didn't come back before I was ready for him.

I opened bullets each day when Moms was at work, using Pops's pliers and wrenches. I kept the operation in Pops's closet since the gunpowder was messy and got all over everything and Moms never looked in there. The hard part was keeping the bullet shell from slipping out of the wrench while I gripped the lead with pliers and twisted and pulled. Based on what the instructions said about gunpowder, I had to slide the lead out slow, or else the powder could ignite and blow off my face. Every time I wiggled another one out, I held the shell up to my nose so the fresh smell of gunpowder shot straight into my brain like a rotty sharp fart. It was like a million matchsticks squeezing my skull. It smelled good.

I could do almost twenty bullets each day before Moms came

home. I poured the powder into a jar I kept hidden behind Pops's old boots. I pretended each bullet was a piece of Pops. The powder was his blood.

Sometimes I took breaks and stared at the bright bulb above me, then yanked the string so I was suddenly in the dark and my eyes filled with swirling explosions of fire and light. When the explosions disappeared after a few seconds, I pulled the light back on and did it all over again, making one explosion after another.

Other times I didn't imagine anything. I left the light off and sat in the blackness and pretended I was blind like Midnight. I liked the dark then. The dark killed colors. In the dark I wasn't colorblind. I wasn't a whiteboy. I wasn't anybody.

I finally had enough powder. I followed the instructions for making a fuse, funneling the gunpowder into the pipe, and packing the powder down. According to the instructions, the packing part was the most dangerous:

PRACTICE SAFETY WHEN BUILDING A PIPE BOMB! USE EXTREME CAUTION WHEN PACKING PIPE WITH POW-DER, AS ANY FRICTION OR HEAT WILL CAUSE DETO-NATION. YOU DO NOT WANT TO GET HURT!

When the bomb was done, I weighed it in my hands. I lifted it over my head like a barbell. I held it out in one hand like a stick to throw. Then I let it rest in my lap and just stared at it, wondering if I really was brave enough to blow it up.

I had to show B.L.T.

The instructions said that once the bomb was built it was pretty safe to carry around with you, as long as you didn't go dropping or denting it or anything. I wrapped it in my Raiders sweatshirt for padding and slipped it into my backpack, then I checked the address in B.L.T.'s note and headed out on my deck to Naval Housing.

It took me a long time to find where B.L.T. lived because each building in Naval Housing had four apartments and looked the same: peeling wood walls, concrete porches, no trees. Kids were playing on the cement sidewalks between buildings, and I had to pick up my deck and walk. I finally spotted 2000 D, the address B.L.T. had given me, written by hand on a piece of tape stuck to a door. You could see a stain mark where the old address had fallen off. On the porch, ashes from a cracked barbeque had spilled onto a dirty wet tennis shoe lying on its side. I knocked.

B.L.T. didn't look very happy when he came to the door and saw me. He still seemed mad about what me and Loop had done to him in the bathroom. I told him I was sorry.

He scratched his arm. "For what?"

"For how you had to go to the bathroom in class and all."

His eyes narrowed on me, and I could see he was remembering it all over again and getting mad about it all over again too.

"Look," I said, pulling my backpack off and opening it up so he could see the bomb wrapped in my sweatshirt.

"Man," he said.

"Cool, huh?"

"Yeah." He stepped out onto the porch and closed the door behind him. "Better close it up so my mother doesn't see it." I zipped up my pack and put it back on. "You gonna use it?" he said.

"Yep."

A smile flickered across his face. "Hey. You want to go skateboarding?"

I looked at him, surprised. I'd never thought of B.L.T. as being able to deck. "Okay. I guess."

He went back inside and closed the door and came back out with a beat-up skateboard. Then he dropped it to the cement and rolled out.

What was I supposed to do? I got on my deck and followed.

Unlike me, B.L.T. had no problem decking through Naval Housing—he just yelled at the kids to get off the sidewalk or he'd hit them. They all seemed used to it, and either jumped to their feet and stepped to the side, or just scrambled out of the way on their hands and knees.

Soon we were rolling fast down the rough cement sidewalk. I looked over at B.L.T.—he was humming to himself. His thick neck jiggled, and popping noises vibrated out of his wide wet mouth. He was a throat.

We decked out of the Housing and down Atlantic toward Webster Tunnel to an alley behind a new business park. He crawled under the cyclone fence and stood at the edge of a canal.

"C'mon!" he yelled. He put his deck under one arm and climbed down a rusty iron ladder into the canal.

I followed him, being careful not to catch my pack on the fence. The canal was all white cement with a trickle of brown sewage muck oozing down its middle. It smelled snacky. B.L.T. was already heading toward the opening of a huge tunnel that went under Central Avenue.

"Where you going?" I called out.

He just waved for me to follow.

"This is the C-Street Pipe," he said when we made it to the opening.

The pipe was ten feet tall and perfect for skateboarding. There wasn't any muck inside either. "Cool," I said, taking off my pack. I dropped my deck and pulled some moves. The smooth surface was fast and free and it made me laugh. I shouted into the tunnel. I ollied into my own echos.

Then I stopped to watch B.L.T. take his turn. He didn't laugh like me. His eyes focused on the pipe like it was a test to take—the curves were critical and the cement was serious. He worked the walls with his weight, building momentum, until he was flying higher than my head. After a while, he didn't seem to weigh anything. I thought he might roll right up the roof of the pipe. He was a bat in a cave, soaring the sides.

When he quit the pipe, I couldn't speak.

"Help me clear a slalom course," he said.

We found a dead frog with no eyes. I spotted a lightbulb and said it was a race to pop it first, but B.L.T. didn't even go for it. I tried inflating a twisted inner tube with my mouth but my cheeks got blown out. "My ears hurt," I said.

B.L.T. found a wet board full of nails and we flipped it over and pissed off a posse of brown worms. I covered them with a wet sock and one of the worms slithered up out of a hole in the toe. B.L.T. lined up black chunks of tire, orange peels, shotgun shells, a piece of dirty rope, and a yellow golf ball—spacing them all three feet apart from each other. "We have to slalom in and out of these," he said.

We messed around in the canal for about an hour. Then B.L.T. said it was time to move on to other things. He told me that I seemed to know the basic skateboard moves, but now I had to take a larger approach. He said I'd been a flatland lowgrounder my whole life and I needed to elevate my thinking if I ever wanted to amount to anything other than a street gritty. If I'd read the books in his brother's room like he had, he said, I'd already know what he was talking about. "Do you want to be just like any other gritty?" he said.

I shook my head, confused.

"Then you have to think like a *real* skater," he said. He pointed at the canal. "Look! Skaters are like bacteria, infesting the sewage systems of America." He flipped up his deck. "Come on!"

I went and got my pack and we climbed out. We rolled through the business park and he taught me how to scout for security guards and how to ollie over bushes when escaping cops. B.L.T. had methods. He pointed at Webster Tunnel, at canals and overpasses, at roads and ramps and rails. He said that the government could outlaw skateboarding, but as long as they kept building these things, we'd find a way to deck them. Wherever there was concrete, that's where we'd go. He said skateboarders were invaders. He called us mutant multipliers. We were cockroaches. After about an hour of educating me, he said we were ready to infest Alameda.

Webster, Central, Broadway, Lincoln, Park, Shoreline, Washington, Atlantic, Grand, Encinal, Clement, Otis, Clinton, Oak. Kickflip backside lipslides, frontside nosebones, tweaked-over tailgrabs, five-O's, feeble transfers, half-cab blunt fakies, alley-oops, noseblunt slides, mid-stalefishes, crooked grinds.

B.L.T. said, "I'm tired."

"Me too."

30

I liked the way B.L.T. came at decking so much that I went back to Naval Housing the next day to see if he wanted to infest Alameda again. But when I walked up to his building, there was a moving truck parked outside, and two men in uniforms were carrying a gray couch out of his apartment. The barbeque had been knocked off the porch and lay on the ground to the side. A woman followed the movers out and I could tell right away from her face that she was B.L.T.'s moms—she had the same puffy cheeks. She saw me standing there with my deck.

"Are you one of Brian's friends?" she said.

I just stared at her.

"Yes," I finally said.

"Well, he's helping his father pack boxes right now."

"Why?"

"Didn't he tell you? They're transferring us to Seattle. We want to get up there while it's still Christmas vacation, before Brian's new school starts up again."

"Oh," I said.

She left to go speak to the movers and I just stood there, staring down at the pushed-over barbeque, my lungs pulled in so tight I could hardly breathe.

I never got to say good-bye to B.L.T. I waited almost an hour that afternoon while the movers carried furniture out to the truck. I was hoping B.L.T. would see me through the window and come out, but he didn't and I finally went home. The next morning, I went back but nobody answered my knock. When I looked in the front window, the house was stone-cold empty.

School started two days later. Before I left the house, I put my bomb in my backpack and one of Moms's old lighters too. Pops was coming back sometime and I was gonna be ready for him.

As I got close to school, I realized I was about to see Loop for the first time since he called me a whiteboy. For some reason, it felt like it was gonna be harder seeing him again now that B.L.T. had moved away. I tried pushing Loop out of my brain but he kept coming back. He was a boomerang. He seemed as inside of me as bone blood.

When I walked into the classroom, Loop was at his desk. He had a black eye. It was swollen shut, the skin puffy and shiny. I heard Chocolate Chip and Douglas whispering that Jerome had slugged him over the break. I knew I should feel sorry for him, but the news sent a warm wave through my whole body. Loop and Jerome were enemies now. I almost smiled at the shiner on Loop's cheek when I sat down.

He looked at me for a second, then emptied his face of any expression. He was trying to erase me.

Mr. Garabedian walked in and everyone quieted down. He said we probably had noticed a number of empty seats in the room. We all looked around—it was true. Sadly, he said, quite a few students had moved with their families to Seattle and San Diego over the break. "Both those cities have large Navy bases," Mr. Garabedian said. "As most of you know already, *ours* is closing down."

Nobody said anything. Loop caught me staring at B.L.T.'s old, empty desk. We locked eyes, then we both turned to the front.

Mr. Garabedian explained that in two weeks we had a Back-to-School Night, where our parents came back to school for a night to learn about what we were doing. He wanted us to create displays to put around the room to show off for them. "How many of you have ever been to the wilderness?" he asked us. "To a place where animals rule, and not people." We all looked around at each other, trying to remember if we'd ever gone to a place like that, but most of us came up with nada, nada, and not a lotta. Garabedian said he wasn't surprised. That's why our assignment for Back-to-School Night was to pick a wild animal, make a display, and show what the hell it did all day. "Focus on the two H's—*habits* and *habitat*," he said. "Does everybody understand what I mean by *habits* and *habitat?*"

Without even thinking, I shook my head, and Mr. Garabedian caught it. "Was that a 'No,' Mr. Clay?"

I lowered my head. "No."

"Then why don't we demonstrate what I mean to the class?" He went to the blackboard and picked up a chalk. "How would you all feel about using Conrad as our example?"

Everyone yelled "Yeah!" and I sunk low and flat in my chair, wishing I was a halibut.

Garabedian drew a stick-man and wrote *Conrad*. Then he made two columns: *Habits* and *Habitat*. "All right," he said. "Let's talk about our specimen's habitat. Certainly, our specimen spends a lot of time in school." He wrote *Jack London Prim.* under *Habitat*, then turned to me. "Now, Conrad. Where do you usually go after school lets out?"

I was all embarrassed. "Slime Canal?" I said.

He raised his eyebrows. "*Slime* Canal?"

I nodded.

He turned to the board and said the words as he wrote: "*Slime . . . Canal.* All right, is there something I'm forgetting? Something we should write above *Jack London Primary* and *Slime Canal?*"

Rashelle said, "Alameda?"

"Excellent," Garabedian said, writing *Alameda* above. "Good. Now Conrad, after Slime Canal, my guess is you go home?"

"Or else I go to 7-Eleven," I said. "Or else KFC too."

Garabedian quickly wrote what I said.

"I seen him at Hideout Liquor!" said Chocolate Chip.

"*Hide . . . out . . . Liquor,*" Garabedian said, getting it up on the board. "Okay. So here we have Conrad's habitat: *Alameda, Jack London Primary, Slime Canal, 7-Eleven, KFC, Hideout Liquor,* and, obviously, *home.*" People were giggling. "Now," Garabedian said, "let's compile a list of our specimen's habits. You will all be doing a similar exercise when you choose an animal to base your projects on. Conrad, what do you eat in a typical day?"

Everyone stared at me. I said, "Extra-large Pepsi."

"Extra-large Pepsi? *That's* what you eat?"

"Yep."

I told him some more food I ate, and he asked me about my other interests, like decking and watching the Raiders, and then he wrote it all on the board and stepped back to take a look. "There we go!" he said, smacking his hands. "There's Conrad."

My habits and habitat splurged across the chalkboard, and everybody leaned forward, staring at them with open mouths and big eyes, like a school of fish.

I looked too, but it wasn't *me* up on the board. It was *Conrad Clay*.

Garabedian said we had to make lists just like this for our animal, plus describe them: species, size, color—stuff like that. For the actual display, he said that in the past most kids brought either a stuffed animal or a skeleton or bones, or just a picture of the animal. We could display a nest if we were doing a bird. One girl had built a groundhog hole out of mud and hay. Nobody could do the same animal. Since he'd embarrassed me in front of the class, I got to have first pick.

I picked a wolf.

When I called it, Loop and Douglas and a bunch of other gritties said, "Damn!" and "Dang!" and "Tuh!" They had to choose lame-ass animals like rabbits and bees and bullfrogs.

When the buzzer buzzed for recess everybody got up and ran out, but I stayed in my seat for a moment. I wasn't done looking at Conrad Clay:

CONRAD CLAY

Habitat	*Habits*
Alameda	Xlg Pepsi
Jack London Prim.	Ding Dongs
Slime Canal	Processed Meat Slices
7-Eleven	Hot Tamales
KFC	Swanson's Chick. Pt. Pie
Hideout Liq.	Decking
Home	Sleazing
	Raiders

31

I went to the library after school and got deep into breaking down wolves' habits and habitat. I found six different books and I cracked through every single one of them until my mentals were mush. The most important fact about wolves seemed to be that the man and woman stayed together until they died. Every book said it.

It was getting late and I headed home to tell Moms about my project. I decked down the middle of Webster Street while trucks and buses roared past me on both sides. The low sun swam hard through the cold thick air. The sky was a ripe peach hanging low and dirty and I reached up to touch it like skin. At the corner of Pacific I ollied up onto the sidewalk and held my breath through a cloud of bus exhaust and wished Moms and Pops were wolves.

The living room was filled with new plants when I walked in. "You like them?" Moms asked me from the couch.

"Yeah."

She held up a channel changer. "Look what I bought." She aimed it at the television and flicked through a few channels. "We're turning over a new leaf, Con."

"Okay. But I have to do a display for Back-to-School Night."

"First I want to tell you about our new resolution." She clicked off the television and patted the couch. "Come sit with me for a second."

I sat down beside her. She fiddled with her bottle of Pepsi, turning it around and around on the coffee table, then she said we weren't gonna sit around anymore and be sad about Pops leaving. It was his choice to do what he did and you just had to let people make their own decisions. She gave me a big speech about not letting what had happened ruin our lives. Her friends at work had helped her and given her some books to read. She knew now what she needed to do, and she wasn't dependent on Pops anymore to be happy. She was applying for a better job and was going to leave the Naval Station for good. She felt strong again and she was going to move on with her life. As far as she was concerned, it was all behind us now. "That's all I wanted to say," she said, lifting the Pepsi bottle to her lips.

"Then, Pops really isn't coming back?"

She suddenly lowered the bottle. For a second, I thought she was gonna break out crying. Then her body seemed to shrink into the couch. She pressed on the television and her eyes glazed over with a glue that kept them open and stuck to the screen. She didn't say anything after that.

Two hours later, she was still sitting in that same sunken way on the couch. The living room was dark and the television was on, but she wasn't really watching it. She was just staring at the flickering light.

"I'm hungry," I said to her.

No answer.

In the kitchen, I made a couple of peanut butter and jelly sandwiches, one for me and one for her. I brought hers out on a plate and set it down in front of her. "Here," I said, watching her face, but she didn't budge. "Can I tell you about my Back-to-School Night project now?" Her eyes didn't even blink. I sat down next to her. "I'm doing a wolf and—"

"What about a wolf?"

I turned to her, surprised. "I have to get a wolf skeleton."

"Who says?"

"Mr. Garabedian. I have to show its habits and habitat, like if it drinks Pepsi and likes KFC. And I only got a week."

"Wolves don't drink Pepsi."

"I know. That's *my* habits and habitat, not the wolf's—"

"I don't want you drinking my Pepsi anymore. They're mine."

She didn't say anything after that. She just stared at the television and I gave up and went to my room. It was all Pops's fault. I hated him for what he'd done to her. He'd made her so she wouldn't look at me.

A few nights later Moms surprised me when she came home with a cold dead chicken. She'd gotten it from one of her suppliers in Chinatown. It was bald and white and still had its head. She laid it on the kitchen counter for us to look at. The eyes were almost closed and the beak was wide open, like it had been making an important point when they killed it.

"It isn't a wolf," I said.

"This will be better, Con. Why can't you do a chicken instead?"

"I told everybody I was gonna do a wolf."

"Look, do want me to help you or not?"

I did want her help. I wanted it a lot.

"It's all the same, anyway," she said. "One skeleton is like the next. Call it a wolf if you want to."

She grabbed the chicken and dropped it into a big pot.

"What are you gonna do with it?" I said.

"We're going to cook it whole until all the meat falls off the bone. Then you'll have a complete skeleton left over for your project." She filled the pot with water from the sink and took it to the stove and turned on the flame. I put my face over the pot. The chicken was already sending oil-swirls out into the water.

"What do we do with the meat?"

"Eat it."

"Can we make chicken pot pie out of it?"

"I don't know, Con." She put a lid over the pot and adjusted the flame, first to a high yellow hiss, then a low blue blow. "It has to simmer. Keep an eye on the water level. Make sure it stays above the chicken. It'll probably take a day at least." She turned to leave.

"Aren't you gonna help me?" I said.

"I need to relax. You watch it for me."

"Okay."

She left the kitchen and I lifted the lid to check the chicken.

I said, Chicken, now your name is Wolf.

• • •

Wolf began to turn yellow. It was getting late, but I stayed with him, adding water when it got too low. I had to show Moms I could do it. I wanted to make her happy.

When she came to wake me up I was down on the linoleum. I opened my eyes to bright kitchen light and a fungus-gray potato peel in front of my eyeball.

"You fell asleep," she said.

"No I didn't."

I jumped to my feet. Wolf lay belly-up in the pot. He was dried out and glued to the bottom of the pan, stuck by his own stick.

"I didn't let the water get too low," I said.

"It's okay—I turned off the heat. Time to go to bed."

"What about Wolf?"

"He'll be all right. He's sleeping in the pot."

I cooked Wolf all day Saturday. By midnight he was stringy but still hanging onto his meat. I hid the pot in the back of the refrigerator for the night. I didn't want Moms to see him until his bones had all come out.

Sunday morning I put him back on the stove and cranked up the flame. The church van pulled up out front and honked, but I didn't leave the kitchen. Moms woke up a little later and didn't even notice I wasn't at church.

I boiled Wolf the whole day long. When I lifted the lid that night, the pot was filled with yellow and white ooze. I put Wolf back in the fridge and went to bed.

In the morning, I checked the pot again. I couldn't see Wolf anymore. In the cold, he'd sunken and hardened into his own ooze, which filled the pot like cracked yellow mud. The only sign of Wolf was his beak tip, rising out of the ooze like he was trying to breathe. He was a buried bird. I tried pulling his bones from the hard pot ooze, but I snapped two ribs in a row.

I didn't have no wolf. I had chicken melt.

Moms came in to get a Pepsi and I covered the pot quick. "Let me see," she said.

"No."

She pushed me aside and lifted the cover. Her face sank when she saw the mess. She just stood there, staring into the pot. Then she let out a sigh, put the lid back on, and walked out of the kitchen.

Before I left for school, I took the pot outside and dumped Wolf and his ooze into the trash can.

During that week, Moms got a new job over in Oakland at a hospital. She was doing pretty much the same thing, ordering food and keeping stock for the cafeteria, but it was a busier place and they expected her to work more. She came home around eight o'clock each night, and when she finally sat down on the couch she didn't say anything or even look up from the television. Her eyes were always puffy and swollen and her face looked dark and distant, like it was in shadow. I tried asking about her new job but she just told me to leave her alone.

Which I did, except about Back-to-School Night. I was working on a secret new display that was gonna make her proud. I handed her Mr. Garabedian's invitation to all parents, which explained the time and place, and I made her promise to come. I reminded her about it each morning before she left for work, and every night when she came home.

On the morning of Back-to-School Night, I got up to watch her put on makeup. "Are you gonna get off work in time?" I said.

"Yes."

"It starts at seven."

"I'll be there, okay? Jesus!"

She squinted, brushing black makeup onto her lashes, and I couldn't see into her eyes to know whether or not to believe her.

32

That night, I waited in the classroom as parents filed in and hovered around the displays, bragging all proud about their kids. Garabedian kept asking me if my parents had come yet—he really needed to talk to them about my display, which I'd brought in earlier that day.

By seven-thirty, Moms hadn't shown up. Loop's moms, Mary, walked over and said she wanted to finally meet both my parents. I told her Moms wasn't there and Pops wasn't coming. She looked confused and started to say something, but Garabedian came to talk to her about Loop, and they left to go look at his display.

Everyone kept asking me where my parents were. After a while I started feeling like a squid so I headed out onto the blacktop to a lone tether pole with no ball hanging on it. The sky was a black bruise and the cold air whipped across the ground. I slid my hands into my pockets and faced the classroom. The windows glowed yellow and people stood inside talking and joking. I turned my eyes to the corridor, lit up in spots by bare light bulbs. No sign of Moms.

People began to leave the room and head home. I watched one family after another walk outside and pause near the door, the momses talking all excited, the popses quiet and thinking to themselves, before they disappeared down the corridor. None of them looked in my direction. Through the window I could see Garabedian nodding and looking serious as he talked to LaTonya and Rashelle's pops. The two men shook hands and then the twins walked out with their parents and headed down the hallway too.

Only a few families were left in the room. If Moms didn't come soon she was gonna miss talking to Garabedian and miss my display.

Mary suddenly walked outside by herself and stood next to the door. She looked both ways down the corridor, then out at the black-top in my direction. I turned away.

"Con?" came her voice. "Is that you out there?"

I didn't answer. The field was black and quiet and empty. I heard heels clicking on the asphalt and I turned just as Mary walked up, shaking her head. "Con, it's really cold out here, why don't you come in?"

I lowered my eyes. Her feet were stuffed into two brown high-heel shoes.

"Your mother hasn't come yet?"

"No."

I felt her hands on my shoulders. "Con, I know you and Loop haven't been close lately, but why don't you come over to the house tonight?"

I didn't answer.

"You can have some hot chocolate, warm up your bones. The wrestlers will be there, and Bobby and my new friend Sandra too—remember? She's that nice lady you met at the shop?"

I kept my eyes on her feet.

"It's so cold! I'm goin back inside. You comin with me?"

I shook my head. She let out a sigh. "I hope we'll see you later, then."

Her shoes spun around and I watched her walk back toward the classroom, rubbing her sides with her arms. A few moments later she came back out, holding Loop by the arm. "You come over, Con, you hear?" she called out to me. Loop looked at me, surprised, as his mother pulled him away down the corridor.

The last set of parents walked out and Mr. Garabedian came to the door and waved to them before going back into the room and shutting off the lights. He locked the door and headed down the hall.

I stared at the blackened windows. Inside that dark room, on a table against the far wall, sat the display I'd made especially for Moms. It wasn't about a wolf. It was about Gramma. I'd written her habits and habitat on the side of a box, which had an open top covered with Saran Wrap so people could look down inside. In the bottom sat a pile of ashes, a circle of bone chips. And a bottle, her Sea of Galilee.

I clung to the tether pole and waited for another half hour just in case Moms showed up. One by one, the glowing windows of other classrooms went black. Finally, the lights in the corridor clicked off and the building was dark against the sky. I let go of the metal pole and stood there, breathing cold air in and out.

She wasn't going to come.

33

I ran from the blacktop, letting the wind whip me through the gate and down the sidewalk until I was out in the middle of Webster Street traffic. Cars swerved and honked but I didn't care. Pops had taken Moms from me without even being around. He'd ghosted her away.

On the other side of the street I found One-Eye the Pigeon puffed up on the pavement. I reached down and grabbed him and threw him up into the air. "Fly!" I yelled. He flapped and fell back down to the ground. I picked him up and flung him into the air again. "Fly!" I kept throwing him up into the air, over and over, until he lay on the ground without moving, his dead eye open. Then I dropped down next to his quiet dead body and cried.

I got up slowly. Everything was a blur of headlights and traffic signals and street signs. I walked and walked until there were no signals and no streetlights, just quiet houses and dark cars and buzzing telephone lines. Before I knew it I was standing on a porch and leaning over a big dog and knocking on a door, and suddenly I found myself in a bright living room, alone and afraid and surrounded by happy people getting ready for a party. Mary was straightening some magazines on the coffee table. Moon Dog was putting out chips. Cinci was mixing dip in the kitchen. Loop was watching television. And Midnight was in his corner, cracking open sunflower seeds and popping them in his mouth.

"Con!" Mary said. She stopped what she was doing and looked surprised to see me.

Midnight aimed his sunglasses in my direction. "Hey, Con. 'Bout time you showed up here."

"We missed you," Moon Dog said. He looked at Cinci in the kitchen. "Didn't we, Cinci?"

"Mm-hm," Cinci said, stirring the dip.

They were all looking at me, except for Loop, who I could tell was purposely ignoring me by keeping his eyes locked on the television.

"Well," Mary said, "have a seat and get yourself some chips. I'm just finishing cleaning this place up before Sandra gets here."

I stayed right where I was, near the door.

Midnight turned in Mary's direction. *"Sandra?* Who is Sandra?"

"A girl whose hair I straighten. A friend." She pointed at Loop's deck lying near the television. "Loop, put your skateboard away in your room."

Loop did as she said and came back out. His eyes started hawking me and I felt stupid just standing there. Half of me wanted to run back outside. The other half of me just needed to be in that room with everyone. As long as I didn't have to talk.

Mary picked up a Termite sock near my feet. "You all right?" she said, eyeing me.

I nodded.

"Don't you want to sit down?"

I shook my head.

She smiled at me and let out a sigh, then went over to Midnight and picked up some bottle caps that had fallen to the carpet. She slapped them on his worktable.

"What are you in a rush to be all Betty Crocker for?" Midnight said to her, his arms out wide like wings. "If this girl Sandra is your friend like you say, she won't care if there's some dirt and some dust in here."

"She's different, *that's* why," Mary said to him. "Sandra's got *class*—what you don't know about. She's decent and sophisticated, and I'm not gonna have her seeing my place looking like a pig heap."

"Shit," Midnight mumbled. He spit a shell out into the middle of the living room.

Mary watched the shell land on the carpet. *"What* did you say?" she said, her head moving all around on her neck.

"Nothing."

Cinci turned to Midnight. "Shouldn't talk to your mother like that, homes."

"Yeah?" Midnight said, getting angry. "What do *you* know about it?"

"I know you should respect your mother. She's a good woman."

"How would *you* know anything about a woman?"

"'Niiite," Mary said, mad at him.

Midnight held out his open hands. *"What?"* He pointed to his sunglasses. "I call things out like I see them."

She shook her head. "Don't you dare ruin this party for me. Sandra is feeling blue and needs some good company. Bobby oughta be over soon, and I want her to meet his friend Slow-drive."

Midnight cracked open another seed. "Why would she wanna meet a friend of *Bobby's?"*

Everyone knew Midnight didn't trust Mary's new boyfriend. When Mary first met Bobby, he'd told her he was a poet from Jamaica, and she thought she was gonna quit cutting hair and move to a tropical island and eat coconuts the rest of her life. Then she found one of Bobby's old driver's licenses—Bobby was from Jamaica, Queens, in New York. She'd also found out that he once dumped an old car of his down in Tijuana and claimed it was stolen so he could collect the insurance. Midnight said Bobby was an East Coast hustler who'd pawn his own teeth if he could. But Mary believed that Bobby had a good heart and for some reason she went easy on him. She was tough with most everybody else, but Bobby could somehow get past her.

Mary glared at Midnight. "You leave Bobby and his friend alone. Besides, I don't know any *other* eligible men."

Midnight mumbled something to himself, and I could see he thought *he* was eligible. Mary saw it too. "Why?" she said to him. "Don't tell me *you're* interested in Sandra?"

He waved a hand in her direction. "I ain't interested in no uptown sistah."

"No, you wouldn't be. And don't you dare spit another shell out onto my carpet!"

I took a big breath and finally sat down on the fireplace ledge. Somehow their arguing was the best thing I'd heard in a long time.

When Sandra showed up, Mary brought her over to say hello to me and I felt my face get all hot from embarrassment about the twenty dollars I'd taken from her. She didn't seem to remember it and just smiled at me. The wrestlers both stood to shake her hand and Moon Dog told her how beautiful she looked in her tight black dress. Mary apologized over and over about her house being so small and messy, but Sandra looked around and said it was a lovely home. She went to the television where Mary still had Jesus in the manger. Before Mary could stop her, Sandra reached to pick up Baby Jesus and got some of Termite's old pumpkin sauce all over her hand. Mary almost had a heart attack, but Sandra broke out laughing and so did everybody else except Midnight. Sandra saw he wasn't laughing and held her hand out to him: "You must be Midnight."

"She's extending a hand to you, 'Nite," Mary said.

Midnight just sat there, refusing to shake her hand. He still didn't seem to like the idea of a betty with class coming into his house. Or maybe it was because she was there to see Bobby's friend Slow-drive.

"Don't pay any attention to him," Mary told Sandra.

Sandra paid *a lot* of attention to Midnight. She asked him all about his bottlecap furniture and even told him she was interested in buying some of it. Her eyes kept moving down to his hands, which were busy breaking open sunflower shells. She seemed so interested in Midnight that I wondered if she had actually come to see *him* and not Bobby's friend. Midnight gave short rude answers to her questions and he spit sunflower shells onto the carpet in her direction. Mary couldn't believe her eyes but Sandra seemed to think it was cute.

Mary brought a sleepy Termite out and Sandra took him in her arms and spun him around, smiling down at him and saying how beautiful he was. They took Termite into the kitchen to give him some juice and I noticed Midnight's face following their voices. Sandra was telling Mary how jealous she was that she had so many children. Mary stuck a bottle in Termite's mouth and they both watched him drink.

Sandra lowered her voice: "So who's this guy you want me to meet, *Slow-drive?* What kind of name is that, anyway?"

I'd met Bobby's friend Slow-drive a few times at Mary's shop. He owned a white low-rider Monte Carlo that he and Bobby called "Sirus." Slow-drive never seemed to talk much, but the betties in the shop always got twitchy and talky around him. Loop said Slow-drive got his name because of how slow he drove Sirus, but Roz, who'd dated him once, said his name didn't have nothing to do with no car.

"I know it's a funny name," Mary said. "He's got green eyes, though."

"You are *kidding* me," Sandra whispered. She rubbed her nose against Termite's. "Oooh, I always dreamed about having a baby with green eyes."

Sandra and Mary both giggled. Midnight called out from the living room, wanting to know what was so funny. Mary raised her head. "None of your business!" she said, turning back to Termite.

"I'm serious, though," Sandra said, keeping her voice low. "I'm just about ready to call it quits, find me a man and start having babies."

"Now you're talking nonsense," Mary said. "Girl like you with a real job. A *career*. Hell, you don't wanna end up somebody's rag doll, getting knocked-up, staying home. Take it from me, woman, because I've done it."

"Maybe," Sandra said, "but I've been thinking lately I really want to have a kid." She lifted her eyes up to Mary. "You know?"

Mary didn't answer her.

Sandra adjusted Termite's bottle. "It's like, how long am I gonna wait to find some perfect husband?"

There was a knock at the door.

"That's them," Mary said.

Sandra took Termite into the living room. As Mary went to the door, she looked at me with a concerned face. "You doin all right, Con?"

I nodded. As long as everybody kept talking, I was doing fine.

Mary opened the door, and Bobby and Slow-drive were crammed in the doorway as a joke. Bobby was tall and thin and had a high-top fade—hair high on top, but faded down to close-cut on the sides. He smiled wide at Mary, his eyes twinkling. He always looked like he was about to say something funny. "Hey, baby!" he said, kissing her on the lips and stepping past her. "Damn, whose Lexus is that out front?"

"Sandra's," Mary said.

Bobby's face glowed and he walked into the house like sunshine slipping in the doorway. Loop ran up and threw some boxing punches at him. "Yo!" Bobby said, wiping off his jacket. "Watch what you dealin wif!"

Mary smiled at Slow-drive, who was still standing in the doorway at a slant. He was smaller than Bobby, and brown like a root. "Come on in and close the door," she said to him, "before all the cold comes in."

"Yeah, don't be shy, S.D.," Bobby said.

Slow-drive pulled the door shut, and took two steps into the living room. His body was thin and flexible and it swayed so loose and easy that he seemed to be made out of graphite.

Bobby looked around at us. Except for Midnight, we were all standing up now. "Damn," he said, "everyone all conversatin here in the living room around the fire. It's like goddamn Norman Rockwell an' shit."

Mary pretended to slap the top of his head. "Don't swear, Bobby—we have guests."

He turned and kissed her cheek. "Sorry," he said. He headed into the kitchen. "I need a drink—I'm an unemployed man again."

"*What?*" said Mary.

Bobby was already searching a cupboard. "Hey, you got any more of that kitchen Scotch?"

"What happened to your job, Bobby?" asked Mary.

He pushed a Quaker Oats carton aside. "Job? Shit . . ."

Mary gave Sandra an embarrassed look, then went to Bobby in the kitchen. "They fired you already? You were only there a week."

"Naw, baby, they didn't fire me—I *quit*. But it's all to the good. They were trying to de-soul my ass, forcing me to sit at that drill machine and listen to Karen Carpenter and Chicago and John Denver all day." He patted the top of his hair. "I was losing the color in my skin, and my fade was starting to get all feathered."

Loop laughed out loud. I stayed quiet. I liked listening to Bobby. He talked different than anybody else in Alameda.

"Slow-drive had to call an ambulance," he was telling Mary, "and haul me down to Doug's for some barbeque just to get the soul back into me. But the real me is back. I'm 'bout it, 'bout it!"

"Yeah?" Mary said. "Well, why don't you walk your soul back into the living room and say hello to everyone like a decent human being."

Bobby stopped and looked at all of us. "Huh? Oh, yeah, shit—I'm sorry." He came out and shook Moon Dog's hand. "Dog!"

"How you doin, Bobby?" Moon Dog said.

"Hey, I'm livin in your world!"

Bobby moved on to Cinci, who gave him a serious eyeballing. Cinci didn't trust Bobby either. He claimed he'd seen Bobby stealing pie in Joan's Coffee Shop down on Park Street. He said Bobby was an embarrassment to his own kind, being the only black man in the restaurant and there he was stealing. Cinci nodded at Bobby with a straight-line mouth. "Bobby," he said.

"W'sup, my man? What's crackilatin?" Bobby held out his hand to slap Cinci five, but Cinci sat back down.

Bobby was already eyeing Sandra, who stood up and smiled, but Bobby turned to Midnight, and I could see he was saving Sandra for last. "Y'all hanging cool, Midnight?" he asked.

Midnight raised his face in Bobby's direction. "Cool as LL Cool J."

Loop rolled his eyes. "'Niiiite, LL is *played out.*"

Bobby looked at Loop, then back at Midnight. "Yeah, didn't you know that?"

My skin went warm watching Bobby move among everybody, cracking it cool. Then suddenly an old thought sunk into me and stuck just beneath my ribcage like a lead weight: I wanted this to be *my* house. The more noise people made, the more quiet and lonely my own house seemed. The sounds coming from my house were the sounds of leaving: doors slamming, engines starting, even Gramma yelling *"Hell!"* Here, people were *coming.* Here, I was stone cold surrounded.

Bobby eased over to Sandra with a big smile. "Look atchoo!" He held out his hand: "I'm Bobby."

"I know. I'm Sandra," she said, giving him a shake.

Bobby looked down at Termite in her arms. "Hey there, lil' homey." He reached out with his finger to touch Termite's nose, but Termite bit him. *"Ow!"* Bobby yelled, shaking his finger.

Sandra put her hand over her mouth and laughed. "He's on to you already."

Bobby pointed at Sandra and turned to Mary. "What have you told her?"

"About all the crap you get up to, *that's* what," Mary said with her hands on her hips. "So don't be getting any ideas. Sandra's here to relax and have a drink."

"Damn! *That's* what we forgot!" Bobby looked back at Slow-drive. "We dropped the ball and forgot the schnapps!"

Slow-drive wasn't paying attention to Bobby. He'd been standing near the door this whole time with his light lizard eyes on Sandra. And now Sandra's eyes were on him too.

Bobby clapped his hands. "All right, we got to go out and coordinate this time. Hideout Liquor is just around the corner. We'll be right back."

"Why don't you take Conrad with you?" Mary said.

I felt my heart almost leap out of my chest. I wasn't ready for that. "No," I said, my voice cracking.

Bobby turned and looked at me, confused. "Huh?"

"Take Conrad with you," Mary said to him, like it was a command. She smiled at me. "You want to go for a ride with Bobby and Slow-drive, right?"

Everyone was staring at me. Now I just wanted to leave the room. "Okay," I said.

"Cool!" said Bobby, going to the door. "Con's comin with us to get the schnapps."

I followed him and Slow-drive out the door and the house heat hatched us like eggs back out into the black cold. What did it matter where I was anyway? As long as I wasn't going home.

34

Bobby took one look at Tugboat laid out across the porch and decided we were gonna give him a quick run before getting the schnapps. If you were in a car, Tugboat chased you because he wanted in—that was how he got walked. The three of us piled into Sirus, Bobby and Slow-drive in the front seat, me in the back. Slow-drive started the motor and Bobby leaned out his window and whistled. Tugboat jumped to his feet and started barking—he knew he was about to get run.

Slow-drive eased Sirus out into the street and we ran Tugboat down Cypress, across Second, and up Brush Street. Through the back window, I watched Tugboat running after us, barking *Let me in, you squids!* His eyes kept popping up over the trunk with each gallop, peeping at us pissed. The car's exhaust kept him in a steady cloud, and his steamy breath mixed with it before streaming back into the dark like train smoke.

"Faster!" I said. "He's catching up!"

Bobby turned to Slow-drive. "Yeah, speed it up, cuz. Why you always drive like you on holiday?"

Slow-drive ignored him and kept his same slow speed. At Third Street, Bobby decided Tugboat's walk was over and threw open his door to let him in. Tugboat pretended he wasn't in any hurry and took a leak on a fire hydrant. When he finally hopped in, he gave Slow-drive a look and said, *What kind of ingrown run was that?*

Tugboat breathed up all the air in the car and I was glad when we finally pulled up at Loop's to let him out. He hobbled up the walkway and plopped back down across the doorstep.

Bobby eyed Sandra's Lexus across the street. "Damn, look at that G-ride!" He grabbed Slow-drive's arm. "You gonna have to elevate your shit, bro, if you wanna get wid *that* woman—she's a player. She's saucy. She's like . . . an *emergency*, noamsayin?"

"Mmm," said Slow-drive, pulling away from the curb.

"You notice the way she dress?" Bobby said. "Telling you, that's some *foundational* booty. Give me some of that on toast! That ain't no second-floor shit, noamsayin? That's from the Motherland! That shit's strictly *foundational*. I'm talkin, that's some basement booty."

Slow-drive turned onto Webster. He stayed quiet as Bobby talked.

"That ain't no Clothestime shit. That ain't no Ross Dress-For-Less. There's some serious *flow* behind that shit. I'm talking Dom Perignon, noamsayin? She ain't one of them Colt 45 hos. The woman gots bank. And once they got the money, you know they want the honey." Bobby turned to Slow-drive. "Don't tell me you don't wanna chew on some of that loose cabbage." Slow-drive wasn't answering him, but Bobby didn't even notice. "She's sweet too. It's like, put that shit on a waffle."

Slow-drive drove right by Hideout Liquor, where I'd thought we were supposed to go. "We passed the liquor store," I said.

"We ain't going there," Bobby said. "We goin to an Oaktown bar where we know some peoples at, and gettin us some quick warm-up drinks before headin home. Get us a little *Cogn-i-ac!*" He looked at Slow-drive: "My friend here is looking a little pale. I think he's feeling a little outclassed by Sandra and if we don't get some vodka in him, he ain't gonna do *nothin* with her. Besides, there's a liquor store right there that sells cheaper shit than Hideout. That busta-ass nigga over at Hideout be charging almost double for his Hennessy, like he all Monte Carlo and shit just for being on the Island."

Slow-drive eased us down into the Webster Tunnel.

"We won't be long," Bobby said. "It's just the other side of the tunnel. We won't even tell Mary." He turned around and looked at me. "You ain't gonna drop a dime on us, are ya?"

I shook my head.

"Good," Bobby said. "We just gonna have us a fast one, then head back so Slow-drive can get ignant tonight—get a piece of that Buppy tail. Some of that Bombay Booty."

Slow-drive slid his right eye over to Bobby, then slid it back to the road.

Bobby pointed at him. "You *know* you ain't turning her down. Only thing you turnin down is your *collar.* You better enjoy it while you got it, bro, and swallow it with a Tic-Tac 'cause it ain't gonna last. But I seen that look in her eye tonight—that Sandra woman wanna take it off and shake it off. I'm talkin, it's gonna be some of that deep love, you know? The motion of the ocean. Some of that deep-ass stuff where your shoulders be sayin"—Bobby made his shoulders dip and rise like an ocean wave—"like Eddie Murphy said when you in love and it ain't sex no more but you making *looove.* You know: *shoulders* an' shit." He looked back at me. "Ain't that right?"

"Yeah," I said.

He turned back to Slow-drive. "That's right. It's your *duty* as a brutha. I once knew this white girl who discovered a box her husband was hiding under the bed—had pictures in it of little naked girls and boys. *Little naked boys!* She was like, 'Whaaat??' She left his ass straight out and went strictly for the bruthas after that. She said, 'Fuck that weird-ass white shit, I want a *brutha!*'" Bobby pushed his finger into Slow-drive's shoulder. "'Cause bruthas be knocking it out—no bull-shit—just BOOM, hello!" Bobby slapped the dashboard. "BOO-YAH!"

Bobby turned back to me and held out his hand. "Ain't that right, Conrad?"

"Uh huh."

"Yeah, you know it is." He slapped my hand, and I was glad he was checking with me. That meant I was part of it.

That meant I was a brutha too.

We parked in front of a bar called Dori's 20. It was a tan building with no windows and a dark door with a neon SCHLITZ sign. Some men were standing outside the liquor store next door. "Look at that," Bobby said, eyeing them. "Don't matter what part of the world you in, bruthas be hangin out on a corner waitin for the booty to come by.

New York, Atlanta, Oaktown . . . I'm talkin, you could be in the African bush, and bruthas be hangin out under a tree, crackilatin like worldwide players, waitin for the tang. It's in the blood."

Bobby told me to come inside the bar with him and Slow-drive. It was a small, dark, crowded place with a wood floor and booths on one wall and a bar counter on the other. A jukebox in the corner blasted music and people were shouting and laughing in THX. The air smelled deep and sour, like the taste of sick stomach mixed with varnish. Bobby seemed to know everyone in the bar. A woman in a silver dress grabbed his neck and kissed him on the mouth. "Hi Bobby," she said, "you lookin fresh-dipped." Bobby kept going. I was still feeling dazed and didn't know what to think, except that Mary wouldn't have been very happy if she'd seen that.

The bartender pointed me out to Bobby and shook his head. Bobby had a talk with him and the man finally nodded and Bobby slapped him on the back. "We cool for one round," Bobby said walking up, and the three of us finally sat down at a booth.

A white waitress with short hair and a square jaw came over and pointed at me. "He is not allowed here." She had a funny accent.

Bobby's eyes moved over her body, all the way down to her dirty white shoes, then back up again. He thumbed toward the bar. "John said we could stay for one drink."

That seemed to make her mad and she left to go talk to the man behind the bar.

"Damn," Bobby said, watching her. "She been working those honky-ass joints too long. This here is a *black* bar."

The waitress came back looking upset, and pulled out her order pad. "What are you having?"

Bobby smiled at her. "Yeah, there we go. It's all to the good." He pointed at Slow-drive, himself, then me: "Vodka for the man. Cognac for me. Coke for the homey. I'm buying." She wrote everything down and Bobby stared at her rear as she walked away. "*Damn.* You see that? That's a *mo'ass.* She got mo' ass than a pig got ham." He winked at me. "Right?" His eyes returned to the waitress. "She's thick, noamsayin, big case of the thickems. I love that. A little jiggle and jubilation . . . *boom!* That's some of that goulash Hungarian shit, man." He looked at Slow-drive: "I'm tellin you, go *East*, young man, go East! Eastern *Bloc*—that's where it's at. Take me to the Motherland!" He lit a cigarette and used it to point out different women in the bar. "Don't matter if they black, white, yellow, or brown—they all sistahs, they all from the Motherland. Sistahs be everywhere too"—Bobby pressed his finger into the table— "Take Australia, for example: you go down there, it's filled with those big thick Anglo-Scottish-Irish whale blubber-eatin ex-prisoners'-daughters wenches. Thick, white, mayonnaise-assed sistahs, you know? Some of that Aussie, get-DOWN UNDER-that-ASS-type of shit."

"You never been to Australia, B," Slow-drive said.

I turned to Slow-drive, surprised—it was the first time he'd spoken. He looked like he'd finally gotten tired of Bobby's talk.

"*So?*" Bobby said. "I know all about it. Take my pops: he was in Vietnam, up in the hills, and who you think he discovered up in there? *Sistahs!*"

"Give me a break," Slow-drive said.

"Man, *put* your head out the window and quit bein a hater! You know it's true! Ask my pops. There was a whole tribe of sistahs deep in the jungle—frizzy old afros and big booties. He spent the whole war up there, procreating and shit. Invited his homeys to join him too. No need to hide it, *divide* it—that's what Pops'd always say."

Slow-drive shook his head.

"*What?*" Bobby said, looking hurt. "Tellin you, the Motherland is where you have to go. Someday, I'm gonna get there too."

Bobby dipped an eyebrow at me and I couldn't help smiling. I was glad to be with him. He was funny and he looked at me a lot.

The waitress came and plopped the drinks down. "Twenty-eight," she said.

"*Twenty-eight?*" Bobby said, staring at the drinks. "Well how much is each drink?"

"Vodka five, Coke three, cognac twenty."

Bobby picked up his tiny shot of cognac. "*Twenty* dollars? What the fuck is this, gold-plated?"

"Imported," said the waitress.

"From where, *China?* 'Cause I never paid twenty for no cognac before. Must be some Chinese dragon dick powder in there." Bobby held it out to her. "Take it back."

"Can't. Already poured."

"Well, I ain't payin for it, whether you take it or not. Just bring me a vodka."

She stared at him for a second, then took the drink and set it back on her tray. "Thirteen dollars," she said, waiting for the money.

Bobby reached into his wallet and pulled out a hundred-dollar bill.

We all stared at it. She swiped it out of his hand, making a slapping sound. "I'll get change."

Slow-drive glared at Bobby. "You had a C-note the whole time?"

"L-I-G-it, bro—*let it go*," Bobby said.

The waitress brought Bobby's vodka and change, and we sipped on our drinks. I finished my whole Coke and told Bobby I had to take a leak. He stood up to let me out, and pointed at a door. "You go through that door into the hallway, then down the hall and make a left. The Men's will be on your right."

I walked to the door, my head a little dizzy, then went into the hall, except there wasn't any hall—Bobby had tricked me: I was already in a stinky bathroom. I let out a lazy laugh and a white man in a suit who was peeing at a urinal turned and stared at me. I tried to look serious. The man turned back to the wall.

Just then Bobby walked in and pointed at me with a smile. "Fooled ya!" Then the smell hit him and he grabbed his nose and turned to the stall. "Damn, somebody be sendin it south!" He pulled up to a urinal and unzipped his pants. "Oh, yes . . . *Goddamn!*" He turned to the white man. "Been holdin it all day."

The man stared at the wall, pretending he hadn't heard him. For some reason I thought that was funny, and I let out another laugh. My whole body felt light, like I was gonna float.

"Ohhh, yeah!" Bobby said.

The white man jiggled himself, zipped up, and walked out of the bathroom. I joined Bobby at the urinal and took a leak. He looked over at me. "See how quickly he left? They always afraid to profile wid us bruthas, right?"

"Right," I said.

"Well," he said, stepping over to one of the sinks to wash his hands, "we best be getting back with that schnapps—Mary is probably sitting at home waiting for us, all worried by now."

I felt my heart pinch under my ribs as I got a flash of waiting for Moms to show up at school, and that lone cold tether pole out on the blacktop. I wasn't ready to go back to Mary's yet. I wanted to stay and hang out more with Bobby. I stepped up to the sink next to him and ran the faucet to wash my hands, but then I saw Bobby check himself in the mirror and I stopped to watch him. Whatever he was doing, whether it was pressing his high-top hair up with his fingertips, taking a drive, or talking about betties and bruthas, he made it seem important to be doing just that.

His eyes turned to me in the mirror. "Ready to go?"

I waited a moment longer. "Okay," I said.

35

We picked up a bottle of schnapps at the liquor store and drove back to Loop's.

The living room was warm and smoky and Mary was smoking mad, but everyone was still there and that saved us from getting too much lip from her. She pulled me aside. "You have a good time with Bobby?"

"Yeah."

She smiled and rubbed my head fuzz. "Good."

She turned her eyes to Bobby, who was getting glasses in the kitchen, and I could see the worry in her face. It was a part of Mary I didn't remember seeing before—a part that needed someone, but maybe someone better than Bobby. When I thought of it like that, Mary didn't seem that different from Moms.

Bobby brought the glasses into the living room and poured schnapps for everyone except Cinci, who seemed upset with Bobby and said he wouldn't be drinking. Bobby and Slow-drive joined Mary and Sandra on the couch. Midnight aimed his sunglasses at them, listening, and the wrestlers sat facing them too, like they were a show to watch. Me and Loop sat apart from each other on the carpet. We still weren't talking.

The schnapps quickly seemed to get everyone bent. Bobby stood up and wobbled on his feet, trying to keep his balance, and said he had something funny to show everybody.

"What do you got?" Mary asked him.

He looked around, smiling. "Y'all wanna see it?"

A bunch of yesses came from everyone. Even Midnight said, "Yeah, show it to us."

Bobby grabbed Mary's hand and lifted her to her feet. "What are you doing?" she said.

"Show them your secret smile."

"No!" She took her hand away from his and tried to make a mad face, but she was too filled with schnapps and let out a giggle. "Are you *crazy?*"

"C'mon," he said. "Let's show 'em."

"No." Mary smiled at Sandra, but before she could react, Bobby lifted her shirt up.

A silver scar sagged across her entire belly, with a smaller scar on each end. Her stomach was smiling at us.

"Whoa," Sandra said.

With one hand holding up Mary's shirt, Bobby pointed at Loop and nodded his head at the scar: "That's from having *you.*"

Loop suddenly didn't look very happy with Bobby, and Mary noticed it. "Enough," she said, pulling her shirt down.

Loop got up and went to his room.

Bobby lowered the lights and popped an old-school Maze CD into the stereo. "Franky Beverly is in the house," he said. "It's all good."

Slowly everyone began talking and drinking again. When Mary went to check on Termite in the back room, Bobby got into a conversation about Macy's with Sandra. He kept pouring more schnapps into her glass, and she laughed and giggled between him and Slow-drive, like she was baloney and they were the bread.

Moon Dog and Cinci had stopped talking. They were staring at Bobby and Slow-drive, and they didn't have very happy expressions on their faces. Neither did Midnight, who was moving his head back and forth, concentrating hard on hearing everything.

Mary came back and noticed Bobby giving more schnapps to Sandra. "That's enough, Bobby."

Bobby's eyebrows flew up. "Come on, baby—we just relaxin some." He turned to Sandra, "Ain't that right?"

Sandra smiled and pressed her glass to her lips. "I haven't done this in *so* long." She threw her head back so the schnapps sank into her mouth. Her head fell forward again and wobbled toward Bobby with a laugh, then flung itself over to Slow-drive. "This is fun!"

Slow-drive kissed her then. He leaned in fast and put his lips over hers. She twisted toward him and threw her arm around his neck.

Bobby looked surprised. "Yo, S.D.—you got to slow your roll, bro. Don't wanna move *that* fast."

Slow-drive ignored him and pulled Sandra's dress up off her legs. Sandra dug her heel into the carpet and pushed up against him.

"That's enough, you two!" Mary said, glaring at them. She gave Bobby a look. "Do something!"

Bobby tapped Slow-drive on the shoulder. "Yo, man, you got no shame to your game. Chill for a second."

Slow-drive suddenly pulled away from Sandra and turned to Bobby with glassy eyes. He looked like he'd just been woken up.

"Con, go see what Loop's doing in his room," Mary said. "You shouldn't be out here."

I didn't move. I was still mad at Loop. And he wasn't talking to me. How could I go into his room?

"What's going on?" I heard Midnight call out behind me. "Mom, what's happening?"

"Nothing," Mary said.

Slow-drive and Sandra started kissing again.

The wrestlers both stood up. "Well, I think we should be going," Moon Dog said, zipping up his sweat-jacket.

"Bobby!" Mary said, glaring at him.

"*What?*" Bobby said, holding out his palms.

They went into the kitchen and started arguing. Mary couldn't believe Bobby was letting Slow-drive take advantage of her friend in her living room. Bobby said they were adults and what the hell he was supposed to do about it?

Sandra and Slow-drive didn't seem to hear any of it and kept pressing against each other on the couch, their mouths locked together. I saw Cinci give them a mean look before he and Moon Dog walked out the front door without saying good-bye.

"Some shit's goin down, I can tell!" Midnight called out.

I looked at him and almost let out a scream. His head was caught in a rectangle of light that poured in from the street through the cracked curtains and made his head look like it was chopped off and floating in space. His mouth was open and scared. Beneath his dark glasses, his cheeks were trembling, and his ear was turned in the direction of Sandra and Slow-drive.

I stood up, my heart racing, and went to the front door. One last time, I looked at Sandra pressing against Slow-drive on the couch. Her shoe had come off and her bare foot kept pushing against the carpet, slipping, then catching itself again. She seemed to want to get her green-eyed baby tonight.

While nobody was looking, I snuck outside and shut the door behind me. Tugboat was curled up asleep on his mat, his mouth open, his breath floating up toward the sky.

I walked into the street. For the second time that night, I was alone out in the cold.

I didn't know what to think now about Loop's house. His family had always been perfect to me and they still were, kind of. They argued, but not about anything too big or bad. They knew how to joke and laugh and have a good time. But tonight, even Mary had gotten drunk. And Bobby talked about other betties in a way I knew she wouldn't like. Then there was Slow-drive and Sandra. I was still all hot and puffy over that. My blood was buzzing through my veins and my bones ached and it had me feeling like a big bee sting. No matter how hard I tried, I couldn't figure out what to make of it all. Too many thoughts had sunk into my brain.

Lights sparkled up in the Oakland hills, and icicles hung from the edges of the houses like fangs and fish teeth. I was ready to slip into my nice warm bed, and I picked up my pace.

When I got to the corner of my street, I froze.

Pops's truck was in front of the house.

36

At first all I could do was stand on the corner and stare. I hadn't thought that maybe the reason Moms didn't show up at Back-to-School Night was because of Pops. I pounded my foot into the ground as hard as I could and called him a bunch of swears.

The more swears I said, the more scared I became. I'd had so many visions of what I'd do when I saw him again, and now he was back in the house. And my bomb was under my bed.

I moved toward the house. The windows were dark. When I pushed against the front door, it opened, and a whisper of hot air escaped like the breath of a ghost. I stepped inside, surrounded by darkness, and stopped to listen.

Nothing.

Had he hurt her? Had he taken her away?

My eyes adjusted to the inky blackness as I moved down the hallway to Moms's open door.

I saw them lying together on the bed, asleep. Light seeped in the window and shined off the skin of their tangled arms and legs, off their bare chests, rising and falling with their sleeping breaths. Their faces were turned toward the far wall, and their matted hair seemed pushed in that direction too, like a giant hand had come down and smacked both their faces at the same time.

I didn't feel scared. I didn't feel anything.

I went to my room, and got out the bomb and one of Moms's cigarette lighters that I had stashed. Then I sat on my bed in the dark. The pipe felt cold in my hands and filled my whole body with a cool calm.

After a while, Moms's bed creaked. I heard footsteps shuffle into the bathroom, and I could tell by their heavy sound that they belonged to *him*. The toilet seat clanked, and I listened to the tinkle of a leak, then a loud flush, and the swirling sound of the tank filling with water.

When it was quiet again, I heard him in the kitchen, popping open a can. The television clicked on and went mute, until it was only a high-pitched whine. Through the crack in my door I could see light from the television flickering in the hallway. The couch squeaked a few times. The heater shut itself off in the hall and made ticking noises.

I waited and listened, until the only sound I could hear was my own heart pounding. Then I stood, holding the pipe and the lighter, and walked down the hall to the living room.

He was asleep on the couch, arms at his sides, completely naked. He looked so thin and wrinkled. His cheeks and eyes had sunken into his head and I could see all his bones.

The television kept making the room go dark, light, dark, and each time light fell on his sleeping body, he looked less alive and more dead to me. His legs stuck straight out of his hipbones like sticks. I felt a sudden shiver and saw a vision of him lying dead and white like Gramma. The couch was his coffin, and I was standing over him saying good-bye for the last time.

The television blasted his face with yellow light, then sent him back into shadow. I remembered Midnight's chopped-off head, and each flicker of light brought flashes of Sandra and Slow-drive, of Bobby kissing the woman in the bar, and Mary's glaring eyes.

I focused with all my strength until finally it was just Pops's sleeping face. But I didn't like what I saw—my face was there in his. The nose. The chin. The white skin too.

I held the lighter up under the fuse of the bomb. Good-bye, Pops, I hate you. I hate you. I hate you. . . .

He let out a long snore, and fell so still I thought he really was dead. Then his lips parted and gently rose to blow out air. For a moment, I saw something I'd never noticed before. His bottom row of teeth were tiny. Tiny and white as a baby's.

I sank down to the coffee table and let out a long breath, watching him. His penis was shriveled and small. His chest quivered as it lifted and struggled to suck in air. He was trying to stay alive.

My dad.

37

Pops left the next morning before I was even awake. I went into the bathroom. His razor in the soapdish was gone.

He wasn't coming back.

Moms woke up to get ready for work, and I went into the hall while she was putting on makeup in the bathroom. Before I could even ask her what had happened the night before, she turned to me and said she didn't want to talk about anything.

For two days, I waited for her to say something, but she just went to work and came home and watched television without a word. It was as if there had never been a Back-to-School night. It was as if Pops had never shown up.

On Saturday, I slipped the bomb into my backpack and decked over to see Midnight. I had to talk to someone, and he always talked to me straight. Besides, I'd been having visions of his chopped-off head floating in the lamplight.

Midnight was listening to a basketball game when I showed up. No one else was around. He said he was glad I'd come over—he needed to talk to me—and he had me sit in the sleeper chair next to him. I took off my pack and held it in my lap.

"First off," he started, "I know why Loop ain't been talking to you— I made him tell me 'bout that nigga Jerome and what they said to you and all. See, Loop—he won't cop to it, but he all embarrassed. He know he disrespected you, and he got his due when Jerome hit him in the eye. Every time he sees you he remembers what he did, and he don't wanna remember that. To him, you a squid-reminder."

"I don't think he's a squid," I said.

"Yeah, but *he* thinks he's a squid. Give it time, let him lamp a little. His pride all bruised up, that's all. And what he said to you—'bout being a whiteboy . . . All that shit—you gotta swat it down 'cause it's nothing. When you blind, that shit don't mean nothing to you. See, I can imagine you're green, white, blue—it don't matter." He pointed to his head: "It's all up here, noamsayin?"

"Yeah," I said. I *did* know what he was saying. I had colors for people too.

"It's all in everybody's head," he went on. "It ain't real. When you break it on down, it's nothing but some colors. People arguing about some brown, some black, some white—it's a seeing man's problem."

"Then I wish I couldn't see," I said. "Like you."

His eyebrows flew up. *"Yeah?"*

"Yeah."

He nodded. "I'm wid ya. I used to fly that plane myself. But let me tell you—you don't wish that for yourself."

A tremble rippled across his face, and I suddenly felt scared. I'd always thought Midnight was glad he was blind.

"No," he said, his voice cracking, "you just don't want that. I'm the first one to tell you that seeing things can bring you a lotta pain, make you feel real, real bad. Make a brutha angry too. But then you see something that just fills you up, makes you feel *good* inside. And from where I'm at now, seeing the good and the bad—they're one and the same, noamsayin? One and the *same.* It's all wonderful."

My fingers were squeezing the straps on my backpack. Midnight cleared his throat.

"Not a day goes by," he said, "when I don't think to myself that I'd give my arms *and* legs to see again." He pointed a finger in my direction. "Don't you tell *nobody* I told you that."

"I won't," I said, swallowing.

He turned toward the television. "The thing I miss seeing the most—it's the ladies. I never got to see a lady, all grown up like I am now. When they come through and I can smell their skin—that's when it hurts."

I remembered the way he'd acted when Sandra had come in that night. "Like Sandra?" I said.

He turned to me, his face full of surprise. "Who told you that?"

"No one."

His face softened and seemed sad now. "No, not like her," he said, sounding hurt. "You gotta be careful with ones like her—they just out to make your heart broke, see, 'cause women like her lookin out for themselves. They play pool with two white balls and you just get knocked around, you know?"

I didn't know what to say. He flicked through a couple channels, then put the changer down.

"This Sandra," he said. "What she look like?"

"What?"

"You know, describe her to me."

"Oh."

I tried to remember Sandra the way she looked that night. "She had a black dress."

"What about her hair?"

"Straight . . . and long."

"Color?"

"Black. Dark black—like ink."

Midnight nodded. "Sweet."

"And she had sparkles over her eyes—"

"Her skin," he said, his face tilted down, deep in concentration. "What about her skin?"

"Brown. No, tan. Like inside a cracked-open almond."

"Huh," he said. He smiled and nodded. "Yep."

"Her mouth looks nice when she smiles. Her bottom lip."

"Mm," Midnight said. He sat there, thinking long and hard about it. Finally, he said, "She beautiful?"

"Yeah."

"I knew it."

He dropped his head, and it was clear he really *was* sorry he couldn't see. We sat there for a while, him listening to the basketball highlights on television, me watching.

"If I ask you something," he said, "I want you to give me a straight-up answer, okay?"

"Okay."

"What did you see that night?"

"What night?" I said, choking on the words. I knew exactly what night he was talking about.

"You know, couple nights ago when Sandra come over here—when Bobby and Slow-drive were here and they was all drinking schnapps. Now don't lie to me. I know what I heard. But I wanna know what you *saw* happen between Sandra and Slow-drive."

My heart was pounding. I tried to think. "They were on the couch—"

"Yeah, I know that. *How* were they on the couch?"

I couldn't lie to him. "I think they were kissing—"

"Sandra and Slow-drive?"

"Yeah."

Midnight's head was moving back and forth—he seemed to be picturing it all in his head. "Man," he said, blowing out air.

"But she was staring at you," I said.

"When?"

"Before. When she came in."

"She *was?*"

"Yeah. A lot."

Midnight went quiet again. Then he said, "I appreciate you coming here today and speaking with me. You and I, we traded secrets with each other before. That makes us homeys. Homeys keep their conversations private and secret, right?"

"Right."

"Good. Now I wanna share something else with you. Another secret."

I knew he was gonna tell me he was in love with Sandra, and I was glad he was sharing it with me. "What is it?" I said.

"A color."

I skipped a breath. Before I could say anything, he said: "I never told anybody about it, but it's something I been thinking about a long time. See, before I became blind, all I wanted to see was black. But when the accident happened, and black was all I *could* see, the world got real empty, real quick—started scaring me, actually, and I started feeling sorry for myself too. I realized I had to fill my world with color again, because nobody else was gonna do it for me. I just had to cold color it. And that's exactly what I started doing. I was able to color anything I thought of—cars, trees, animals, people. Then I started coloring my *feelings*. I came up with colors for when I was lonely, sad, mad—you name it, I colored it. I kept that up for a while until one night, I was sitting right here in this same chair, holding Termite. He was sleeping in my arms, see, and I was just listening to his breathing. That's when I tried to color his breath." Midnight slapped his knees. "Well, man, I'm telling you, I came up with something I'd never imagined."

"*What?*" I asked. I was so excited I couldn't breathe.

"A color that no one has ever seen. I'm talking about a color that is impossible to describe because it's never existed in the real world."

"Where is it, then?"

"In my mind, I guess."

Now I was all mixed up. "Then, what does it look like?"

Midnight took a deep breath, then let it out slow. "Like the brightest light you've ever seen."

"The sun?"

"Yeah, only take that, and darken it—soften it a little, until it can flow into your eyes without leaving those echoes of light that always mess your eyes up after you look at the sun."

I tried to imagine what Midnight was saying.

"Then," he continued, "pour that into the clearest water you've ever seen, so it dances and glows. So it hovers, noamsayin?"

"I think so."

"Imagine that water now, with the color swirling through it. Imagine pouring that water into your mouth."

"The color is in my mouth?"

"Exactly!—See, I knew you were the person to share this with. It's in your mouth, and the color is warm and sweet—it doesn't taste like water, it's better than that. It's got honey in it, and when you swallow the color, you feel it flowing all down through your body, and it makes your skin all tingly like when someone takes their fingertips and barely touches the skin on your back."

A shiver went down my back just imagining it. Not only could I see the color Midnight was describing, I could feel it. I could even smell it. Midnight had me *tasting* that color.

"This color," he said, running his fingers over his thighs, then up his belly and chest, "goes straight down to your toes, then up the insides of your legs and through your body, filling your heart, and making you *see*."

He sat there, his chest breathing in and out.

"Anyway, I had to tell someone about it. I don't know where it came from. I probably made it myself."

I was staring at his black sunglasses. "'Nite?" I said.

"Yep?"

"Can I see your eyes again?"

He let out a wide smile. Then he reached up and removed the sunglasses. I got out of my seat and set down my pack, and I bent over him so that my face was right up to his.

His eyes wandered side-to-side, and they were glassy and dark but light at the same time. I looked straight into them and realized they were reflecting light straight back out. I'd never seen eyes do that. Then, for a split-second, I saw a flicker deep inside them, but just as fast, it was gone. I thought it was the television at first. Then it came again—a quick flash—and that was it, I didn't see it again. But it was enough. My whole body was shivering.

I'd just seen the color Midnight made.

38

I said good-bye to Midnight and stepped outside. Heavy black clouds had moved in over Alameda, and the air was cold and wet on my cheeks. I rolled down the street feeling tingly and light except for the tug of a steel pipe inside my pack, which bounced against my back each time I pushed off with my foot. I thought about what Midnight told me, how he secretly wished he wasn't blind. The gun going off had been an accident, but carrying the gun, and shooting out the lights—those were not accidents. A person could do crazy things trying to get rid of what they didn't want to see.

There were things I didn't want to see. But I didn't wanna be blind like Midnight.

I pushed hard and fast, all the way out to the end of Slime Canal, where I climbed down the rocks to the edge of the bay. Against the far shore, waves rumbled and fizzed and went white, then were erased by the flat black water. It was a blackboard bay.

I unzipped my pack, took out the pipe bomb, and hurled it out into black water. It made a small white splash, then that was erased too.

From Slime Canal, I decked straight to Mary's shop without stopping. Midnight had said that Mary wanted to see me. There was a new sign up in the shop window: WALK-INS WELCOME. Through the glass, I could see Mary and Roz at their stations. Mary was cutting an old wilma's hair, and Roz was giving her boyfriend, Dean, a trim. I was surprised to see Mary wearing a dress—it made her look taller and thinner, a little more like a betty and less like a man. She looked good.

The wind whipped down the sidewalk and I had to pull hard on the door just to open it, and then it sucked me in with a slam. The shop was nice and warm and filled with hair spray. I let out a sneeze. Everyone looked up at me, including Tugboat, who was laid out in the corner, and Loop, who sat there petting him. I felt my chest tighten. I hadn't seen Loop from the window.

"Con!" Mary said, her eyes smiling. She put down her scissors and walked over to me and gave me a big hug. "You had me scared that night leaving all by yourself so late." She held me away from her so she could look at me. She ran her hand over my head. "You all right?"

"Yeah."

"Good." She nodded toward the water cooler in the back. "I got hot chocolate packets back there. Why don't you warm yourself up."

"Okay."

I set down my deck and walked past Loop without looking at him. In the back, I emptied a packet of hot cocoa mix into a mug and filled it with steaming hot water from the Sparkletts. I took a sip—even the hot chocolate tasted a little like hair spray. When I came back out, I didn't wanna go near Loop, so I just stood there behind Mary. She saw me in the mirror.

"Careful, Con—I don't want to knock you with my elbow and spill that hot chocolate." She pointed her scissors at the corner where Loop was sitting with Tugboat. "Go wait over there while I finish Mrs. Hookfin's hair."

I walked to the corner but I didn't sit down. Me and Loop locked eyes.

"W'sup?" he said.

"Nuffin," I said.

His face went from looking mad to sad, and then back again, almost like waves rippling across his changing cheeks. He patted Tugboat's belly. "Wanna pet him?" he said.

I felt goosebumps spreading all over my skin. I did want to pet Tugboat with him, but I was still mad at him too.

"Puh!" I said.

"Tuh!" he said.

I sat down. Loop petted Tugboat's head. I took his belly.

The women were talking about nose jobs. Every time Dean tried to say something about it, Roz shut him down. She kept saying he didn't have any manners, but from what I could see he was just trying to get a word in.

Roz was studying her nose in the mirror. "Well, I wanna get one," she said.

Dean looked up. "You don't need to be messin with your nose, honey."

Roz pushed his head forward. "Keep your head down."

"Why should I?"

"'Cause she's gonna bald your *head* if you don't," Mary said.

Dean sank down with a hurt face and mumbled something to himself.

Roz turned to Mary. "I think you should get your nose done too."

Mary stopped cutting the wilma's hair for a second and looked at her own face in the mirror. "Why? I like my nose—I can always smell bullshit."

Nobody said anything. Then Roz mumbled, "Except when Bobby's around."

"Yeah, well"—Mary raised her scissors—"he has a way of stuffing me up."

"He a walking hayfever," Roz said.

The old wilma chuckled and Roz and Mary both started laughing. Me and Loop laughed too. Then Mary turned to us. "You boys didn't hear me say the word B.S."

We petted Tugboat like we weren't listening. It was good to be back at Mary's, where the air was warm and filled with lots of lip.

"Anyway," Mary said, "I'm not allowing Bobby to come around anymore since he and Slow-drive pulled that monkey business the other night."

"Good for you," said Roz.

We were all quiet then. Mary and Roz focused on the hair in front of them, and the clipping sounds of their scissors seemed to slip everyone into their own thoughts.

Then the front door opened and we all turned to see Bobby standing there in the doorway, letting cold wind fill the shop.

"*Shoot,*" Roz said under her breath.

Mary put a pin in the old wilma's hair and eyeballed Bobby. "Either come in or don't, before we all freeze to death."

Bobby's eyes fell down along her dress. He pressed his lips tight and slowly stepped in. He stopped for a second in the middle of the shop, like he didn't know where to go.

"What are you doing here, Bobby?" Mary said.

"The sign says 'Walk-ins Welcome,'" Bobby said, pointing at the sign in the window. "I'm walkin in."

Mary gave Bobby a quick, mean look. He just smiled at her.

"That's funny," Dean said, chuckling. "I like tha—"

"Stop turnin your head!" Roz said, taking his head between her hands and jerking it straight.

"*Damn,* woman," Dean said, trying to look up at her in the mirror.

Bobby kneeled beside me and Loop to pet Tugboat, but I could see by the way his hand pushed too hard on Tugboat's head that he wasn't focused on it.

"W'sup, Bobby?" I said.

"Hey, just tryin to get it done."

He stood up and took a seat in the empty chair next to Mary's station. Now that he was so close to her, Mary wouldn't look at him. He leaned forward so he could see Dean on the other side of her. "Dean," he said, nodding his head.

"Hey, Bobby," said Dean softly, looking at Roz to see if he'd blown it by saying hey to Bobby.

Bobby leaned back in his chair to get a view of Roz. "Roz," he said.

"Hi, Bobby," she said, then let out a sigh.

Bobby spread his legs out wide and looked over at me. "Guess a man can't come an' apologize no more these days, can he, Con?"

I didn't know what to do. He was looking at me, waiting. "Nope," I said.

"Guess not," he said, picking up a magazine from the counter then putting it down.

Mary stopped cutting, put her scissors on the counter, and turned to him. "You got no business coming here. You let your low-class crony take advantage of *my* friend, on *my* couch, and as far as I'm concerned, you're a no good, inner-city, housefly!"

"Yeah?" Bobby said. "Well, not all of us piss perfume and shit chocolate."

Mary's eyes grew large. "What'd you say?"

"You heard me."

She shook her head at him. "You're just like every other busta-ass nigga out there—a coward, a liar, and a cheat. Just like Slow-drive, just like the president, just like every man."

"Wait, you forgot some things," Bobby said, jumping to his feet. He leaned his face toward Mary's and she glared back at him, her nostrils flaring. "Why don't I help you out—tell you how men *really* are. Hey, you right: men are *dogs*. If a man could, he'd have every woman he saw on the street"—Bobby smacked his hands—"*boom!*—right there."

Mary turned and stormed into the back. The bathroom door slammed. The old wilma got up and followed her. Now Dean stood up. He and Roz were watching Bobby, who took a few steps toward the back and stopped. "THAT'S RIGHT!" he yelled in the direction of the bathroom. "IF SOCIETY ALLOWED IT, HE'D SLEEP WITH FIVE DIFFERENT WOMEN EVERY DAY, RIGHT ON DOWN THE LINE! THAT'S HOW I AM"—he shook a finger at Dean without looking at him—"AND DEAN AM TOO!"

Bobby caught me and Loop staring at him and almost seemed surprised to see us. His chest was heaving. He gave a final look toward the back, then spun and walked out the front door, leaving Roz and Dean standing alone in the middle of the room. Roz turned to Dean. They looked at each other for a second. Then Roz slapped him on the face.

"What'd *I* do?" Dean said.

Roz's lips trembled, then she left for the back of the shop and joined the old wilma knocking on the bathroom door. Dean leaned up close to the mirror and looked at his face, then he took his robe off, grabbed his jacket from the counter and walked out. The door stayed open from the wind, and I got up and closed it. I sat back down with Loop and listened to Roz and the old wilma trying to talk Mary into coming out. My blood was beating fast. Me and Loop stroked Tugboat over and over, sometimes petting each other's hand by accident.

After a while, Mary came out from the bathroom, and Roz and the old wilma led her to one of the empty seats, where they tried to calm her down. Yelling didn't accomplish anything, they all agreed.

"Why do men always end up being such jerks?" Mary said, rubbing her face with both her hands. "I mean, I can't believe women always fall for that shit." She dropped her hands and looked at herself in the mirror. "*I* fell for that shit."

"*I* fell for that shit," Roz said.

Roz and Mary both turned to the old wilma, who saw them staring at her and raised her eyebrows. "I fell for *a shit*," she said.

Mary let out a cackle. The old wilma smiled. Then they all started laughing and me and Loop did too. Mary pointed at us. "You didn't hear us say the 'S' word, either." We shook our heads.

Mary finished up the old wilma's haircut and was back to cracking jokes and laughing and everyone seemed happy again. Me and Loop put our heads against Tugboat's warm belly pudge. Loop said to close our eyes and pretend Tugboat was our magic carpet. We floated up over Alameda and over all of Oaktown too. We rode the wind and climbed the clouds, looking down at the houses and hills far below. Loop asked if I could really see it. I could, I told him, and I really could. But for me, it was the sound of women's voices in that barber shop—Mary's, Roz's, even the old wilma's—that lifted me up and set me back down like no flying carpet ever could.

The old wilma thanked Mary, paid her and left. Mary and Roz started sweeping up the shop.

Then Bobby walked back in.

Both Mary and Roz froze with their brooms. Mary eyed him, looking unsure what to do. He flashed her a smile but she just stared at him.

"That dress sure is hittin you in all the right places," he said.

"*That's* what you came back in to say?" Mary said, shaking her head. "You think that does it for me?"

"You tell him, girl," whispered Roz.

Bobby lost his smile and lowered his eyes. He ran a finger along the top of a chair. "It ain't what I came back to say."

"Then what is it?" Mary said.

"I don't know. I was feelin thirsty. Just thought I'd see if you had a Coke or somethin." He patted the chair with his palm and looked up at her. "You got a Coke?"

She was glaring at him. His eyes squeezed out a "please."

"What if I did?" she said.

"Just say you don't," Roz said.

"Well, if you did," Bobby said, "then I'd ask you to bring me one."

"I'm not your waitress."

"I know, but I'd still like a Coke."

"I'm not your slave."

"I'd compensate you for your services."

"With what?"

"Use your imagination."

"*Honey*, I'd rather not."

They eyeballed each other.

"I'm sorry," he said.

She started shaking her head at him, and for a split second, I thought I saw a smile at the corners of her mouth. She turned and went into the back, and when she came out again, there was a can of Coke in her hand. I suddenly felt a warm tingle go all down through me. Bobby was smiling from ear to ear, even when she purposely set the can down on the counter instead of handing it to him straight.

"You're still a housefly," she said. She picked up her broom and started sweeping.

"That's cold," he said. "But that's exactly what I been thinking about—being your housefly for reals."

She stopped and looked at him like he was crazy. "You talking about moving in with me?"

"Hell yeah, that's what I'm talkin bout."

"*Why?*"

"Use your head. It's a matter of *intelligence.*"

She went back to sweeping. "You're living in San Leandro right now. That's twenty miles from here. That's an *intelligent* distance."

He followed her as she swept. "Besides, I think I got a new job hauling pipes over in Richmond."

She stopped and looked at him like she didn't believe him. "You got a new job?"

"Almost."

"*Almost?*"

"I got it!" he said, all proud. "And you can put that in the paper!"

"Nobody would wanna read about your sorry-ass life," she said, starting to sweep again.

"I don't know why you're being like that. If we lived together, I'd cook for you."

She straightened up. "What are you gonna cook? One of your low-rent hotplate dinners?"

"Yeah."

He smiled at her. She shook her head at him again. I knew right then Bobby had made a comeback. Words spilled out of him, causing all kinds of trouble, but he was good on the inside.

"I gotta close up and get home," Mary said to him. "The wrestlers have Termite."

"All right, that's cool. We'll talk later."

She nodded. They looked at each other. He leaned forward and gave her a kiss. "I'm sorry."

"Yeah."

He turned to Roz. "Bye, Roz."

"See you, Bobby," Roz said without bothering to stop sweeping.

Bobby pointed at me and Loop and smiled. "Keep your eye on the sparrow, you two."

"Bye," Loop said.

"Bye," I said.

He smiled at Mary once more, then walked outside and closed the door. She leaned on her broom and watched him waiting to cross the street. "Sometimes," she said, "I think I can't tell the hamburger from the steak."

I followed Loop's eyes out the window to Bobby, who was darting through traffic to the other side of the street. Bobby jumped up onto the opposite curb and headed down the sidewalk and out of view. I had a weird feeling suddenly that Bobby wasn't going to be around much longer. I turned back to Loop and realized something I hadn't thought of before.

Both of our popses were gone.

Loop caught me staring at him. "Why you lookin at me?" he said.

For a second I just blinked at him. "Wanna go decking?"

Me and Loop left the shop and pushed off hard down Central, faster than we ever had before, like it was a race. I was excited but had a lump in my throat too.

We ollied the bushes and bums. We slalomed some people. Whenever we got too close, we pulled away from each other. When we got too far apart something kept pulling us back. We were boomerangs.

Right then I knew that me and Loop were wrestling with each other through the street. We were wrestling with everything we'd done together, like decking, and stealing, and me touching his penis, and with everything we'd seen, like our popses leaving, and Jerome tearin it up with LaTonya, and the wrestlers, who'd gone from being our heros to two men who loved each other. We were wrestling with him calling me a faggot whiteboy. We were wrestling with everything we now knew.

Me and Loop had more philosophy in us than we'd ever wanted, and that made us uneasy tag team partners. We grinded the benches, shredded the curbs, and tore through tunnels. And we rolled our anger into the cement.

39

A week after Back-to-School Night, Mr. Garabedian told us to take our projects home. Moms didn't get to see my display. She still hadn't told me what had happened that night, but from the dead look in her eyes lately, I wasn't about to ask her.

Pops never did come back, but about a month later he called. Moms wouldn't speak to him, not even a hello—she just handed the phone straight to me. He told me he was calling from Virginia, where he was working on ships at the Norfolk Naval Base. I didn't know anything about Virginia and I had a hard time picturing him there. His voice sounded small. He asked me how school was going. I said it was going fine. Then he said I probably wasn't on his side anymore. Neither of us said anything. I wanted to tell him to come back home. I wanted to tell him a lot of things. But he suddenly said he had to go and I said okay and then I heard a click.

When I told Moms he was in Virginia, she said she was sure Ms. Van Pelt, who had sold her house a few weeks back, had gone with him.

We didn't hear from him after that. Sometimes, when I heard the tinkling sound of Moms peeing in the bathroom, I thought of the time he made me laugh with his long fake leak. Or when Moms went to bed without turning off the television and I'd have to walk out and click it off, I'd get a flash of him sitting alone in the dark watching a fishing show. I remembered the way his gold ring clicked against the frame of his glasses when he pushed them back up his nose. And once in a while, when I was drinking a bottle of Pepsi, I'd lift it to my lips and remember the time me and him sat in his truck with our drinks, celebrating the two-thousand-dollar check from the saint.

But mostly I tried not to think about Pops.

Moms seemed to be putting him out of her head too. There were a few times when I could tell he was still on her mind, like one after-noon in April, when warm air had finally begun to ease over Alameda and the sun seemed to laze a little longer in the sky. Moms had opened both the front door and the sliding door in the kitchen in order to get some fresh breeze flowing through the house, and a bum-ble bee got into the living room and buzzed all over the place, bounc-ing off the window curtains. Moms didn't even get up from the couch. She just watched the bee for a while without saying anything. Then she pointed at it and said, "That's your father. Buzzing around. Cheating. Trying to get out."

Otherwise, she didn't mention Pops at all, and the more clear it became that he wasn't coming back to us, the more Moms began to come back to me. We started watching television together and laugh-ing at *I Love Lucy*, like me and Gramma used to do. And one night before going to bed I told her that I was colorblind, but that I could see colors in people anyway. The first thing she wanted to know was her own color, and she smiled when I told her yellow. I told her Gramma was gray and Pops was camouflage. She said that fit him just perfectly. I didn't tell her that I hadn't figured out what my own color was yet.

School ended and everything seemed to shut down in the summer heat, including the Naval Station. One Saturday, the hottest day of the summer so far, I got a letter postmarked from Florida.

It was from Mr. Kalt:

Dear Conrad,

I am glad to return your Otis Sistrunk trading card. It was a good trade. I kept the card on the TV here in my hospital room where I've been able to look at it. Otis Sistrunk's smiling face brought cheer to the room, and the nurses joked that I was purposely losing hair in order to resemble him. The Raider motto of Just Win Baby! gave me courage and strength during difficult times. Unfortunately, it looks like I won't be winning this battle against cancer. The card belongs to you. Cherish it as I have, for it is a gift from a father to a son.

Gratefully yours,
Ira Kalt

I read the letter over twice, wondering how I could have ever thought it had been a fair trade. Mr. Kalt was a stranger to us—a man I'd never met who'd gone out of his way to help us when he didn't have to, and the thought of it spread goosebumps all over my skin. When I read over the part about him not winning his battle against cancer, I felt my lungs pull in. Mr. Kalt was going to die.

I put down the letter and held up the trading card. I couldn't help but feel sad looking at Otis's shining, happy face. It reminded me of how things had been back when I seven, before the Naval Station started to shut down, before Moms and Pops started fighting.

That afternoon, me and Moms drove past the Station on our way to the beach out at Washington Park. We wanted to see what the Station looked like now that it was officially closed. The main gate was chained shut, and there were no people anywhere to be seen. The fighter jet statue sat alone on its stand, its needle nose pointing up at the barren flagpole.

We turned and cruised past Naval Housing and I thought of B.L.T. Curtains had been removed from all the windows and you could see right through the buildings, which stood quiet and dead. The monkey bars were empty and so were the swings. Moms said it felt like a cemetery. A white roller-skate lay on the sidewalk in front of one building. It was like all the kids had suddenly been swept up from playing and taken away without warning.

We drove on. The sun stood above the flat, frying streets of Alameda and shot shine straight down onto the houses and cars, heating the colors right out of them. It was cooking inside the Impala but at least we already had on our bathing suits. We stopped at 7-Eleven to get two sixty-four-ounce Pepsis, and we almost had them finished by the time we made it to Washington Park.

The beach was crowded and the sand stung our feet. We stretched out our towels and sat looking out over the bay. A few white puffy clouds floated down from the Bay Bridge, followed by their dark shadows on the water below. To the west, we could see the piers of the Naval Station. Seagulls cried overhead and kids ran everywhere, leaping and screaming and laughing while their parents watched. I didn't mind—it was a summer sound. We lay down for a while without saying anything. Then Moms sat up and pointed to a gray Navy ship leaving the piers.

"It's the *Nevada*," she said. "Your father worked on that one. I heard it's going to Seattle."

I watched the *Nevada* ease out into the bay. She didn't have to tell me Pops had worked on that ship. The summer before, he and Moose had taken me aboard the *Nevada* and led me to the engine room. Pops wanted to show me a weld he'd done—a weld so difficult that ten other guys, including Moose, had tried it and failed. The engine room was filled with giant piston casings and copper pipes and I still remembered the cold, sour-smelling air. It tasted like a penny in your mouth. The weld was hard to get to, up inside a vertical steel pipe just wide enough for a person to fit in. The bottom opening of the pipe was six feet off the floor. We had no ladder, so I stood on Moose's shoulders, and he held onto my ankles and lifted me up into the pipe. It was pitch black inside, the sides smooth and cold to my palms. Moose and Pops were directly under me, looking up. I asked them how I was supposed to see Pops's weld. They called up that I couldn't—I had to *feel* for it. "Where?" I said. "All around you!" they answered. I ran my palms over the cold metal. I couldn't feel anything. Pops called out for me to close my eyes, and I did like he said and that's when I felt it—a slight dip in the surface. I ran my fingertips back and forth. The dip was no wider than my finger and if you didn't give it all your concentration you'd swear it wasn't there. I had Moose rotate me so I could follow the weld with my fingertips all the way around the pipe. When he finally eased me down into the bright light, Pops smiled at me so big and proud that his cheeks pushed his glasses up.

The *Nevada* was moving under the Bay Bridge now. I dug my heels into the sand and watched until it was only a small dark rectangle disappearing behind Alcatraz, taking with it a piece of Pops.

"I was all dressed to go, Con," Moms said suddenly.

I turned to find her looking at me. There were pained lines in her face.

"I wanted to come to your Back-to-School thing," she said. "I was just about to leave when your father showed up."

An old feeling of anger washed through me. I could feel my heart pounding.

"I had my car keys out, ready to leave," she said, "and there he was on the porch. He started apologizing. I was so angry I yelled at him through the screen door. He wouldn't leave. He stood out there and kept saying he was sorry."

"Then you let him in?" I said, my voice mad. I couldn't help it.

"I grew tired, Conrad. I'd had a long day at work and then I did all that yelling. I got tired of standing there. Yes—I let him in." She looked out at the water. "We ended up talking about everything. It was *horrible*. It felt so bad, we both started crying. We ended up comforting each other. It was confusing. I still don't know what really happened."

"You could have come," I sputtered.

She turned her blue eyes on me. "I'm sorry. I'm really sorry." She bit her lip, and her mouth quivered. Then she opened her purse and took out some money. "Our Pepsis are warm," she said. She pointed at the snack stand at the top of the beach. "Why don't you go get us two more."

I got to my feet and began to move up the beach as slow as the tide. Halfway to the stand, I looked back at her. She was facing the water, crying. She pulled a Kleenex out of her purse and wiped the runny makeup from her cheeks. I watched her lower the tissue to stare out at the bay, and I felt all the anger leak out of me.

• • •

When I came back with the drinks, Moms's face was clean. We sipped our drinks and looked out at the view. More clouds had moved in, partly blocking the sun. It was still hot, but now the light had turned milky, like breathed-on glass.

My head began to whirl from the sugar and the heat. Moms said she felt a little dizzy too, and made me go down to the water with her to cool off. We walked in up to our knees. The water was clear and not too cold. There were lots of people swimming around us and it felt good to see the light coming through the clouds and bouncing off their sunset faces.

For a moment, a hole opened up in the clouds and the sun shined down on us, heating our heads and flickering millions of light spots on the surface of the water. I slapped my hands down on each spot of sun. Then I tried to move into them, but every time I got to one, it disappeared. My head was still buzzing and my eyes echoed with light and I couldn't seem to see things right for a while. The world looked fuzzy as old flannel.

The sun grew so bright it caused the clouds to clear, and light burned the bay. My eyes filled with Moms in front of me, and I stepped toward her to share the shiny water. The air around us seemed to glow. Waves rolled past us like gleaming lips of light. It was so bright I couldn't tell the bay from the sky, and it was all a color I'd never seen, which had me excited and afraid at the same time.

What color *was* it?

I tried to separate out blue and white and yellow, but they weren't there. I shielded my eyes from the sun and squinted hard at the sky, thinking.

The color was too full to be a *what*—it was a *who*. At first I thought it might be God. Then I thought it was Gramma coming back. Suddenly, a warm feeling trembled down through every bone in my body. I *had* seen this color before. I'd seen it in the flicker of light in Midnight's eyes. I'd seen it out of the corner of my own eyes all my life. . . .

It hurt to look at it straight on, but I didn't take my eyes from it in case it went away.

Acknowledgments

I am very fortunate to have Jennifer Rudolph Walsh as my agent and friend, and wish to thank her for her passionate support of this book. I am equally grateful to Greer Kessel Hendricks for her commitment to this novel, and for her careful and intelligent editing. For their enthusiasm and help in guiding this book into the world, I would like to thank Judith Curr, Rosemary Ahern, Karen Mender, Tracy Behar, Seale Ballenger, Craig Herman, Suzanne O'Neill, and everyone else at Washington Square Press. Marc H. Glick is the kind of lawyer every creative person dreams about; my thanks to him and Stephen Breimer for their advocacy.

I am deeply indebted to my mentors in the UC Irvine Program in Writing, who were there when Conrad Clay was just beginning his adventures: Geoffrey Wolff accepted an artist with no letters of reference and supported this book from day one; Michelle Latiolais read two early drafts and offered much intelligent advice; Melanie Thernstrom gave generously of her help and friendship. My heartfelt thanks also to Michael Ryan, James McMichael, Margot Livesey, Robert Newsom, and my peers in the graduate fiction workshop at Irvine for cheering me on and sharing their insightful comments.

For their support and assistance during the writing of this novel, I thank Arielle Read, Matt Shaw, Ayame Fukuda, Cullen Gerst, Tony Barnstone, Aaron Pugliese, Howard Harrington, Thorsten Hoins, T. Jefferson Parker, Justine and Christopher Amadeo, Peter Hedges,

Colleen Craig, Louisa and Glenn Craig, Gloria Gae Gellman, and the Squaw Valley Community of Writers.

To my mother, Jane Louise Winer, my stepfather Larry O'Shea, my sister, Elizabeth, and to Judy Winer and the rest of my family, thank you for your love.

If there is any person on the planet who knows this book better than me, it is Charmaine Craig. In addition to reading more drafts than any sane person ever should, she has been my keenest critic and fiercest ally. For her patience, friendship, love, and support, I am forever grateful.

Finally, I owe the greatest debt to my father, Arthur Winer, who first encouraged me to write. His support, both financially and spiritually, have made this book possible.

Dad, nurturer of my dreams, this one is for you.